SWAN SONG

C. Lymari

TO.victory

SWAN SONG

DANCE OF THE DEAD
BOOK 1

C. LYMARI

ALSO BY C. LYMARI

Homecoming Series

It's Not Home Without You- Hoco #1

(*Second Chance/ Forbidden*)

The Way Back Home – Hoco#2

(*Friends-to-Lovers*)

You Were Always Home -Hoco#3

(*Enemies-to-Lovers/ Second Chances*)

No Place Like Home- Hoco#4

(*Friends-to-Lovers/ Second Chances*)

Home At Last- Hoco#5

(Second Chance Romance)

Sekten Series

Savage Kingdom

Cruel Crown

Brutal Empire

Violent Realm

(Extremely dark & full of triggers)

Standalones

For Three Seconds

(Forbidden/ Sports Romance)

Falcon's Prey

(A Dark bodyguard Romance)

In The Midst Of Chaos

(MC dark romance)

Swan Song

(Dark age gap/daddy romance)

Gilded Cage

(Dark Fairytale Retelling)

Press Play

(Dark Romantic Thriller/brother best friend)

Boneyard Kings Series (with Becca Steele)

Merciless Kings

Vicious Queen

Ruthless Kingdom

(*Reverse Harem*)

Bonus Stories

Hollow Vow

(A Halloween special taking place ITMOC world)

Home Sweet Home

(A Homecoming prequel)

Homecoming Bonus

clymaribooks.com/bonus

AUTHORS NOTE

Swan Song is not your typical love story. The main characters are somewhat crazy and all kinds of broken. If you have read my books before, you know they can be triggering. If you have triggers, this book might not be for you.
For more information you can go to my website:
clymaribooks.com/triggerwarnings

Enjoy the crazy ride.
Love,
Claudia.

SWAN SONG

Welcome to the dance of the dead.
Come on, little swan, get up and dance. For you have feet,
for you shall bleed, for no good deed shall be left unseen. It's
time to atone for all your sins.
Dance.
Twirl.
Spin.
Your master shall be waiting patiently.
Dance with your demons, spin with your doubts, and twirl
till you drop, for this is the beginning of the rest of your life.
This is your swan song.

Here's to finding beauty in our dark side.

FOREWORD

"I became insane, with long intervals of horrible sanity." –
Edgar Allan Poe

PART 1

DENIAL

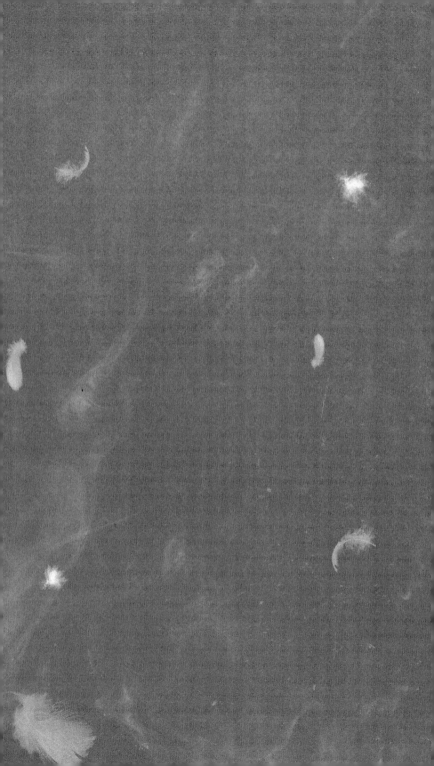

PREFACE

"Benvenuto nella danza dei morti."

"Welcome to the dance of the dead," the MC said, speaking into the microphone. His Italian accent was smooth, like fine-aged whiskey. It put the whole theater at ease, and people breathed easy.

How could something called the dance of the dead be announced by someone with the voice of an angel?

I looked upon the lights, letting them blind me because it was game over once they went off. Not for me, but for some.

My back still ached from last night's practice. There was a soreness between my legs that wasn't there before. It was like one little act now defined me. My eyes scanned the room, looking for him—for my saint—but like always, he was nowhere to be found.

I looked across the stage, and my eyes landed on my counterpart. Our company was famous for our macabre piece of art. I was dressed in all black. My tutu was puffy and the corset extra tight. At moments I felt as if I was suffocating, but all I needed to do was look to my left and remind myself why I couldn't fall.

Delia Silvestri.

She was my understudy. She was life while I played the lead role of death. She was gorgeous, and she knew it. Her skin was sun-kissed, with lush lips. When she smiled, people stopped and stared. Her eyes were a bright green like emeralds in the sun. At times I hated her, but then I realized I had the one thing she wanted the most.

I was the prima ballerina; I was the one people came to watch from all over the world. I was death with the face of an angel, or so they said.

My head was starting to hurt from where I had my bun. My hair was brushed and tied that you couldn't even tell I had curls. My skin was olive but nothing special. I was just another tanned Italian girl.

The lights started to dim, and I looked everywhere for my father. Thinking the word felt illicit, but it still thrilled me.

I craned my neck to look upon the stage once again when a lone figure caught my eye.

The lights were almost off, but I saw the man standing in the middle of a row. He was in a black suit, with one hand inside his pants pocket, while the other hung with ease.

He was looking right at me.

Then it was all dark, but it was like I could still see him, even more vividly than I did before. My nose scrunched, and suddenly I could smell burned flesh.

The violins started to play, and I took my position. It was time for the second act and my grand finale. My legs shook a bit as I put one in front of the other and got ready to go on my tippy-toes.

My head turned, and I was met with Delia's cold stare. She looked pale as if she'd seen a ghost. I didn't question it because I didn't care much for her, and a bad day for Delia meant a good day for me. Ignoring the look she gave me, I raised my hand, ready to dance my way across the stage like the angel of death—pirouetting havoc in my wake.

The orchestra started to play, and as soon as the cellos got louder, it was like I was no longer in this theater but another.

Suddenly I was dancing; I was no longer twenty-three, but I was sixteen. My white tutu was not stained but soaked in blood. I looked like a newborn devil rather than the white swan.

My body shivered uncontrollably, goose bumps covering my arms. I looked around, but I was alone. I couldn't remember who was here with me anymore.

When I twirled, I was back in the present. My heart thumped with the beat of the drums that now echoed in the auditorium. My face was a calm mask because death had many faces, but a scared one wasn't one of them.

One of the male dancers came and put his arms on my waist. I whimpered because I was sore from last night's events. I couldn't call it lovemaking because we weren't in love, and we weren't making anything. If I had a word for it, I'd call it an awakening.

As soon as we stopped dancing, he dropped to the floor as he pretended to die, another innocent victim left in my wake.

When it was me in the dark dancing with my eyes closed on the stage, I could pretend like the horrors I had lived through weren't real. When my demons danced alongside me instead of being in my head, I could be temporarily free.

I let go of all my worries about the fact that I had finally gotten what I wanted last night. I put on my brave face and smiled at the crowd. They ate it all up—the innocence on my face, the smile that was worthy of a toothpaste commercial. They didn't know I was only soft on the outside; on the inside, I was made of scales and claws. Something beautiful to be guarded but was already shredded to pieces.

I twirled again and glided my way across the floor until I made it to the other end and did an arabesque. My hand was stretched with my chin straight, my left arm and leg behind me as I supported all my weight on my right leg.

The man in all black was back, and he was watching me, and next to him was none other than Nicolas "Nico" Dos Santos.

It was like time ceased to exist as past and present merged together. I ignored the fact that my father was not even looking at me. He always made me feel like I wasn't in the room. He would look at everyone except for me, but he said it was too painful to stare at my face.

Bile rose up my throat because he had no trouble looking at Delia. When I put my foot flat again, I immediately went into a fouetté as I finished spinning, and only once I looked up did I see the face of the man who was next to my father.

His face was burned, the scarred flesh spread across his cheek down to his mouth. I knew I wasn't close enough to see, but I brought it from memory. I turned again, and Delia was right there with the same look on her face.

For the first time in my life, I fell—death succumbing to the demands of life.

I didn't turn to look at Delia, for I knew she would be triumphant. Instead, I lay on the floor, and I remembered it all.

"Dance, my little ballerina. Dance for me."

My lower lip trembled, and my legs shook, but I knew that depending on how well I danced, it would change the outcome of what would happen to me afterward.

I got into position, and then I started to move, giving the men in the room the show they wanted to see. I moved left, and then I went right, but there were men twice my age or maybe even more at every turn. I was barely sixteen, but being here was all I'd ever known.

I guess you could say I was a modern slave. My family sold me for a bit of gold because to some people, the only thing they traded was in flesh, and nothing sold quicker than that of an innocent child.

After a while, I could pretend like none of the men could see me. Like they didn't imagine doing things to me that no grown men should ever do to a child.

Then my eyes met the most beautiful azure orbs. Bellissimo like Mar Tirreno. *Eyes like the sea.* His eyes were guarded but not lustful, and I cocked my head studying him because, indeed, this was rare.

He was tall and dominating with hair like a crow's feather and skin that was olive but was blessed with a hint of gold. Even at my age, I knew he was beautiful.

"La mia piccola ballerina," my master said in a warning tone. So, I made my way to him in haste, and as I got near, I did a grand jeté, then landed in a split at his feet.

Unlike the beautiful man, my master's eyes weren't guarded or bright like the sea. His were dark like the tart found in hell. He was old, perhaps the oldest in the room, and he was vile.

I hadn't been subjected to his hell, but that's because I danced, and he liked to watch me dance. We both knew that once he touched me, his little ballerina would be no more. He knew that if he did, he would break me, and my dance would cease with my innocence.

The men talked as I sat in my master's lap. They all watched in envy as he caressed my naked thighs. How he played with my long curls. I hated the white tutu he made me wear. Hated how exposed it made me feel. They all gazed with envy, all except one.

"You owe me," he spoke, the beautiful man with eyes like heaven. His voice was deep, but there was a softness to it that made you feel protected, cherished, like he would wrap you around steel velvet.

His voice angered my master so much that he got braver as he touched me. I bit the inside of my cheeks so I wouldn't make a noise, because Master wouldn't like that.

I tuned out all the voices around me and blocked the way the men stared at me from my mind. Instead, I focused on that soft spongy skin inside my mouth and how it was going raw between my teeth. The way blood coated my tongue, and I wanted more because it was the only thing stopping me from feeling the hand between my legs.

Then I smelled it, the burning that was coming from the building we were in. My master was one of the first ones to run. He threw me on the floor as he ran away. In the frenzy, I ran away too. I briefly wondered how far I could go with clipped wings. The men started to shout and run, but at every turn, there were more men. I made it past the stairs, going anywhere but the room full of men. I needed to get to the upper levels so I could outrun the fire.

Just as I landed in the stairwell, my hair got yanked back. I started to scream in pain, but a hand covered my mouth. He was one of the men in the room. Not nearly as old as my master, but older than the beautiful man with blue eyes. He *dragged me to the first door he found, and it was the door to the backstage of the opera house we were in.*

"Por favore," I begged in my native tongue.

I don't know why we were taught to beg, kneel, and plead if it never worked. Why begging was something all humans learned how to do, when all it did was just waste your energy and breath.

The man wasn't alone, and I was destroyed. The little sane piece I held near and dear ceased to exist.

When I woke up, my body ached, and the once white tutu I wore was now all red. I heard whimpers coming from the other end of the room. There was enough light that I could make out the other person there. She was young, about my age. When our eyes met, she smiled at me. I wanted to recoil because there was something so terrifying about the feral smile she gave me.

I craned my neck so I could look at her better because I didn't have the energy to move. She was scratched and had blood all over her hands. Master kept many girls, and I guess she was just another one of them.

"W-w-what's your name?" I barely managed to say.

"Delia," she said.

Before I could try to introduce myself, the door opened, followed by a cloud of smoke.

The man with the beautiful blue eyes stood before me, and I closed mine because I couldn't stand to look into a piece of heaven as someone took me to hell.

"Dio Mio," he growled.

I cried as he pulled my body off the ground. I felt the wetness in my back from the blood, but I didn't have it in me to see where it came from.

When I felt that he put me to his chest, only then did I

open my eyes. He looked down at me, and I saw no malice in them. At least not toward me.

"I'm sorry," he said in a gruff voice.

A tear slid down my cheek. He had me in his arms as he started to walk away.

"Wait," I told him.

He stopped immediately, watching me with caution.

"We can't leave Delia," I told him.

He looked at the spot where I had pointed and scrunched his eyebrows, but I knew it was because the fire was getting closer.

"She's scared too," I told him, refusing to beg.

He looked down at me for a second, and he nodded. Then as he made his way to get Delia, I passed out.

Now the entire crowd was watching me as I lay there, unmoving, on the floor of the theater." And all I could think about was Nico, my savior, with the man who raped me.

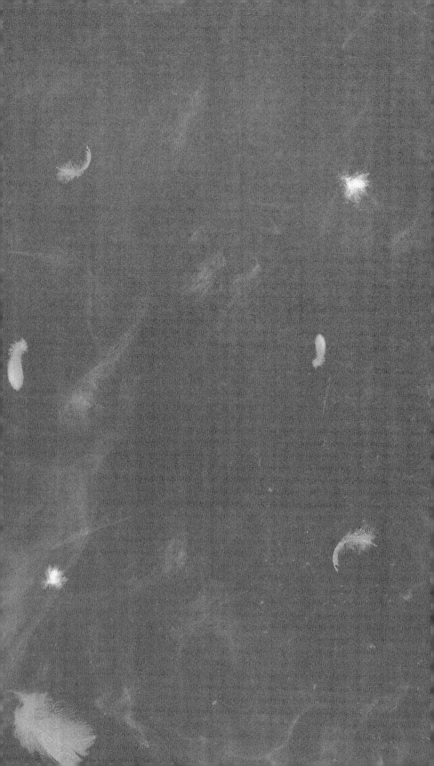

BURNOUT

Oh, little girl. You shine so bright,
not from gold, but wildfire in your eyes.
You came from hell, but you survived. Now, what will you
do when the fire ceases out?

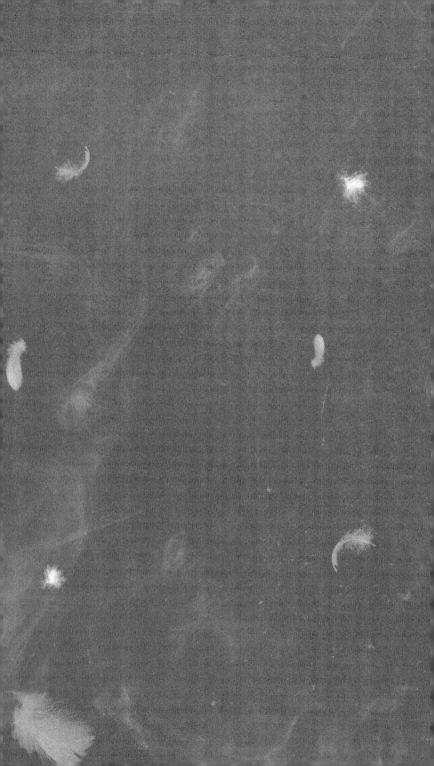

1

OFELIA

It was a laugh that gave me chills all the way to my bones and swept its way into my soul. A blinding white smile reflected through the mirror, but it wasn't me who I was looking back at—it couldn't be.

"You did this," she told me with glee before she brought her index finger to shush me. Blood dripped from her broken fingernails.

My eyes sprang open as soon as the morning light hit my face. I rose from my bed quickly, my chest rising and falling rapidly. My breathing took a second to even out. More often than not, my mornings started this way with the rush of adrenaline running through my veins.

It was always the same with my dreams. They haunted me. It was like a two-way mirror trying to get me to see what was on the other side. I might not know what was on the other side, but I knew it was covered in blood. I didn't dream in colors; I dreamed in bloodstained reds.

I took a second to calm down and then put a hand to my heart, making sure the beat had normalized.

There was something so comforting that came from the

unknown. To not know where you were going as long as it didn't take you to the place you came from.

I turned my head, looking outside my window, and smiled. I loved spending my summers by the sea. It had always given me peace. I loved watching the waves of the raging sea come crashing into the shore. How something so vast and untamed like the ocean came to a halt with the land.

It reminded me that no matter how volatile things could be, they came to an end sooner or later.

Out of all of our houses, I liked this one best. Here, I didn't need a cage to feel contained. Sliding out of my bed, I made my way to the balcony. My eyes didn't go to the sea but went to the outside patio, knowing who I would find. My heart sped a bit when I saw that breakfast had been served.

My room was done in grays, blacks, and soft pinks; it had a calming effect on me. My bed was a California king, with a blush canopy all around. I usually left that down. It gave me comfort and a false sense of security. I was the little girl of the house. Or I had been at one point, even if I wasn't a girl.

Some cultures believed you became a woman with your first bleed, others at fifteen, and then the last was when you rid yourself of your virginity.

Mine had been taken from me.

I would have died in the old opera house if it wasn't for the man who had taken me in and treated me like I was one of his own.

My eyes caught my reflection in my mirror, and I bit my lip. Without thinking much on if it was appropriate or not, I made my way to the patio.

Our summer house was not huge but more than big

enough for two people and the staff. It had a dock to park the yacht and a small landing for a helicopter.

I ran through the halls, waving good morning to all the staff. I stopped when I made it to the door and took a deep breath. It always failed. Not when the man behind the glass was so imposing, he seemed to take out all of the oxygen in any room he walked into.

Nicolas "Nico" Dos Santos was an enigma, a businessman with some questionable dealings. Scratch that—it was all questionable; I just did not ask about any of them. You didn't bite the hand that fed you, and in my case, you didn't bite the hand that saved you.

He heard my footsteps as I walked in, but he didn't look up from the newspaper he was reading. He sat at the head of the table with one leg bent at the knee and a Cuban cigar between his lips.

The way the sun shone at his hair made it seem like pure oil. He wore a white long-sleeve shirt rolled at the forearms, light gray pants tailored to perfection, and brown Hermès loafers.

On the floor on either side of him stood his two Dobermans, Joker and Bane. The dogs perked up when they heard me coming.

"Morning, Ofelia," he said without looking up in that deep voice I had loved since I was sixteen. I loved the way he said my name. The way he rolled his tongue when pronouncing the letter L. It gave me shivers.

To the world, I was like his daughter.

To me, he was my hero.

To him, I was an inconvenience.

"Hello, Daddy," I said in a low-pitched tone.

Nico took another drag of his cigar and turned the page

of his newspaper, and when he went to ash his cigar, only then did he look at me.

His eyes still looked like heaven. He looked much the same since I had first met him, except there were some crinkles around his eyes, and he now sported a full goatee.

And like everything he did, he made it seem classy and refined.

He wasn't amused by my choice of words. He was not my father, even if people thought he had adopted me.

He was thirty-three when he saved me. He could have taken me to a shelter or given me money to fend on my own, but instead, he brought me to live with him. Maybe he thought a daughter would make his corrupt empire seem less threatening.

"Little swan," he bit out with no malice in his voice. Whenever I resorted to calling him Daddy, he called me little swan so I wouldn't forget where I came from.

He found me a broken, bloody swan, and he made me into what I am now—a world-class ballerina in the most sold-out show of the modern era.

"Did you sleep okay?" he asked as he started scrolling through his phone.

"Sure."

He always asked me that question. When I first came to live with him, I had night terrors. I would wake up screaming bloody murder at night. I would end up being bruised and had even cut myself. Waking up with blood wasn't new nor odd.

It all stopped the moment Nico started to watch over me. He put a desk in the corner of my room, and he would work all night and keep an eye on me. His presence had soothed the demons that lived inside my soul.

More than once, he ended up hurt because I would try

to hurt him. To this day, he didn't like to talk about the things I did when I sleepwalked.

"Are you ready for tonight's show?" he asked casually.

Every year we came to relax by the sea, and we ended our vacation with a special performance from the company. Then our tour would begin. People came from all over the world to watch our play. Tchaikovsky had the right idea when he wrote *Swan Lake*. People were fascinated by a bit of darkness. They followed it like a moth to a flame. A dark heart was just a dark heart, something evil and rotten, but add a little bit of gold and it was suddenly art.

"Are you ready?" I retorted. "You call this a vacation, and I've hardly seen you take some downtime," I told him as I reached across the table to pick up the butter for my toast. My hand outstretched, and if he were to look up, he would have a perfect view of my cleavage.

As always, he ignored me. Without glancing my way, he grabbed the butter knife and handed it to me.

"Don't worry about me, Ofelia. I've told you this before."

"Isn't that what good little girls are supposed to do? Watch over their *daddies*?" The *daddy* rolled out of my mouth, laced with seduction.

"You're irritable this morning," he muttered, and I rolled my eyes.

"Will Delia be there?" I asked as I made a face.

One night sealed the fate of the three of us. At least Nico took me in; as for Delia, she went her own way. She wasn't as fucked-up as me. She didn't need him watching over her. I didn't mind her when we were younger, but she made it clear she was fascinated with Nico as we got older. It made me angry because he was my father figure, but my feelings for him went from platonic to sexual as I got older.

Nico looked up again and gave me another of his looks. He had a few, and all of them varied from slightly amused at me to irritated or angry.

"If Delia shows up, I just assumed you have invited her," he said.

My lips twisted in disgust at the idea. The only reason I tolerated Delia was because we danced for the same company—for *his* company. She'd been trying to take my spot since the day I met her.

"Trust me, Nicolas, if Delia shows up, it's not by my doing," I said as an afterthought.

"Now that I believe," he muttered as he reached for his black coffee. He made no comment of me calling him by his first name. The man was like Stonehenge. He was unshakable.

"Nico." Estevan, Nico's right-hand man and closest friend, walked outside toward us. "Missus Dos Santos."

I raised my left hand and wiggled my fingers at Estevan.

"Oh, look, no ring on my finger. Guess I'm not the missus of the house."

Estevan smirked at Nico as I said that. Nico glared at me. Like everything he did, it just made him seem that much sexier.

"Ignore her. She's throwing a tantrum."

I gaped at him.

"How?"

"You don't want to leave, but you also don't want to stay, so you do what brats do best, and you annoy."

"I'm going to kill you," I said as I pointed the butter knife at him.

Nico's face was stoic, not giving anything away. I felt the weight of his gaze on me. Those blue eyes blinded you if you gave them a chance.

He got up and fixed his shirt.

"Aren't little swans supposed to love their daddies?" he bit out with just a hint of humor.

My belly dipped, and I shifted in my seat, wondering if I was crazy or a total whore for getting just a bit damp between my legs because he was teasing me.

Estevan coughed a laugh into his hand, and I wanted to kill him for interrupting a precious moment.

"Where are you going?" I asked.

Nico was checking more emails on his phone as he answered me.

"You're not the missus of the house."

I raised my finger and flicked him off.

"Next time you flick me off, I might just break your bony finger," he said without looking back at me.

"Asshole."

To say Nico and I had a complicated relationship was like saying a tsunami was just a storm.

NICO WAS OFF DOING WHATEVER SORT OF THINGS HE did while he worked his day job. I didn't ask, and he never freely gave me an answer.

My feet hurt from practicing for hours straight with no break. Sometimes the thoughts in my mind were so loud the only way to drown them was with body-numbing pain.

I practiced every day because I wanted to be the best. I did it until my toes bled because it reminded me that everything came at a price, and I had already paid the ultimate one, so a little bit of blood wouldn't kill me. It wasn't like I hadn't done it before. The scars were there to prove it.

It wasn't until I fell from exhaustion that I noticed I

wasn't alone in the room anymore. Sitting in one of the chairs in the studio was Nico.

He sat there like a king, watching me fall at his feet before him. One of his legs was crossed over his ankle, resting on his other knee.

"You are overworking yourself, Ofelia," he said, his voice sounding docile, but his eyes were full of rage.

"I'm fine," I lied, even though I felt like throwing up from the rigorous exercise.

"That's why you're crawling on the floor? If you over-work yourself to the point where you can no longer walk, I will not have any need for you."

I glared at him, wishing I could say something back that could hurt him as much as losing lead role would hurt me.

"You'd love it, wouldn't you?" I spat back at him. "If Delia took my place?"

Nico gave me an impassive look. He tended to get annoyed whenever I mentioned her, and it made me wonder why.

Why did his face change when she was mentioned? Even if it was in annoyance, he never did that with me. When it came to me, he was like a blank canvas—something empty, boring.

She got a reaction out of him, even a negative one, and me, who had been by his side like a faithful dog, couldn't even get a fucking bone.

"And what would I like about that?"

He uncrossed his legs and sat forward. I felt the magnitude of his presence holding me down and not letting me gather enough strength to get up.

"You want her," I said between gritted teeth, hating the way my voice went low with jealousy.

Nico threw back his head and laughed.

My anger was forgotten only momentarily. I was mesmerized by the way his eyes crinkled at the side. How his age showed in those carefree moments when he wasn't all blank stares.

"*La mia ballerina*," he mocked. "I could be your father."

That was a lie; he was old, but not enough to be my father.

"But not Delia's," I stated.

"Same shit," he replied as he rose to his feet.

He walked until he was standing directly over me, and then he crouched. He was at eye level with me, so close, yet it felt like I could never reach him.

"Ice your feet, Ofelia, and don't overwork yourself."

I held my breath as he reached for me, my heart stopping to see what this man would do next. He touched my face, and I became aflame.

His fingertip grazed over my cheek, gliding down to my chin, and all I could do was pray that I didn't become a puddle of goo at his feet.

"Don't overwork yourself. You're of no use to me dead."

Nico wasn't soft, so he left me alone in my studio. He walked out without looking back. If I wanted to work myself to death, he would let me but not without a reminder of what I could lose by doing so.

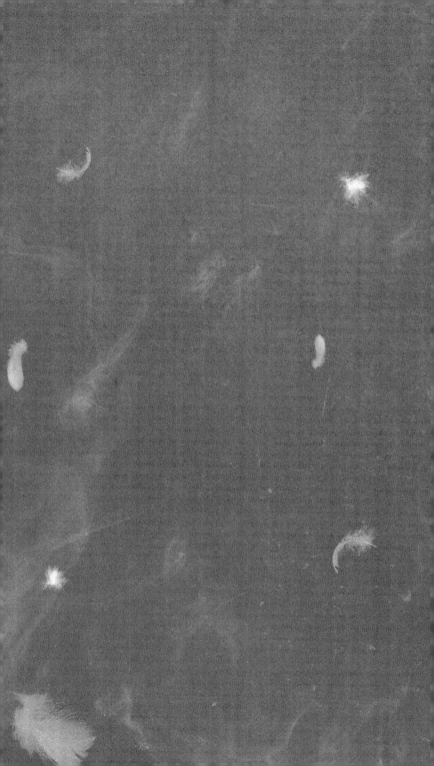

BLIND

See with your eyes and not with your heart.
For the mind is not blind to the feelings inside.

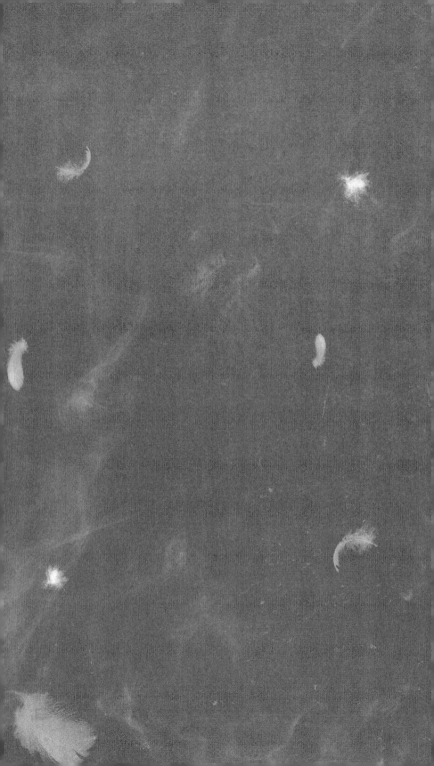

2

OFELIA

THE STARS ILLUMINATED THE NIGHT SKY, THE DOORS TO my balcony open as I changed for tonight's event. No one could see me from here; our house was the last one in the harbor, and all I could see was the sea.

I looked at myself in the mirror, and as always, I focused on my imperfections. It was easy to overlook the beauty in something so flawed.

My champagne dress made me look tanner. The sequins made me look like a shiny toy. The sleeves flared out below the elbows into long bell sleeves with tassels. There was a slit that stopped just below my right hip bone. My heels were champagne-colored from the sole, and the straps were see-through. Not your average stripper shoe, something a bit classier and more refined.

My long curls were tamed, and pink lip gloss stained my lips. My eyes went to my collarbone at how it stood out. I looked at myself a bit longer and forcefully smiled. There was no denying I cleaned up good. I just didn't enjoy looking at myself for long periods of time. I was sometimes scared at what stared back at me.

Looking at the clock on my wall, I knew I was already running late. Grabbing my wristlet, I made my way to the foyer where Nico would be waiting for me.

As soon as I made it to the first step, I saw him standing next to Estevan, a few of his men surrounding him.

We couldn't go anywhere without backup. The devil didn't have demons guarding hell for no reason, right? Same with Nico Dos Santos. He had a group of men ready to lie down and give their worthless lives for his.

I guess you could demand that from people when you were the king of the underworld.

The men all looked at me in awe as I made my way down the stairs. I was used to attention; it came with the territory of performing, so it was second nature to feel eyes on me. Still, it sometimes got uncomfortable when it was close to home or a group of men.

All of them looked at me except for Nico. He bent and started to give Joker and Bane commands.

He was their alpha—he was everyone's alpha around here.

"Aren't you going to say I look beautiful, da—"

Nico cut me off before I could finish my sentence.

"*Bellissima*," he said without looking at me.

"Awesome. I figured going naked was the way to go," I said as I put my right leg right in front of him.

I watched in fascination as he craned his neck and looked up at me. I felt his gaze like a soft caress running from my ankles up to my thighs, then my waist and the deep V between my breasts.

Nico's blue eyes were dark. His eyes didn't look like heaven anymore but like they were ready to storm.

I felt thrilled. Sometimes I felt like I lived for his reactions.

"Are you ready to go, or should I wait another hour for you? I'm sure we can postpone," he drawled in a lazy tone.

I bit the inside of my cheeks.

God, this man was infuriating. I'd get more of a reaction from a blow-up doll.

Smiling sweetly at him, I extended my hand for him to take.

He shook his head, but I could almost make out the ghost of a smile.

This time I bit my lip as I waited for him to get up.

He did and fixed the button on his black tux. Since he had yet to take my outstretched hand, I used it to pet Joker and Bane. The dogs loved me. Nico gave one command to the dogs, and they took off like two hounds of hell. Probably to go check the perimeter before we did.

Nico looked at my outstretched hand and ignored it. He motioned for me to take a step forward. Sighing, I did as he asked. Just as I had taken a step, he put his hand on the small of my back.

"I don't have to remind you to be on your best behavior, do I, little swan?" Nico asked as he led me to the front, where there was a limo waiting for us.

He gestured for the driver to stay put, and instead, he opened the door for me.

"Ofelia?" he said my name between gritted teeth, waiting for my answer.

"Don't I always behave?" I shrugged it off.

Nico put pressure on my back, causing me to fall into the limousine face-first.

"If you did, we wouldn't be having this conversation."

I scoffed but smiled when I realized my ass was in the air, giving Nico a perfect view of it.

"You do realize your men can see my ass, right?" I asked as I slid inside and made my way across the seat.

Nico didn't speak until he closed the door.

"My men get paid to watch our backs, not your ass," he answered confidently.

"My ass is in my back." I turned and smiled sweetly at him.

He pressed the button and put the partition up.

"Unless they want to lose their eyes, they don't look at you—ever."

My mouth parted open in surprise. I mean, I always thought Nico's men were too scared of him to talk to me. Now that made a little more sense.

"There's a man..." Nico started to say, and my stomach dipped.

This was it. This was going to be the moment he was going to ask me to pay him back for everything he had done for me by getting on my knees.

Nico stopped what he was saying and turned his profile so he could look at me.

"What's wrong, Ofelia?"

I swallowed and shook my head.

"Nothing," I said in a tense tone. "What do you want me to do with this man?"

He gave me an odd look, not getting why I was suddenly uncomfortable.

"I want you to charm him," he said, and my heart stopped for a second in relief.

"Charm him?" I asked.

"He loves the play, but more importantly, he loves you in it."

This was no surprise. I was everyone's favorite ballerina.

Dance for me, my little ballerina. Show me that I made the right choice in saving you. "Ofelia."

"Ofelia." Nico's voice was harsher this time. I blinked a few times and shook my head before I got lost in a voice from the past. I swear I could still feel him when I danced. Felt his praise on my skin like acid.

"*Stai bene?*" he asked if I was okay.

"Everyone likes a little ballerina," I spat as the car came to a halt. Something passed over his features, but I didn't stay long enough to figure it out. Instead, I opened my door and walked into the building.

It was always the same with the rich. They tended to gravitate toward each other like blind little sheep. They liked to pretend that they wanted danger and living in the fast lane until the speed of it scared them.

People waved and smiled at me. When a waiter passed by, I grabbed a champagne flute and nodded. Life in the spotlight wasn't always what it seemed, but at least this way, people were blinded by the light. They couldn't see the stains that it covered up.

Nico walked in, and people stopped and stared at him, admiring him from afar. I rolled my eyes at the amount of attention he got from women. All of them would give up the dates they had come with for a night with him.

"Ofelia," Nico said in a warning tone as he came and put an arm around my waist. His fingers dug into my hip. Asshole. "There's a friend I would like you to meet."

We smiled at the guest as we passed by them. We were a formidable father-and-daughter duo. A power couple, just not the one I had envisioned.

"Is everything okay?" He leaned his head down so he could whisper in my ear. His lips brushed against the shell, causing me to suppress shivers.

"Everything is fine," I lied. "Let's go pimp me out."

I didn't even get a step out when Nico pulled me back. His fingers were now digging even more into my hips that I could feel the nails biting into my skin.

"Is that what you think I am doing, Ofelia?" he asked between gritted teeth.

"Yes," I was quick to reply.

Before I could take another step, Nico's grasp on me was like steel. His face came down with a smile so party-goers wouldn't get alarmed.

"My little swan, I don't know what has gotten into you today, but know that the short leash you have around that fragile neck is held by me. I've never asked you to do anything degrading."

My face twisted in remorse because he was right; however, when Nico Dos Santos wanted to, he could be a ruthless asshole.

"Now, if I asked you to kneel down and suck dick, your response should be how long, and should I deep-throat?"

"You're an asshole," I said as I took a step back, ready to go meet his associates.

"And you're a bitch assuming I'd ever ask that of you."

That's when I heard the hurt in his voice, but before I could say more, he led me to the back where a lone table stood. Two men and a woman were already sitting down.

There was one more chair, and Nico motioned for me to take it. I sat down and bent as I did it, letting the men at the table get a good look at my cleavage. The woman at the table was in her forties. Face full of fillers and Botox, a total cougar if I may say so.

"You are a very beautiful woman," the older of the two men said with a heavy accent. He was a bit round and his hair already graying. He looked at me like a leech looked at blood, ready to strike and start sucking the life out of me.

I hid my disgust and smiled at him.

"Thank you for coming," I said in a sweet innocent voice.

Nico positioned himself right behind me and put his hands on either side of my neck, standing behind me like the guardian he so desperately tried to pretend he wasn't.

The other man was younger, maybe around my age. With bronze hair and matching eyes, dare I say he looked almost kind. He gave me a small smile.

"Ofelia," Nico said as he motioned for the older man. "This is Emilio and his wife, Fernanda."

I extended my hand so I could shake theirs. I had already guessed from Emilio's accent that he was a Spaniard.

"This is Alejandro."

"My pleasure," I told them. "Are you excited for the play?"

"We never miss it," Mrs. Botox said. "Every time I watch you on the stage, I get chills. The emotion, the rawness... How can someone so young and beautiful be something so ugly and scary."

"Death has many faces," I replied automatically. "A spider, a snake, a frog, a scorpion; all of them are different sizes but are capable of killing you."

"You forgot Homo sapiens," Alejandro said with a chuckle. He turned his profile, and something in me stirred. I blinked a couple of times before I carried on. This was not the moment to have revelations.

"True, but animals kill when they feel threatened. Humans more often than not do it for sport."

Nico put his hand on the back of my neck in warning.

He probably wanted me to steer the conversation else-where. It probably hit too close to home for him.

"Pardon me for staring, but I am in awe of your beauty," Emilio said. I maintained a small smile as his wife glared at me. What a fucking pig. "How can you even call her your daughter?"

I had to suppress a snort. I could feel the tension coming from Nico, and I couldn't help but mess with him. I brought my hand up and grabbed one of his.

"Nico is the best *daddy* I could have asked for."

Alejandro did snort, and when I looked up at Nico, I could see he was gritting his teeth.

"It's time for you to get ready, Bambina."

My throat constricted. I hated when he called me child more than when he called me little swan. At least when he called me a swan, he said it with some form of respect.

"I hope you enjoy the ballet," I said as I got up to leave.

"Trust us, we will."

I glared at Nico as I walked as fast as I could away from that sicko.

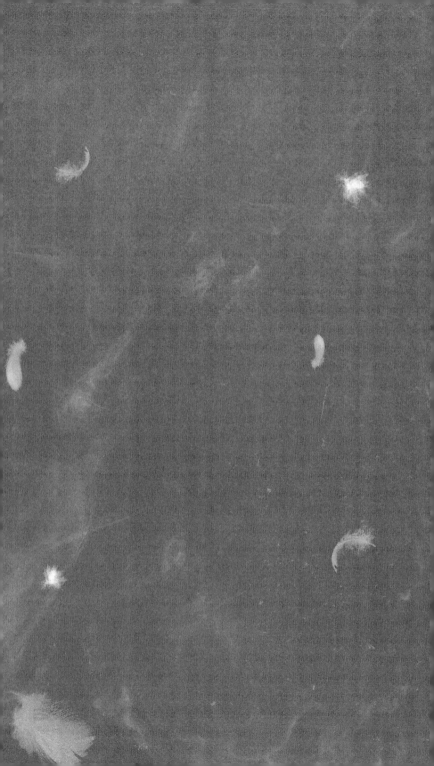

FACES

She is soft but not fragile.
She is death but not deadly.
She is wild but not crazy.
She is just one of many faces.

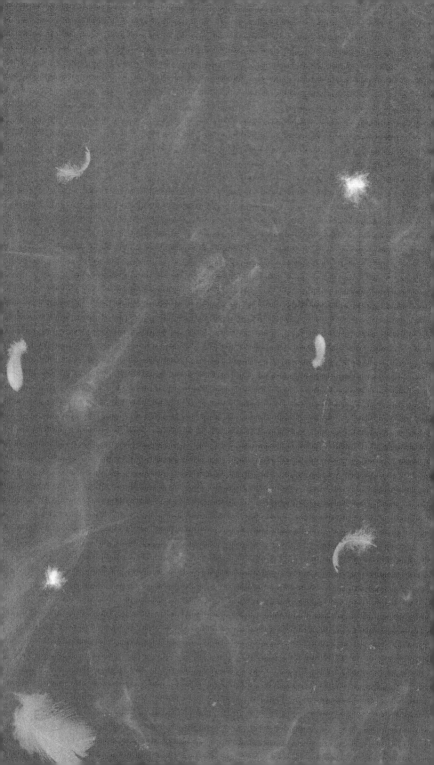

Since my night was already going to shit, I wasn't surprised when Delia walked in. I was standing by the sink and had just poured a bit of cold water on my face. My lips instantly curled in disgust. While I went with something more tasteful with my dress, she dressed in all white.

The V of her dress was deeper than mine.

"Ah, you look adorable," she said in a mocking tone as she made her way over to me.

"You look like a whore," I told her.

"You wished you looked this good, Lia, don't kid yourself."

"Unlike you, I have class. It might do you good to get some."

Delia smiled at me. Her red lips were perfectly even on the top and the bottom. If she wasn't so good-looking, I might hate her a little less.

"Maybe I will buy some when I finally take your spot," she said as she turned around. "And while I'm at it, I'll fuck your daddy too."

My hands moved furiously, trying to find an object to

throw at her. When I finally had an item in my hand, she was already gone.

It was not my fault Nico chose to take care of me over her. That he fought to keep me under his care while he was content to watch her from afar. Then my thoughts took a dark tone, but I shook it off as soon as it entered.

There was no way he would want her over me. We were both children, and Nico wasn't like the men who had been at the opera house.

I don't remember much from my time with my master, just what Nico told me and the things that were ingrained in me that I had never forgotten. I had been a slave, and I had not lived a happy childhood. It would explain my fascination with all the morbid things, why I found beauty in things that were barely beating.

Taking a deep breath, I made my way outside and wandered to where they had made the makeshift stage for today's party.

Rich people always paid an excessive amount of money for their entertainment, and here I was, a hamster in its wheel.

When I arrived at the room where we would change, I was pleasantly surprised to see that most of the crew was already there.

I got along with mostly everyone; the people I didn't get along with were because they were Delia fans.

Most of the dancers kept their distance from me because of Nico. He was the founder of this company, so to most of the dancers, I was sure my spot wasn't earned but given to me because of the man whose house I lived in.

I didn't let that get to me. When it came to most humans, there was never a right answer, so we might as well do what we loved and ignore the hate.

Once I was changed, I walked out with my head held high. Everyone was wearing different shades of whites and beiges, while I was the only one in all black.

This was just a small preview, not the whole play—just something to go along with while they ate their dessert.

When we walked back out to the ballroom, the lights had been turned off, so when they turned on again, we would be on the dance floor.

"Break a leg, Ofelia." Delia's whisper echoed in my ears.

My hands fisted, and anger spread through my veins. I was surprised with the amount of rage I carried had yet to poison my heart.

She would just love it if she could take my life. She would no longer live in my shadow.

I took my spot in the center of the cast and waited for them to introduce us. The lights slowly turned on but stayed dim enough that we didn't have to see people's faces.

What doesn't kill you makes you stronger, but there's just some toxic shit that instead makes you addicted. At least that's how I felt about my dancing. It was something I'd been doing for as long as I could remember. It was part of who I was, but my dancing cursed me.

Spin, my little ballerina, spin.

You could say I'd been spinning ever since. My legs moved, and I made my way across the floor, smiling and grinning because this was a more intimate setting, and I got to interact with them in hopes of donations.

The rich loved helping "a good cause." The sad thing was that the causes that actually needed the money never saw a dime.

I felt itchy the moment I made it to Nico's table. Unwanted gazes felt like fleas on your skin. I made sure to give them my best moves. There was now another man at that table, and my head cocked, trying to see him better.

I would have kept staring at him longer, but my eyes met Nico's, and he did not seem pleased. His jaw was hard, and he was glaring at the old man, who kept watching me like I was his appetizer, main course, and dessert.

Nico's head turned to me, and his eyes scanned me from the top of my head down to where I was in a deep bow.

With his eyes, he motioned for me to go to the next table.

It was rare, but sometimes when he commanded things, I listened. If he asked me to kneel down and suck his dick, then I would ask for how long and if he wanted me to gag on it.

One could dream.

We finished our set quickly since this was just a preview to entice them for more. I stood in the center as everyone around me was already "dead" when the applause broke.

As soon as we were done bowing, I made my way back so I could change.

The show ended, and people clapped. They cheered and thanked us for being here with them and giving them the first show of the season.

Delia glared at me, but I ignored her.

After the show was over, many of the dancers went to mingle with the people, and before I could go and do the same, I got pulled back.

Estevan was right there with a *don't fuck with me* attitude.

"It's time to go, little dancer," he told me.

I tried to pull away, but he didn't let me. I couldn't be

the darling of the ball if I wasn't there thanking every person.

"What the hell is going on?" I asked.

"Nothing for you to worry about," he replied as he continued to drag me with him.

He took me out through the back, and I was surprised to find the car already waiting for us.

When Estevan opened the door, Nico was already waiting in his seat.

He did not look any happier than Estevan.

"Is something wrong?" I asked.

"We're leaving," Nico said.

"Yeah, I get that," I mocked, gesturing to the theater.

"No, we are leaving the island right now."

I stood up straighter, my gaze intently on Nico while he typed furiously on his phone.

"All my stuff is still at the house," I said, even though I wasn't attached to anything.

"We can get more. The staff is clearing out, and someone is already grabbing Joker and Bane."

I nodded and sat back on the seat, trying to relax and wondering what could have gone wrong. It seemed like we were running, but the Nico I knew wouldn't run away from anyone.

When we got to the airstrip, his men were already waiting. Estevan pulled the car to a stop and then dragged me out while Nico headed for his men.

They left me alone on the plane, and after everything that had gone down today, I crashed.

EVERY PART OF MY BODY ACHED. I COULD BARELY MOVE, pain radiating from my legs. My neck was sore, and even moving my arms burned.

I didn't remember much about what happened in the theater. It seemed like it had been only yesterday, but the doctor informed me this had been a few days ago.

When I closed my eyes, I saw things I would rather not see and heard things I wished to never have directed at me.

I thought the saddest day of my young life had been the day my parents sold me, but that had not been the case.

Something had happened to me, but I didn't quite recall. I just knew that every time I closed my eyes, I would see red. My ears rang with curses and screeches.

The door opened, and I brought the soft cotton blanket I had been holding up to my mouth. The smell of lavender that was being emitted from the cotton soothed me.

I recognized the man who walked in. He had been the dark angel who had been in my master's room—the one with the blue eyes.

He spoke to me in our native tongue. "Are you okay?"

I looked at him, not knowing if I should speak. I wondered if he was my new master.

"You are safe now," he said as he took a tentative step forward.

Safe? What was safety? My old master took me away from a life of poverty and hunger, but at the cost of my family. In the end, they weren't very loving, but they were all I had.

Dancing was all I had. I was a poor girl with talent, and my master gave me the tools to become better, but he made sure I had to bleed for it. He made me dance until my toes bled and blisters covered my feet. He got a sick thrill from the pain dancing cost me.

The man stopped until he was next to me. He crouched down and got at eye level with me and cocked his head, examining me.

"Don't worry, little dancer, you are safe now," he said, but it sounded like a vow.

I nodded at him because I wasn't sure if I could muster enough energy to speak.

When he left my room, I vowed that I would be the best dancer the world had ever seen. If dancing saved my life, not once but twice, I was willing to kill myself to prove to the world I was worthy of being saved.

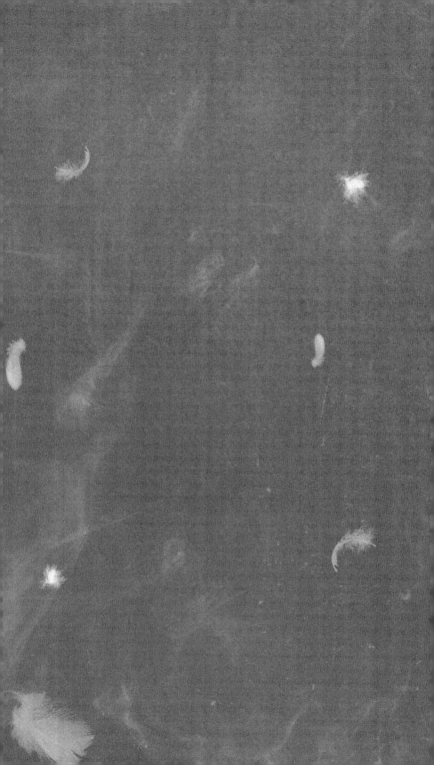

BREAKPOINTS

All of the worst moments of our lives have a starting point.
They have a beginning and sometimes an end,
but the truth is the more you revisit it inside of your head,
the closer you'll get to it being dead.
When you reach that breaking point,
then that horrible moment will finally fade.

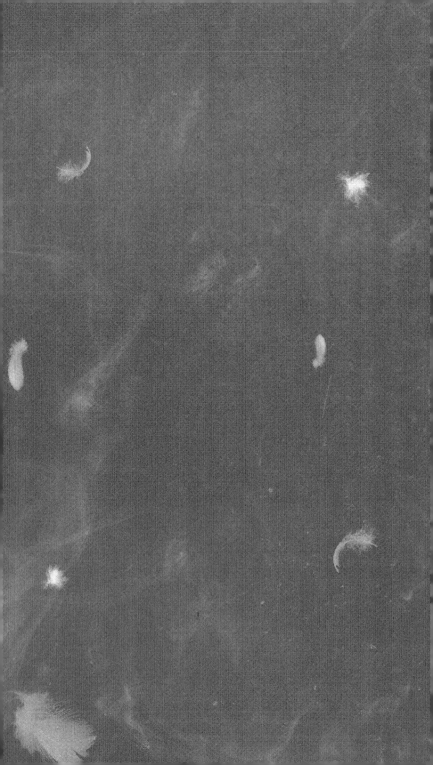

4

OFELIA

I woke up covered in dog saliva. When my eyes sprang open, Bane was licking my face while Joker nudged my side so I could wake up. The dog's master was standing, and he looked down at me.

"We are here," he said.

"Where is here?" I asked, my voice still sounding groggy.

"We are starting the tour in Italy this time," he said as he fixed his jacket.

"But we always end it here? What's changed?"

I pretended not to look at Nico, for I knew he hated being questioned because his word was law at the end of the day, and we all did what we were told to do. Instead, I petted Bane since he was the friendlier of the two dogs.

A couple of years ago, we got them when I had an incident, and Nico felt like I needed something more than a human watching my back. Joker and Bane had been part of our little fucked-up family ever since.

"You worry about dancing, and leave the rest to me," Nico said. It was something he had to remind me of from time to time. More now that I seemed to question every-thing he did.

I rolled my eyes at him, and Nico shook his head and walked away.

"Home sweet fucking home," I whispered.

You could run as fast as you wanted, but the past always caught up to you. That's how I felt every time I came back to Italy.

Everything that went wrong with my life started here, and I hated being reminded of it.

"Off we go, boys," I told both the dogs.

When I got up, I remembered I was still in my dancing clothes. I scoffed but kept making my way out of the jet.

The Tuscany sun was already scalding.

I glared down at where Nico was already standing with a few of his men.

Here in this light, in this place, he looked like a god.

The thing no one liked to talk about deities is that they too eventually faded. And something was bothering Nico enough to have us rearrange all of our plans.

"Estevan, Ricky, Dino." I smiled at the men who stood next to Nico.

They had been part of Nico's security detail since I could remember. At first, I was shy and hesitant around them, but since they never gave me the creep factor, it became easy to trust them.

They all greeted me without actually looking me in the eyes. They rarely did. Nico's word from yesterday now made more sense. His men didn't get paid to pay me any attention.

"Let's go, Ofelia. We have a few things to discuss before we get to the house."

Because I still hadn't had my morning coffee and felt like being sassy, I saluted him.

"Yes, Daddy."

His men scoffed, trying to hide their laughter, and Nico glared at them and then at me.

"Do not toy with me, my little ballerina. I am not in the mood for games today."

The thing was, I wanted to toy with him, and bad. I bit my lip for a second, wondering what would happen if I did push him over the edge?

"That's too bad. I was in the mood to play," I said in a sultry voice.

Nico didn't miss a beat. He opened the door to the black sedan. The only reason I knew I had affected him was by the way his fingers dug into the skin at my back.

"Daddy, you're hurting me," I whined.

Before I could slide in the car, I got pulled back, and the door slammed shut. Lust spread through my veins, and I wondered if this was the day Nico finally snapped.

My back hit the door hard, making me ache. That was nothing compared to the way Nico held on to my jaw. He had me in a tight grip to make sure I was looking at him.

My heart was trying to beat out of my chest; all the while I tried to remain aloof.

"Listen up, Ofelia, because I won't be saying this more than once," Nico spat through gritted teeth. "As of right now, you become the loving little daughter you always taunt you'll be."

I raised my brow in surprise but had to remain quiet since Nico made sure I couldn't speak.

"Some...complications arose, and that means I have a few eyes on me, which means you'll have even more eyes on you on this tour. What I don't need is your smart-ass little mouth questioning every move I make."

I never thought I'd see the day Nico Dos Santos was rattled, and I liked it. It made him seem human—attainable. It made me feel like he was finally within my reach.

"You understand?" he said as he brought his head down but not close enough to make our foreheads touch.

That was like Nico. Showing enough affection but not enough that I could bask in it.

When I didn't answer, he loosened the hold he had on my jaw.

"Are we safe?" I asked, even though the answer scared me.

Nico stared at me, and his blue eyes flashed, but then his face softened for a second. I stopped breathing the moment I saw his hand reach out to me, but this time much gentler than before.

He cupped my cheek tenderly, and with his thumb, he traced the path he had gripped earlier.

"No matter what happens to me, I'll make sure you are safe."

My stomach dropped.

"I don't want anything to happen to you," I said in a low voice.

Nico grinned at me.

"Don't worry about me, my little swan. You just keep dancing, and everything will be alright."

EVERYTHING WAS NOT ALRIGHT. As soon as we arrived at Nico's house, I noticed the detail he usually carried around had doubled. To this, Nico acted like everything was alright. Since our talks were getting us nowhere, I decided not to comment on what I had observed.

"Will the schedule be the same, or will we be staying here longer?" I asked as we made our way inside his home.

Nico fixed his suit and then turned to look down at me. "It doesn't matter at the end of the day. You do as you are told."

My blood boiled, and anger simmered through my body. It was one thing for him to speak to me like a child when I was one, but I was a woman now. Regardless of his feelings for me, he needed to start treating me with some respect. I might not be his daughter, but I had been with him almost as long as some of his most trusted men, and I deserved the decency to know what was going on in my home.

It could be that Bane and Joker knew more about what was going on around here than I did. I got it. I was the poor little girl he rescued, but this poor little girl had made him millions of dollars in sold-out shows.

Without thinking, I yanked him back by his shoulders. Nico was surprised by my actions. He looked at my hand and me, not quite believing I got physical with him.

"Ofelia," he said slowly, almost in a warning tone.

"Don't Ofelia me, you jerk!" I spat at him. "Something is wrong, and I think I deserve to know what it is."

Before he could say anything, Estevan stepped out from behind me and called to him.

"Nico, your guest has arrived."

"Fuck," Nico said as he ran a hand over his hair.

"Are we entertaining company?" I asked as I batted my lashes at Estevan.

Estevan grinned at me. "I think the bossman would prefer it if you went and unpacked for now."

"That won't be necessary," Nico said. "We won't be staying here for long."

This actually thrilled me. I hated being back home, and the less time I spent in this shithole, the better.

"You know, Daddy, you should have said that to begin with," I said with glee.

Nico gave me a dry look, and Estevan chuckled.

"You—" Nico looked at me. "—go practice. It will be a big night next week, and I want everything to be perfect."

I rolled my eyes.

When wasn't I perfect?

"Estevan, bring my guest to my office once Ofelia leaves."

Estevan and I stayed rooted in the same spot while Nico walked away. I turned toward the foyer, wondering who had come to the house.

"Is it anyone important?" I asked Estevan.

He smiled at me. Out of all of Nico's men, he was my favorite. He was dangerous but always kind to me, and then there was the fact that he always teased Nico, and no one ever really did that. It was nice seeing Nico have friends. Since most of our time was spent on the road, I think it had been proven I was not Nico's favorite company.

"I don't think that's something Nico wants you to worry about."

I made a face at him.

"Nico would love it if I did nothing but pirouette my way around the house."

"Ofelia," he said, sounding serious.

I looked up at the man. He was built like a damn truck with broad shoulders and thick thighs. He was the one who was always with us. When you had him, you really didn't need anyone else.

I looked into his hazel eyes.

"Yes?"

"I know you're not stupid, so don't go pushing Nico further than he's willing to be pushed."

Before I could give a smart-ass comment, he spoke again.

"Just remember that everything that man does, he does it for you."

Confusion was written all over my face.

Estevan tapped my nose and smiled at me.

"Now run along, little swan. The grown-ups need to talk."

I backed away as I flicked him off, to which he just chuckled.

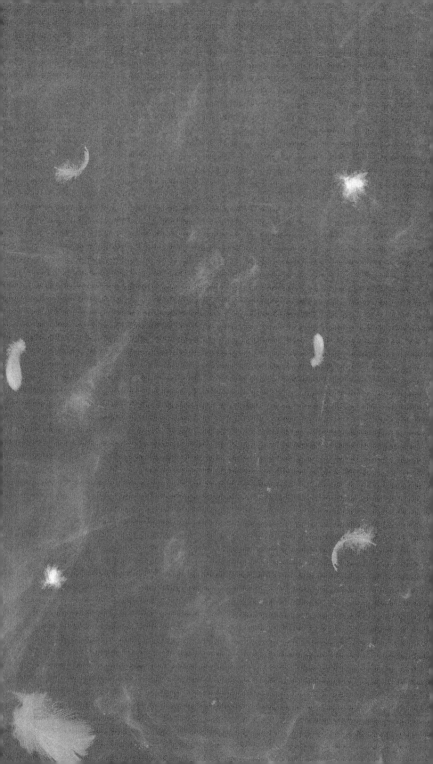

5

NICO

My body was calm at the moment, but my mind was a raging sea of emotions. My life consisted of being on my toes twenty-four seven, and if I was being honest, it was getting quite exhausting.

The higher you climbed to the top, the more you had to watch your step because any little slip made you fall. I'd worked my ass off for years, and I was so close to reaching the peak, I could almost taste it.

Much like Ofelia, I hated being back in Italy. This was our home, but it had brought nothing but pain and deception to us both.

When I got the order to change my course, I immediately had a feeling something was already wrong, and I hated unknown variables.

There was a knock on my office door, and I knew it was Estevan letting me know that he was here. I stood behind my desk, appearing the poster boy of aloofness.

"Geraldo," I greeted the young man. He looked at me like I was beneath him, but this was nothing new. He looked at everyone like they were scum beneath his shoes.

He thought he was better than everyone else because he came from an old Italian monarchy that somehow his blood was now blue. His would-have-been titles were meaningless.

He was younger than me, but he was not wiser. His arrogance was his biggest flaw and my biggest advantage.

"Nicolas," he greeted me in a bored tone.

I grabbed the bottle of my best whiskey and two ice cubes from the tray I had brought up here earlier.

"To what do I owe this pleasure?" I asked him. "It is not like you to want to change the dates of our tour."

"Some things arose, and I needed my shipment out of the country much sooner than expected."

I sat down and swirled the ice cubes in my drink.

"That's going to cost you double," I told him.

"You know money is not an issue for me," he spat.

That much was true. Money was not an issue for him, but as someone who had to claw their way up to the top, I knew money was not everything. This boy had been eating with a golden spoon since birth. He didn't know the meaning of life.

He was the media's golden child, but they didn't know what really lurked behind those dark eyes of his.

"Where do you want your shipment to go?" I asked, humoring him.

I had one goal, and I would do whatever it was to get it.

"Not far," he replied.

I raised a brow and cocked my head for him to continue.

"Just London."

My interest was piqued.

"If I do that, I have to start my tour backward and end it in Russia, and I'm afraid that won't make them happy."

"Don't forget how you got to where you are!"

Estevan's body twitched. He was ready to strike if I gave the order.

I didn't let Geraldo's tone get to me.

"If my memory serves me correctly, it was your father who granted me clearance once to cover up for your indiscretions. Now I have my own means to fly around the world undetected. But alas, I have a child too, and I know you all tend to speak before you think. So, make it worth my while, and I will do you a favor." I took a sip of my drink and smirked at him. "Of course, payment will still be required, but it's a favor nonetheless."

Geraldo was shooting daggers at me, but he needed me. Eventually, everyone did.

There were certain people and organizations that everyone knew about, and, well, I was one of them. My ballet company got funded off blood money. And if you were wondering if it bothered me, the answer was no. I'd been scalded by blood all of my life, so if I was going to get hurt, I'd rather decide the way it was going to burn.

"I'll pay anything," he said, sounding desperate.

"Bring the merchandise to the theater. We will be leaving immediately right after the show."

Geraldo smiled at me.

"Well then, Shipper, it was a pleasure doing business with you."

I ignored his comment.

It was what most people liked to call me—the Shipper. I didn't mind it, nor did I care for it. It was just a name, and I knew names held meaning. I could get anything delivered anywhere in the world without getting back to the person who was sending it. It meant I was putting my life on the line for them.

I nodded at Geraldo and motioned for Estevan to see him out. Meanwhile, I planned what would happen next.

The sins of our past are what shapes us, and mine had scarred me beyond recognition.

Before Geraldo walked out of the door, he turned to look back at me and smiled. "I heard Alejandro met your prized swan."

Anger spread through my veins, but I forced myself to not make any type of reaction. If the world knew I had a weakness, that would be it. I would be signing my own death.

"And if you stop annoying me, then maybe you'll get to meet her too," I forced myself to reply. Like those words didn't cost me to say. Like the mere thought of anyone putting their hands on Ofelia didn't make me go apeshit.

"Now I can't wait for the play." The slimy fucker smiled.

Estevan already knew I was about to fucking lose it, so he pulled him away before revealing that I had one weakness.

I poured myself another drink when something in the backyard caught my attention. It wasn't the garden that cost thousands to upkeep or the marble statues that surrounded said statues.

My hand gripped the cup tighter while my eyes feasted on the way Ofelia moved around the patio.

There was no word to describe her. She looked magical —like a fairy or an angel just gliding around my home.

In these moments, I felt like shit because if she was an angel, then I was the devil, and I should have felt guilty for keeping her trapped in my hell, but I couldn't bring myself to get rid of her.

I remembered the day I met her. She was so small, bony,

and scared, but there was something about the way she danced. How she fed off her own fear and made it seem beautiful. The first time I saw her, she reminded me why I was in that room with all of those men. I wanted revenge, and seeing her gave me some sort of peace that I was doing the right thing.

Now I told myself the same thing repeatedly that I had Ofelia's wings clipped so I could keep her safe, but the more time she spent with me, she was at risk.

At this point, setting her free would only get her killed.

I brought the amber drink to my lips as I watched her twirl. My gaze drifted from her hands down to her shapely legs, and I hated the way my stomach coiled.

In some moments, I saw the young broken girl I had brought back with me from that horrible meet. At other times, I saw the woman she had become, and then there was the last side of her that I rarely liked to think about.

"He's gone." Estevan walked in and closed the door to my office.

I gave one last look at Ofelia, but it was pointless. I had already committed all her features to memory.

"Do any of the men have any information on why that little shit wants me to make a flesh shipment?"

Estevan sat down on the chair across from my desk. He had been with me since the beginning. He was as invested in this as I was. We both had a score to settle, and he was more than happy to let me be the face of our front while he did most of the dirty work.

"You know how he likes his girls," Estevan said with disgust, because "girls" was the appropriate terminology to use when it came to Geraldo. "Rumor is he touched someone he shouldn't have, and her family will cause a media storm. He wants her to disappear."

"And what better way to do it than funneling her through his other business. No body for him to worry about, and when and if she is found out, it won't be in this country."

That was how my ballet company got started. I had the talent, and I just needed the money and the passage. The idea seemed crazy at first, but Geraldo's father had been desperate to make a problem disappear. And I was more than eager to finally have a way to get my revenge that selling my soul didn't even faze me. No one would ever think that the famous *danza dei morti* was just a lucrative front to what really happened behind the scenes.

Estevan nodded, having come to the same conclusion as I had.

"What about his interest in Ofelia?" he asked, cocking his head to better look at me.

"What about it?" I said, sounding aloof.

Estevan scoffed.

"What happened to Diana was a long time ago. You are allowed to heal."

I glared at him.

"I get laid just fine."

"And you're still a miserable piece of shit."

This time when I looked at him, he was grinning.

"All I'm saying is that she's not a little girl anymore, and you ain't her father."

"I've raised her."

Estevan got up from his seat and walked over to the window where Ofelia was still practicing.

"Well, I hope you keep that same attitude in a couple days. I know you have seen the signs already, and it's coming."

"I want everyone to clear out at a moment's notice when that happens," I replied without looking at him.

The fucker left my office laughing.

He was the only one who could get away with it. He was like my brother. Our sisters used to be best friends. When we were little, they tried to take us on playdates together, but we despised each other on the spot when we met.

Now I couldn't imagine doing all of this without him.

Revenge was almost here. I could taste it, and Ofelia was one of the pieces to the puzzle; she just didn't know it, at least not yet.

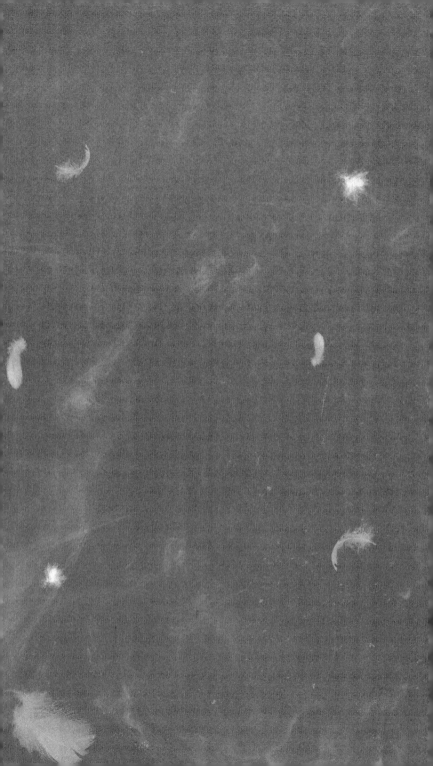

CONTROL

WHY DOES IT SOMETIMES FEEL LIKE OUR BODIES FAIL us? In those moments that we are at our weakest, we feel like we are crumbling. There's not enough air in the room, not enough space, to contain all those raging emotions that are coming in waves. Why is it that when we most need a solid pillar to hold on to, we end up losing control?

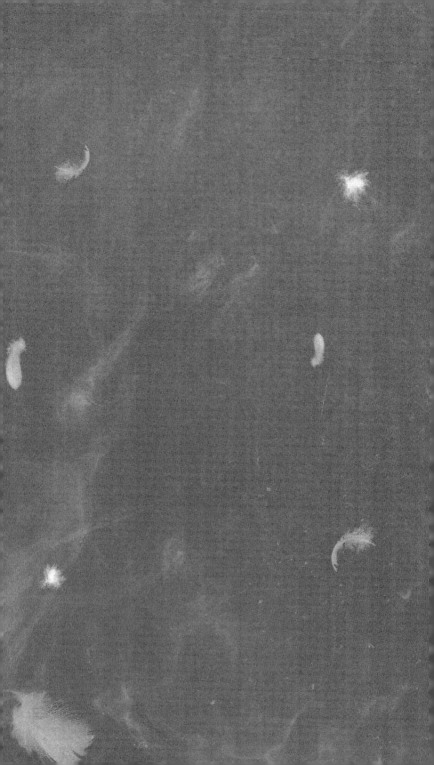

6

OFELIA

EVER SINCE I COULD REMEMBER, I'D HAD THESE anxiety attacks. I knew they were getting worse when my insomnia would flare, and my days were filled with dread. Then my body would get so exhausted between no sleep and practice that I tended to crash.

I hated that feeling because it felt like I slept for days, and I always woke up disorientated.

Right now, I sat at the dining table on the outside patio that overlooked the ocean. My leg was crossed at the knee and bouncing uncontrollably. In my right hand, I held on to a cigarette and a coffee cup in the other.

Probably not the best choice to drink coffee, but my nights were getting restless. If I wanted to get some practice, I would need all the energy I could get, even if it came with a side of feeling like I might fucking die.

I had just taken a drag off the cigarette when Nico walked outside.

He glared at me as soon as he saw the stick between my lips.

"That's going to kill you," he said.

"I learned from you, *Daddy*," I said in a snippy tone.

His head turned, and he gave me a look. I wouldn't exactly call it heated, but it was something. Not entirely fatherly but not full-on lust, and that made me smile at him.

My eyes trailed down his back as he made his way to his chair. He wore a white linen shirt and navy blue shorts with another pair of brown loafers.

Nico exuded raw masculinity. He didn't look douchey. He looked like he belonged on the cover of magazines.

"If it gets out that you smoke like a chimney, your spot will be given to someone else," Nico said dismissively.

I choked on the smoke at the mere thought of that happening. I could imagine Delia smiling at me from the center stage for stealing my spot.

"That's never going to happen," I vowed.

Nico ignored this as he poured himself some water.

"Are you having trouble sleeping?" he asked in a calm, docile voice that made my insides melt.

It was rather confusing what I felt for him at times. Sometimes I wanted to ride him in the chair where he sat, and other times, I just wanted to bask in his warmth. I blamed my lack of parental guidance.

"It will pass," I said. "I think it's the change in the schedule or being in this fucking hellhole."

Nico was barely taking a drink, but I think my answer caught him off guard. He brought the cup down with more force than necessary, and those blue eyes pinned me down.

"Are you unhappy, Ofelia?"

This time it was me who was at a loss for words. In all the years, he'd never taken into account my opinion or my happiness. I guess I just followed along because he was all I had.

I took a drag of my cigarette before answering his question.

"No," I finally said. "I'm not anything. I don't take those types of feelings into consideration. I am grateful. I have a roof over my head, a pillow to rest my head on each night... and I have you."

Those azure eyes beamed with my last statement.

"I know I annoy you and you probably detest me at times, but the truth is that you have done for me more than anyone who was blood-related has ever done."

Nico took a moment before he replied.

"I don't detest you," he said in a low tone, as if he hated saying that aloud.

His words eased my anxiety for a second. His words stilled time. I hated myself for being so desperate for affection that I became transparent in my emotions when it was given to me.

"If you want to leave the company, you can. You don't have to dance anymore. I will still provide for you. I'll always provide for you."

We had never talked about this, about my hopes and dreams or anything that had to do with a future.

"And what would I do? All I know is how to dance."

"You're still young. You can do whatever you want to do."

He meant it. He was willing to let me go and find my own way in the world, but that scared me. I lived my life like a ballerina in a music box, only coming alive when its master wanted it to dance.

"What about you? You have more than enough to retire by now, don't you?"

A serious look crossed over Nico's features.

"Leaving is not as easy for me as it's for you, little swan."

"We can always run away," I said, eager to have any fresh start, mainly if it consisted of him coming with me.

"I'm not leaving," he said, his tone sounding final. "I can't leave."

It was my turn to stare at him. To really look and read what he was saying between the lines. He looked tired like he would rather not be living the life we did. I knew what he did was dangerous. You didn't carry bodyguards with you without reason, but I had been selfish enough not to pay it much attention. Except it was harder to do the older I got, and my life stared at me right in the face.

I grabbed my cup of coffee and raised it toward him. "Here's to another tour."

His shoulders seemed to lose some of the tension, and I could swear it was in relief at hearing that I wouldn't be going anywhere.

"To my little swan," he said with a smile.

Right away, I felt my legs quiver, with dampness ruining my panties. I bit my lip as I imagined how it would feel if he whispered that in my ear while he drove deep in me.

"You okay, Ofelia?"

My head snapped up to where Estevan had now joined us. He had a smirk on his face.

"Yes, sorry, got lost in my thoughts," I said as I felt my face flame.

"What were you thinking about there?" Nico asked with an equally amused smile.

"Blood," I replied, not entirely lying.

It was always blood when my insomnia and anxiety came at me full force.

Both men stood a little straighter.

"The nightmares are back?" Nico asked casually as he reached for some bread.

I nodded as I looked at the sea.

"This place will always haunt me. It's in the salty air of the sea that clings to my skin. It claws out memories I'm not sure I want unburied."

Estevan was the one to speak this time.

"They might not even be memories, just nightmares."

I took a drag of my cigarette, then ashed it.

"A nightmare is scary, but deep down, you know it's not real. No one can harm you in it. A memory, that shit you can feel days, hours, or years after."

I knew I did. It was always the same thing. I was back with my old master, and he had me caged in a dark box. My skin was warmly covered in something thicker than water, but I couldn't see what it was, but I could smell it—blood. Sometimes I still felt my feet sting from where he would whip them when I didn't dance to his satisfaction.

Then he would open the door, and the light would blind my eyes, and he would smile at me delightfully, like he couldn't believe what he was staring at.

"La mia bella ballerina."

I could still hear his hoarse voice praise me. It was something the wind would carry; it didn't matter in what corner of the world I found myself in.

"Have you remembered anything new?" Nico asked.

"If I had, I would have told you," I snapped.

He always asked me about my past, trying to get me to open up, but he always refused to tell me how we both ended up in that same theater on that day.

"Can someone take me to the studio? I want to practice with the others today."

Nico nodded. "I'm heading that way. Get ready."

HALF AN HOUR LATER, I WAS SEATED IN THE FRONT seat of Nico's silver Ferrari Portofino. The engine on the car was a beast, and when he drove it, I had to stop myself from coming in my seat.

He weaved his way into town to where the rest of the crew would be practicing. Nico double-parked in front of the building, but we both knew no one in this town would tell him anything.

I still wasn't sure what his role was in all of this, but I knew it went beyond owning a dancing company because dance never got people to owe you favors, and people all over the world seemed to owe Nico something.

"Will you be picking me up, or are you sending someone for me?" I asked before I tried to open the door.

"I'll come back," Nico said as he got out of the car.

I waited in my seat as he made his way around the car and watched as every female within a mile radius stared at him. To this, he didn't pay any attention. He came to my side and opened the door for me.

It was another one of those things that made my belly feel all warm. I hated it, yet it thrilled me in the little ways he took care of me.

I was about to say something to him when a woman walked up to us. She was gorgeous. Older than I was, with shiny blonde hair. I immediately despised her. Instead of leaving, I cocked my head and smiled at her.

"Mr. Dos Santos," she said in a breathy voice. "It's so nice to see you around town with your daughter."

She emphasized the word "daughter" as a way to put me in my place. My smile broadened at her petty words.

Nico, being the gentleman he showed the world to be, greeted her and gave her a warm smile. Fake, but it looked real. I knew it was fake because the light didn't reach his eyes. He was so used to playing this game I didn't think he even realized when he was acting or being real.

"We are getting ready for another tour. Will you be attending the show?"

The blonde bitch batted her eyelashes at him. "I wouldn't miss it for the world. Maybe I could sit in your box?"

Over my dead fucking body.

"If you'll excuse me," I said politely at her. "Talent gets me the lead role, but practice makes me stay the best."

My words were a dig that while she was ordinary, I had something most people only dreamed of having. I had talent —a gift.

I turned my back to her and used the opportunity to do something I rarely had the chance to do since Nico wasn't the affectionate type.

After all, if he asked later, I could just say I was playing a role.

Nico looked at me with his eyes guarded, wondering what I was up to, but there was nothing much he could do while we were out in public. At the moment, he was at my mercy, and I fed off that power.

Putting my hands on his shoulders, I raised to my tiptoes and kissed his cheek.

Electricity flowed from where my lips met his scruffy skin. I wish we didn't have an audience and I could run my hands over his broad shoulders.

"See you later, *Daddy*," I whispered against his skin, then licked him with the tip of my tongue.

As I pulled away, I let my hand trail down his body, marveling at the ridges in his chest and abs, and wondered if I would get a chance to taste them too. Then I turned around and said goodbye to the woman, but as I did that, I let my hand graze over the top of Nico's pants.

For the first time, I had something that gave me hope.

He was hard, and it was because of me.

I didn't turn to look at him again, but as I walked into the studio, I did it with a smile on my face.

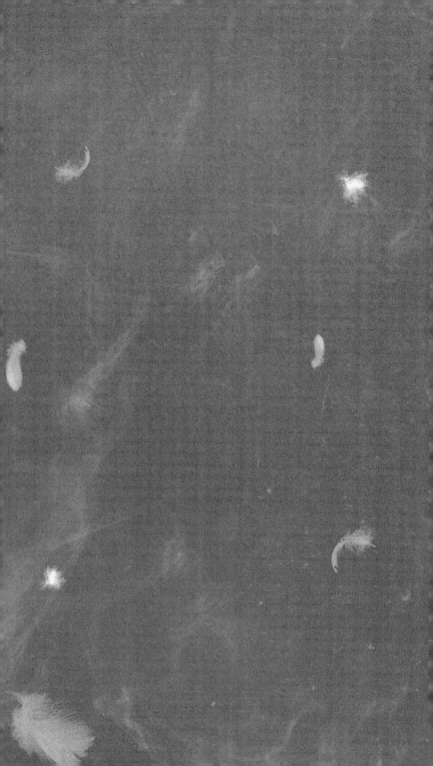

HATE

THERE'S A DARKNESS IN OUR HEARTS THAT BIDES ITS time.

It waits until the first beat of vile pumps through your veins. From there, it takes root, and it spreads.

It thrives on your insecurities and thrives on hate, blinding you with rage.

To hate something so profoundly, the love you once must have felt for it must've been great.

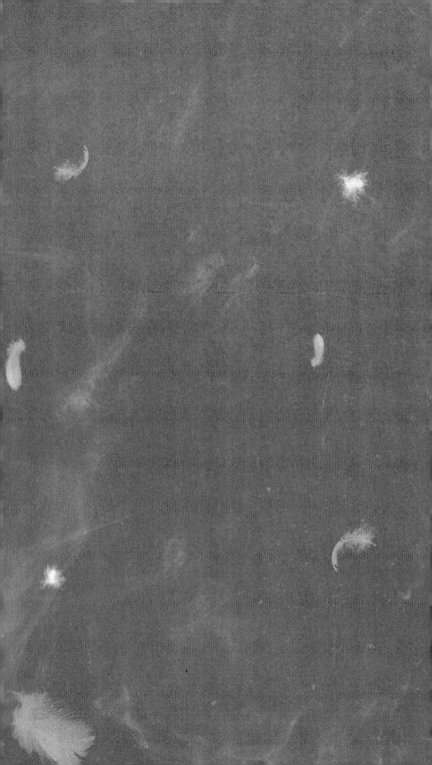

7

OFELIA

WHEN I WALKED INTO THE STUDIO, THE FEW DANCERS that had been practicing halted their conversation upon seeing me.

"Don't mind me. I'm going to go to the room upstairs," I told them.

They nodded. No one tried to stop me, and I was fine by it. If they didn't want to be my friends, I wasn't going to beg them.

My life was lonely. I knew that, but I had Joker, Bane, and Nico. That's a lot more than most people got. My life could have been a dark hole of despair. I wasn't going to let this sour my mood. I knew true darkness, and being here in the light, nothing could bring me down.

As soon as I opened the door, I knew I had spoken too soon. Standing in the middle of the room was Delia.

She didn't mind me, not paying any attention as I walked in. Instead, she focused on her own movements. There was no denying that she was talented.

"What are you doing in my space?"

She didn't answer me. Instead, she raised her leg in the air and stretched.

Fine, if she wanted to play it that way, we could both play the silent game. I went to the opposite of the room from her.

I liked this room the best because it gave me a 360-view of myself at all times. It was the room of mirrors.

Ignoring Delia, I went over to the speaker and set up my music. I could feel her watching me. Her gaze raked over my skin, and it made me feel alive. I thrived in the competition. I learned to claw my way to the top. There was no one bringing me down—at least not so easily.

Once the music began, I started to sway with the flow. I let the macabre music fill my body with life. I began to dance and noticed that Delia started to copy my every moment perfectly.

It wasn't uncommon for her to know my preferred dancing method as my understudy, but the way she danced was like staring in a mirror. As I did a half turn, our eyes met, and she smirked at me.

Dread filled the pit of my stomach as I remembered the first time she looked at me that way.

My body was warm, wrapped in the finest of wools. The cool of the room hit my cheeks, and it felt like heaven the way the two temperatures wrapped around my body.

When I opened my eyes, I saw the man who had saved me sleeping in a chair that was in the corner of the room. His body was too big for the chair; I bet it was uncomfortable for him to be sleeping there.

I looked around the room, and even though this place

was new to me, I had never felt safe nor free. I didn't feel like I had just escaped one cage and gone to another.

Light streamed through the window that was in the center of the room, making it easier to see my surroundings.

This room was nice, much nicer than I was used to. My master had nice things, but those didn't extend to me. He kept me locked away in the basement. I was used to the dark and the shadows that wrapped me in their arms as I slept at night. My bed was inside a cage, and my master brought me out when he deemed fit.

Here, my bed had no bars. It was much too big for me, and it was comfortable, like sleeping on a cloud. I wasn't used to such luxuries, and I didn't think I deserved it.

I was just grateful to have a place to sleep and something to eat. My master provided that for me, and in exchange, all I had to do was dance. I wasn't like the other girls that had to do more.

No, I was his little ballerina.

Even as young as I was, I could tell my time was running out in that place. That paying my dues on my toes was running out. But that didn't matter because here I was, and the man with the face of an angel and eyes like the ocean had saved me.

I tried to sit up to see if I had been restrained any other way when I whimpered in pain.

Everything hurt.

My abdomen hurt when I tried to get some strength to pull myself up. But the worst pain was when I tried to move my legs.

There was pain that radiated between them that had two tears rolling out of my left eye.

"Don't move," a hoarse voice commanded.

When I moved my head to look at the corner, I noticed the man was no longer there.

My beautiful angel was now at my side. His face was harsh, no longer on guard because he had fallen asleep, but there was no denying he was still a thing of beauty.

He leaned into me and then wrapped me in his arms.

Once upon a time, I had a family. I had a mother who would sing us songs so my sister and I could go back to sleep. I remembered my mother crying because we were so hungry. Her lullabies were a plea to let her go to sleep so she wouldn't feel guilty that her children were starving.

I remembered cold embraces and tearful ones when they said goodbye to me. As if letting me go was a sacrifice to them. Like they didn't get rewarded in gold.

I never had anyone care for me in a moment of sickness.

The way this man held me opened up a new world.

Kindness was one of the things we could do for free, and it could change the course of a day for someone, but it was one of the things humans kept guarded the most. Being kind could save lives, but we used that as a weapon of convenience. Nowadays, kindness came wrapped in favors and IOUs.

There was nothing I could offer this man, yet here he was helping me out.

I opened my mouth, trying to speak, but no words came out. My throat was too dry. It had been a long time since I had been thirsty, but that and hunger was a feeling you never forgot.

"Hold on, Bambina," the man said.

He fixed some pillows and left me resting as he walked out of the room.

While he did that, I tried again to move my legs despite

the pain. There had to be something I could offer this man so he would keep me, and dancing was all I had to offer.

The door opened, and he came in with a tray.

I looked at the food and drinks on it, then back at his face.

He sat the tray on my bed, and then he went to get the chair and dragged it to the side.

I watched silently as he did all of this. If he knew I was watching him, he didn't show it.

When everything was arranged to his liking, he took a seat on the chair and reached for the water, then brought it to my lips.

"Slow sips," he said, and I got the feeling he wasn't a man of many words.

Not like my old master, who loved to hear himself talk.

Sometimes he would have me dance around the room while he watched television. I didn't like it when he did that. I didn't know what show he watched, but it always consisted of shouts and moans. There was nothing else the actors would say, and my master would breathe heavily as his eyes went from the television and to me.

Instead of focusing on this, I focused on the way the cool water went down my throat.

The first sip of water after being thirsty for a long time was the worst. It felt like someone was trying to push a log down your throat. Water was a liquid, yet it felt like it was made of thorns as it glided down your throat.

"Thank you," I said as he pulled the cup away from me.

"Where am I?" was my next question.

He leaned back and stared at me. Those blue eyes traveled from my face down to my throat.

"What do you remember?"

That was a good question because I didn't remember much. Everything was a bit hazy.

"There was a room, and my master was there—so were you—and then everything else seems a bit fuzzy..." I took a moment to try my hardest to think of what had happened, but my head throbbed as I did that.

I could see smoke and smell it.

"Was there a fire?"

The man looked at me as if he were sizing me up. Unfortunately, I was used to men looking at me. My master even encouraged it. But there was something different about how this man did it.

"How old are you?"

"I think I'm sixteen," I told him.

"You think?"

I nodded my head. I'd never celebrated a birthday while I was with my master, and being with him, time was nonexistent. We lived for him, and the outside world didn't matter.

"I had my first bleed not too long ago, and one of the girls said I was coming of age."

The man's face transformed at that instant. He was furious. I knew this was the case when the vein in his neck pulsed, and that happened to my master when we did something he didn't like.

"You are safe here," he said.

"Are you my new master?" I asked, hopeful.

The anger was back in his eyes.

"No, I'm not your new master. My name is Nico, and you don't owe me anything. As soon as you are better, I'll take you back to your parents."

I licked my lips. His name was Nico. It was a beautiful name, and it suited him. Even if I remembered where I was taken from, I didn't think I would want to be returned to them.

"I don't think my parents want that," I told him.

He reached for the soup that was in my bowl.

"Why is that?"

"Because they sold me."

The clanking of the spoon dropping on the metal tray echoed across the room.

He cursed and ran a hand through his hair, seeming to come to a conclusion.

"What's your name?" Nico asked in a softer tone.

"Ofelia," I replied, the one thing I had that had always been mine.

All I had was my name and my dancing.

"You can stay under my protection for as long as you want," he said as he offered me a smile.

Despite the pain that started to get more prominent, the more awake I felt, and I smiled at him. As Nico fed me, images started to come back to me. I was on the floor screaming. I was on the floor begging.

I pushed the tray to the side and pulled back the covers.

There were no words to describe the way I saw myself. Scratches and bruises covered my legs.

"I'm sorry, little one," he said, sounding sincere.

With tears in my eyes, I looked up at him.

"Who did this to me?"

"I don't know," he told me. "Do you remember if there were more girls?" he asked tentatively.

"Yes, but he usually kept me separated from the rest."

He seemed content with my answer for now. He started to leave my room when another memory came.

"What about the other girl? The one who was with me?" I asked, remembering her being on the floor with me.

He looked across the room, and that's when I noticed she was on the other bed. She looked peaceful as she slept.

"I can only keep one of you," he said.

Guilt assaulted me because that was one of the reasons my master kept me separated. The other girls tended to get jealous about the way he treated me.

As soon as the door was closed, laughter ran through the room. It wasn't something cheerful; it gave me chills.

Delia was now seated on the bed. I gasped as I looked her over. She was beaten badly. I imagined that was probably how I looked too.

She stopped laughing and smirked at me.

"They always pick you."

SKIN

She danced, she twirled, she spun.
She was his little everything when all she wanted was the
smell of him on her skin.

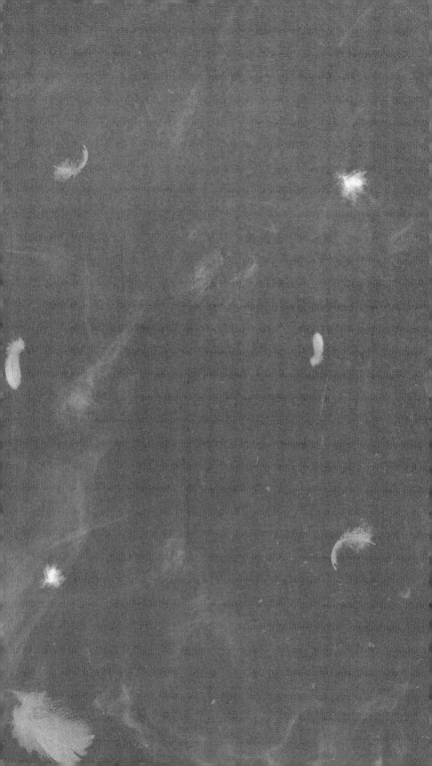

8

OFELIA

By the time we finished dancing, both Delia and I were breathing heavily. Neither wanting to be showed up by the other.

"One of these days, your spot will be mine," she vowed.

Like I would ever let that happen. I would rather die and bring everyone I loved with me than let her have them.

Cutting people was easy. Everyone had an open wound that never healed, and all you needed was to prod it a little bit for it to burn, but I never wanted to stoop that low.

I'd been put down many times in my life, and since Nico had taken me in and shown me a better life, I'd tried to do better.

It wasn't easy, especially when I knew what I could do or say to kill her.

"What would have happened if Nico had chosen me?" Delia asked as she reached for her stuff.

"Unlike you, I bet I would have already gotten him between my legs," she taunted me as she looked me up and down.

"You don't deserve any of this. Nothing that you have

should have been yours, but you know what, Ofelia..." Delia gave me a feral smile as she walked up to me. "It will all come crashing down around you one of these days. And when that happens, I will be there, ready to take your place."

My breathing was coming in pants. I felt like a rabid animal. Everyone knew that when you came from nothing and had a taste of paradise, you would do anything in your power to keep it.

And I would do just about anything to keep Nico.

Delia laughed much like she had all those years ago. When she was almost out of the door, she turned to look back at me.

"Sooner or later, I'm going to have Nico, and when I do, I'm going to turn him against you."

By then, I'd had enough. I stormed after her.

"He didn't want you!" I spat the words I knew were bound to hurt her. "He picked me and not you!"

Delia's face went blank. She didn't want to show how much my words killed her.

"Then why has he kept me around all of these years? Is he waiting for you to fuck up?"

I closed my eyes and heard the door slam.

"Aughhhhh," I screeched.

Everyone often asked me how I was able to play death. How did I play the role so well? The truth was it was easy to do when hate had infiltrated your heart. When you had a dark side ready to strike with no remorse.

I opened my eyes and looked at myself in the mirror. I was unraveling.

There was no denying that lately I felt like I was losing my mind. Sometimes, I looked at myself in the mirror, and I hated what stared back at me.

Maybe it was self-loathing?

When I couldn't take it anymore, I ran to the mirror, my arm extended, ready to strike. Before my fist could make contact with the glass, I got pulled back around by the waist.

Strong hands held on to me. They gripped my hips, making it impossible to move.

"What. The. Fuck."

The hairs on the back of my neck rose when I heard Nico's voice.

"Let me go." I wiggled, trying to get free from his hold.

The more I moved, the closer he pressed me to his body. It was no use. He was stronger than me, and there was no getting out of his hold.

"What the hell were you thinking? You could have hurt yourself," he said softly.

I gritted my teeth because I hated it when he talked to me in a condescending tone. I wasn't a child anymore.

"None of your business," I retorted as I tried to get free from his hold once more.

That was not the correct answer.

Nico spun me around and backed me up until my back made contact with the cold mirror.

"None of my business, little swan?" he repeated in a low, lethal tone.

Since I wasn't looking at him, he used one of his index fingers to tip my chin up so I could look him in the eyes.

"I pay for everything. This studio. Your lifestyle. You are my star, and if you get hurt, I have no fucking show."

His words calmed me. Soothed the insecurities I had. That's when I noticed how close he was to me. How he had me pressed between his body and the mirror.

Then I remembered earlier he had been hard for me.

"You'll still have Delia," I said, annoyed.

"Is this why you had a tantrum? Delia again?" He scoffed. Every time I brought her up, he got annoyed, like what she said to me didn't matter.

Why couldn't he see that by not getting rid of her, he was hurting me?

"Why do you put up with her?" I asked honestly, my voice sounding defeated.

When he hesitated to answer, I scoffed. I took one step closer and pulled at his shirt.

Frustration. That's what I was feeling. The older I got, the more intense the feeling became.

Nico raised his eyebrows in surprise.

Before he could process any of this and before I could talk myself out of it, I pulled him down and kissed him.

This was the feeling I had been missing my whole life. It tore me apart only to put me back together. It clawed its way into my soul, trying to hold on to the shredded pieces.

He tasted like mint and something forbidden.

Nico stayed stoic, but I didn't want that. I wanted him to be the imposing man he showed the world. I wanted him to tear into me. To destroy me and then put me back together, piece by piece.

I bit his lip hard to try and get a reaction from him.

That seemed to do the trick.

Blood coated my tongue, but before I could pull away to see if I had hurt him, Nico moved his lips.

They moved possessively against me. It was like he wanted to smear his blood all over my lips.

His hands went to my ribs and slowly moved down to my hips. Electricity hummed over my skin. I was ready to come undone by one simple action.

My hands wrapped around his shoulders, bringing him

down even more. I wanted to be all over him. I wanted him to think of me wrapped around him the next time he saw me.

With his fingers, he pulled the material of my tutu, making it rise up. I moaned as part of the underwear rubbed against my pussy. The friction felt divine.

Nico's kiss deepened as he did the action again, this time with more force.

I tore my mouth away from him and threw my head back against the mirror as I moaned.

Before I could put my head down, Nico was already pacing across from me.

His hand ran over his hair. Blood smeared his lips. The feeling I had between my legs intensified.

"That shouldn't have happened," he said hoarsely.

"Well, it did," I replied as I took a step closer to him.

"Ofelia," he warned.

"I want you, Nico," I said as I took another step closer.

Nico let me get close enough, and when I was within reach, he pulled me toward him.

This was what I always wanted, and it was finally happening.

One of his arms went to my waist, holding me to his side, making sure I didn't move. It wasn't like I wanted to either way. Then he brought his other hand to his lips, where he proceeded to lick his thumb.

I cocked my head, confused about what he would do when he brought his thumb and swiped it over my top lip.

"You're a child, Ofelia," he finally said.

Then he moved the top of his hand over his mouth, removing the blood.

"Let's go."

Nico pulled me with him.

"You want me too," I said because I needed something to prove I wasn't going crazy.

"I travel all over the world operating a business. On top of that, I have a *child* I have to take care of. It's called sexual frustration."

The building was already vacant, and it was no longer daylight. This made me halt for a second. Just how long had I been practicing with Delia?

I shook my head, ignoring this because I had more important things to handle now.

"Maybe I'm sexually frustrated too," I said as Nico dragged me toward the door.

"Good for you," he said.

"Maybe we can—"

Nico didn't let me finish that sentence.

"I am your legal guardian, Ofelia," he said that like that was answer enough to what I was about to say.

Since I knew no one was in here, I spoke loud enough for my words to vibrate around the room.

"Wouldn't it feel so good, *Daddy*, if you slide inside my wet pussy."

Nico glared at me. His jaw was stiff and his body taut. Three seconds later, he let go of me and walked out.

I rolled my eyes and then walked after him.

The ride back to the house was quiet. He gripped the steering wheel so hard his knuckles were white.

"PLEASE, YOU HAVE TO HELP ME," THE OTHER GIRL TOLD *me. She was in the cage opposite me. She was taller than me, maybe a year older, and despite being stuck in this hell with me, she was still beautiful. Most of the girls my master kept were.*

Sweat covered my back as I awoke, clutching onto the bed comforter. My heart pounded against my chest. My stomach felt empty yet full, and I felt as if I were going to throw up.

I'd had many nightmares about my time in my cage, but I had always been alone. There had never been any other girl with me until today.

I reached for my nightstand, where I always kept a cup of water because nights like this one were often.

I didn't know what had triggered this memory, but maybe it was the stress I found myself in. Something had changed this year, not only between Nico and me, but the whole company.

The change in our routes still bothered me, but I had dropped it for now. There was no point in worrying about something I didn't have answers for. Since the night at the studio, Nico had been distant, and to top it all off, our show was tomorrow night. I felt like I wasn't ready.

Since our rehearsal the other day, I hadn't seen Delia, and I felt like she was also up to something.

I was going crazy.

Maybe it was just sexual frustration?

Knowing I wasn't going to get any sleep staying in my room, I got up. The only thing that helped clear my head was dancing.

As soon as I made my way out of my room, Bane stood up, ready to guard me. After all, that was why Nico got him in the first place. I tended to wander, and Nico wanted me safe.

"Hey, boy." I scratched his head, and he grunted.

When we reached the bottom, Joker was there, and he

whined. Nico kept one dog outside my door and the other one down the stairs. You know, in case something ever happened, one was the failsafe.

Before walking down toward the gym, I went to the kitchen and got my boys some treats. It was going to be a long night, and I didn't want them there without anything to snack on.

After that was done, I made my way to my home studio when a light caught my attention.

My heart sped up, knowing it was probably Nico because no one other than Estevan had access to our gym. He usually did his workouts in the morning.

"Wait," I told the dogs, and since they had better instincts than me and knew that Nico was in the sauna room, they stopped.

The room was to the far corner of our gym. Made of brick and stone, it had pillars that made it look like an alcove. At the end, there were two glass doors that opened to the actual sauna part. I strolled in slowly, making sure that no noise would give me away, glad that the pillars gave me coverage. I felt like a Peeping Tom, but there was no stopping me now. I pulled the door slowly and walked in. The room was hot, and the glass was steamed but not enough that I couldn't make out Nico's naked body.

My mouth watered.

Suddenly, I was suffocating in this damn room.

I stood to the side, watching him. His chest was broad, and sweat glided down his hard pecs. The lines from his abs were defined. He was in better shape than men half his age. My pussy throbbed when I saw his half-erect cock. His eyes were closed, and his head was tipped back.

He looked like a fucking god.

The moment his hand gripped around his dick, I had to

bite my lip to stop from moaning aloud. There was some-thing beautiful about the way he touched himself—strong, precise strokes.

I was ready to make a move when someone moved from my opposite side.

What. The. Fuck.

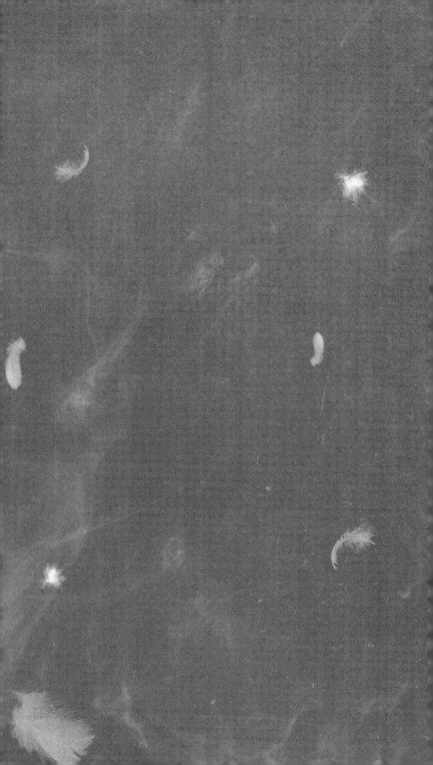

9

OFELIA

I stood rooted in my spot as I watched Delia make her way to Nico. *My Nico.* Her hair was wild and untamed. She walked to him with just a towel draped around her middle.

The moment she opened the glass panel, Nico's eyes snapped open, and I could see the way he looked at her. My heart skipped a beat as I waited for him to kick her out. That didn't happen. He finished stroking himself as Delia took a step closer between his open legs. Delia let the towel drop and then bent forward to touch his knees.

Bile rose up my throat as I saw lust was written all over Nico's face.

"Let me make you feel better," she purred.

I felt like I was going to throw up, yet I couldn't move. It was like I needed to see them take it all the way so I could have his betrayal branded in my brain.

"You should go," Nico said, but even I knew he didn't mean it.

Delia just laughed as she kneeled before him and put

him in her mouth. Her head bobbed as Nico threw his head back, and his hips rose, feeding more of him to her mouth.

My throat clogged; I couldn't breathe.

My nails dug into the skin of my hands as Nico groaned. He wrapped his hands around Delia's hair and tugged it.

I'd had enough.

I looked up, trying to find another way out.

Slowly, I started to walk back because I didn't want them to know I was in the room with them. For someone who was poised, I cursed myself when I took the wrong step and fell backward. I didn't bother to look up because I didn't want them to see the humiliation on my face.

I got up and ran away, tears spilling down my face.

"Ofelia!" Nico's shouts followed after me.

I didn't dare look back at him. I didn't want to see Delia's smug face. Instead, I ran faster with Joker and Bane barking alongside me, each dog at my side trying to cage me in and protect me.

"Ofelia," Nico yelled again, sounding desperate, but I pushed myself to go faster.

"Ofelia!"

It was too late when Nico shouted because I was already falling down. Pain radiated from my head, and one of the last things I saw was Nico standing over me.

———

I woke up again, and this time, dawn was beginning to break. My head hurt, and when I tried to get up, a hand pushed me back down.

"Don't move too fast. You have a concussion."

My stomach dropped as soon as I heard Nico's voice.

All I could see was him and the way his eyes fluttered, and how his throat bobbed, knowing it wasn't me he was thinking about.

I blinked furiously, trying to clear out of my sleepy haze. That's when I noticed I wasn't in my room. The bed was bigger than mine, and the comforters were dark. The room lacked my fruity smell, but it was one hundred percent all Nico.

Any other time I might have been thrilled to be in his bed.

Nico was still shirtless; the only thing covering him up were his boxers.

"Ofelia, I am so—"

I didn't let him finish his sentence. The anger came back when I noticed the nail marks on his thighs. He had liked the way she was sucking him off.

"Did you come all over her mouth?" I spat at him.

Nico cocked his head to the side, his blue eyes inky and intense.

"Ofelia," he said softer like he was trying to soothe a child.

"Did you like the way she sucked you?"

His breathing got heavy.

"You should rest some more. You have a show tonight."

Was he serious right now? He wanted to put me back to bed? That was bullshit. I removed the comforter he had wrapped around me and stopped when I realized I was naked.

"You fell in the sauna room and got yourself wet," he replied upon seeing the confusion on my face.

I was naked and in bed with Nico.

"Where is she?" I bit out.

"Go to sleep or don't. I'm fucking out of here."

He started to move away, but I couldn't let him go, not if he would chase after her. I removed the comforter and blocked Nico by putting my hands to his chest.

My heart pumped against my chest.

Deadly butterflies fluttered in my stomach. I was not too fond of the way they made me feel. Like I was on a high, because once they were gone, you wanted to chase that high again.

"Ofelia?" Nico asked with a grave voice.

I straddled him, and he let me.

My hands roamed over his broad shoulders and then made my way down to his six-pack. His breathing was labored, and his body was tense. I marveled at the way his muscles constricted under my touch.

"Nico," I breathed as my hand moved down his abs, my nails lightly scratching against his happy trail.

When I let myself sit down on him, my eyes fluttered at the feel of his hardness between me.

"We should stop. You need to get some rest," he said between gritted teeth as I started to grind myself against him.

I ignored his comment. If he truly wanted me gone, he would have already pushed me off. Concussion or not, he could still overpower me.

"I want to be the one to make you feel good," I told him as I pushed against his chest so he could lean back against the bed. "I want you to use me for your pleasure."

"Ofelia, get off me and go to sleep," he said, sounding annoyed.

That's when I realized he kept staring at my face and hadn't let his eyes travel down my naked body.

I smiled at him.

Then, I reached for his hands. His chest kept rising and

falling uncontrollably. My smile broadened as he let me guide his hands and put them on my rib cage.

His nose flared the moment his hands made contact with my ribs. I rubbed myself against him once more.

"We should stop." His voice was groggy, like he didn't want to speak because it was laced with need, and he didn't want me to know just how much I was affecting him.

I didn't stop. Instead, I moved his hands lower down my body until he was holding on to my waist. My hips moved furiously, and my eyes fluttered.

"Ofelia," he said through gritted teeth.

"Mhhhmm." I couldn't form a coherent thought.

His hands were now gripping my waist, his hips moving against my own. He could feel how wet I had gotten for him.

"Let me make you feel better than she ever did," I begged.

"I practically raised you," he said as he held on to me. His eyes were on my chest. "I'm not taking advantage of you."

This time there was some steel to his words, and I knew he was about to throw me off him at any second.

"Is she better than me?"

"For fuck's sake, Ofelia, let it go," he gritted out as he sat up.

He moved my body with ease, and I knew that it had only gotten as far as it did earlier because he allowed it.

I was not about to let it go. As much as I hated Delia, she had gotten further with him than me, and that hate and rivalry between us were what allowed me to lose my morality.

Boundaries never let anyone go very far. They worked

as barriers so the weak wouldn't go anywhere, and so we, as humans, wouldn't give in to our most depraved desires.

"Please..." I begged him as I held on to his shoulders with one arm.

"Ofelia, *por favor*, stop being foolish," he ground out.

I ignored him while, with my other hand, I worked to pull down his boxers.

"I want you so bad," I whined.

"You need to stop. I don't want to hurt yo—"

His words died the moment I put the tip of his dick inside of my entrance. It was thick, and it felt so good.

"Fuck," he croaked when I started to sink down on him.

I felt so full to the point that it hurt, but I'd rather it be me who made him feel this way than Delia, so that was the thought that kept me going.

"Please, Daddy, let me make you feel good," I whispered once he was entirely inside of me.

He fucking lost it.

Nico flipped us so it was him towering over me. His hips pushed painfully against my petite frame, but I relished in the feel of him. It would serve as a reminder that he was with me. That all my fantasies were finally coming true.

"Is this what you wanted, little swan?" he spat at me angrily.

He spread my legs even wider, pushing himself to the hilt.

It burned but not like when it was done before, when all the innocent things had been ripped from me. My innocence was gone a long time ago, and now I wanted to embrace all my sins.

"More," I begged in a strained voice. "I need you to make it all go away, Daddy."

His jaw was stiff, and he looked at me with dark eyes full of want and hate. But I think I had finally gotten through to him.

"Stop calling me that," he groaned as he pulled out, only to slam back into me.

It burned the way he stretched me. It had been so long I had forgotten just how painful it had been the first time. Except for this time, there was an obvious difference. I was wet. I could hear the sounds we made as he pulled out of me only to slam back in. That burn I had been feeling was slowly turning into pleasure. It was like the start of a fire; the flame was slowly turning into an inferno.

"Has my little swan had enough?" he asked as he pulled one of my legs and wrapped it around his waist. He looked down at me, maybe hoping I would tell him to leave that this was a mistake, but the only one thinking that way was him.

"I want more," I moaned as I raised my hips to meet his.

His chest heaved. There was still a part of him that was holding back, and I wanted it unleashed.

Nico started to move faster. Every time he rolled his hips, my eyes would flutter. I needed him to kiss me. I wanted him to tell me that I was better than anyone else. Anyone who had come before me didn't matter. I had been with him in all these years, it had only been me, and I wanted it to be that way forever.

"Am I making you feel good?" I asked in a breathy voice.

Nico stilled his movements. He then leaned lower until his nose was brushing against mine. He glided the tip over my cheek until he got to my ear, and then he gently bit the top.

"It was your mouth I wanted wrapped around me, my little ballerina."

My chest spread full of warmth. Delia seemed like a thing of the past. "Did you fuck her?" I asked as I glided my fingers over his hair.

"No."

It seemed to kill the mood, so I lifted my head up and kissed his lips. This time, he didn't push me away but kissed me back. It was slow—hesitant.

"Make me come," I whispered against his lips. "Make me feel good."

His hips started to move once more, but this time, his movements were slower. He was taking his time. One of his hands came to my stomach and held me down as he pushed deeper inside of me.

I broke away from our kiss. "*Ohh.*"

Nico chuckled.

Then, I felt his finger slide down to the top of my mound. He used his index finger and traced it to where our bodies were joined until he touched my clit.

My hips arched.

"You're going to come hard for me, my little swan. Your pussy is going to cream all over my dick. You are going to scream and beg me to stop fucking you, but now that I've had this..." He stopped talking as his finger swirled around me. "There's no going back."

That was the last coherent sentence I heard him say as he started to fuck me harder, his finger making me feel pleasure like I never had before.

"Oh God," I moaned as I started to buck under him.

"That's it," he groaned.

My hands held on to his shoulders, my nails breaking skin. I came so hard my vision went black.

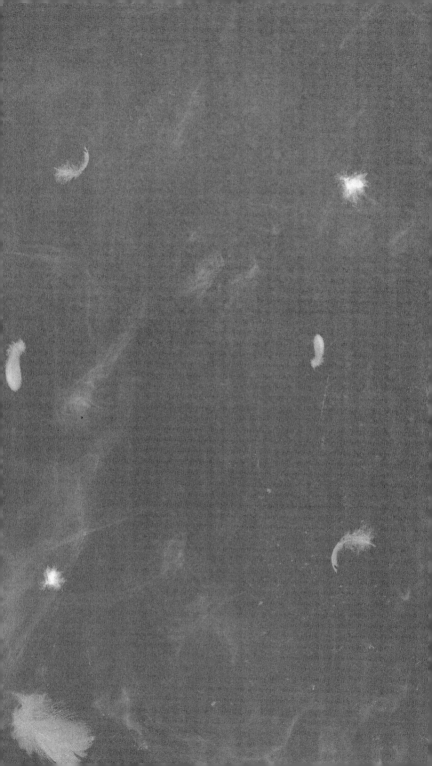

TIME

There's something more precious than money, more
precious than gold.
It's something invisible that holds all.
You could have all the money in the world, but without
time, you won't have anything at all.

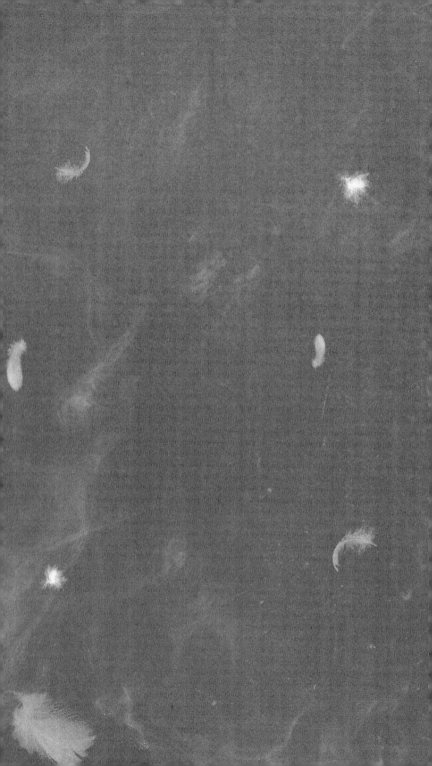

10

OFELIA

The moment I woke up, I knew it was already late by the way the sun was shining. I sat up, expecting to be in Nico's bed, but I was on my own. I removed the comforter, and I wasn't naked, but I was in the clothes I had changed into before I went to the studio.

What the fuck?

The back of my head throbbed. I looked around, but everything seemed just how I left it. However, something inside of me stirred.

What had happened last night felt like a dream. I looked down at my palms, but there were no markings from my nails. I could have sworn I had felt blood trickle on my skin.

I made my way out of my room. Joker perked up as soon as I opened the door.

"Hi, boy," I said as I reached down to pet him. He walked beside me as we made our way downstairs.

No one was around. I didn't see any servants, nor security.

"Hello?" I yelled as I made my way down the stairs.

No one answered back.

There was no sign of Bane either. Last night felt oddly real but also like a dream. I made my way toward the studio, but nothing seemed out of place when I got there. I even made my way to the sauna to see if I could find anything that told me last night had happened. I was looking for a wet towel, a piece of hair on the floor—anything.

Maybe if I had woken up sore between my legs, that would have been all the validation I would need, but that wasn't the case either.

Joker stayed next to me the whole time. He was the only one who seemed to be home, which was odd, because it was always filled with people. I couldn't remember when they had left me alone other than when I was practicing.

"Let's go outside," I told the dog.

The weather was warm, but the breeze was cool enough to stop this day from being humid. My bare feet burned from where the sun had already warmed the pavement.

"Nico?" I yelled.

No one answered.

"Anyone?" I yelled again; this time, my palms got sweaty, and my heart strummed against my rib cage.

What if last night wasn't a dream at all and now everyone had vacated the premises? Nico realized that he saved the wrong girl.

There were times when I felt small and insignificant, and today was one of them. My heart thudded against my chest, and I marveled at the fact that the stupid muscle could ache and could break, and the very next day be put back together again.

That's when it occurred to me that I still had to check

Nico's bed. Life spurred inside of me, giving me the sweet taste of hope. It swirled inside of my chest, spreading warmth through my body.

I was rounding the hall. I could see Nico's bed when my body was met with a wall. My body bounced back but didn't fall because two hands held on to me.

"Nico," I said in awe.

He looked like he always did—tall, imposing, and dark.

"Ofelia," he said, looking down at me. I felt his gaze at my neck, traveling down to my skin to my clothes. "I see you had a late night of practice."

My head cocked to the side, wondering if he was joking. My eyes traveled from his eyes down to the zipper of his pants.

"My eyes are up here, little swan."

My head snapped back up.

Ask him.

That voice in my head sounded a lot like Delia, and my eyes turned into tiny little slithers.

"Something on your mind, Ofelia?" Nico asked as he buttoned his jacket. "I do have to get going, and you need to start getting ready."

"Where's the staff?" I asked.

Not what I should have gone for, but with Nico, you couldn't go straight for the kill. He would cut off your head before you even made your play.

"I know how much you appreciate your peace and quiet before a show, so I gave them all the day off."

I guess that made sense. I did tend to get a little erratic on opening night because I thrived on perfection, and this show set up a precedent for the rest of the tour.

My eyes were on the floor, trying to rack my brain to

find something, anything to hold on to—that last night wasn't a dream.

"Where's Bane?" I asked him.

Nico licked his lips. He looked down to my side, where Joker sat waiting patiently.

"Estevan took him to the vet. He wasn't feeling well this morning."

My mouth parted. I didn't want anything to happen to Bane. Nico started to walk away, but I caught up to him.

"Where are you going?" My question came out like a demand.

"Did I miss the part where you get to ask me those questions?"

"You don't have to be such a dick!" I shouted, aggravated at the whole situation. My head was throbbing, and I remembered leaving my room.

"I'm not a mind reader, Ofelia. If you have something on your mind, then say it." He raised an eyebrow at me, and I don't know if it was an intimidation tactic, or if he was trying to provoke me. I went with the latter.

"Did we..." My mouth went dry, and my cheeks warmed.

"Did we what, Ofelia?" he repeated after me, annoyed.

"Did we have sex last night?"

Two seconds passed, and then Nico threw his head back, laughing.

"Listen, Ofelia, this obsession you have with me has to stop," he said without remorse. He was usually careful not to hurt my feelings, but obviously, that wasn't the case anymore.

"Is this because of her? Because of Delia?"

"I have so much shit I have to do today. I don't have time for this nonsense."

He turned around and started to walk away, but I just couldn't let it go.

"I loved every minute of it," I told him, and he stopped. "Every touch, the kisses. Even when you were hurting, you made me feel alive."

His shoulders sagged, and I took one step closer to him, sure that last night was not in my head after all.

"I'll get your doctor to come see you as soon as possible. You are even worse than I would have imagined."

He left, but his words hung in the air. They were heavy and crushed me. This would not be the first time I'd had vivid dreams where I could have sworn it had been a reality. The last time a doctor came, he said I was under too much stress. I was going into delirium.

So even though this wasn't new, it still wasn't a pleasant feeling to have.

Since there wasn't anything I could do, I walked back to my room and prepared myself for tonight's show.

WHEN IT WAS ALMOST SHOWTIME, NICO DIDN'T SHOW up for me. Estevan did. I was waiting in the living room dressed in a black cotton dress. Our makeup artist would be there, ready to work her magic on all the dancers. The cast and crew would be running around frantically.

Nico, Delia, and my dream were temporarily forgotten with the rush of excitement for a new tour.

"Ready to go, Ofelia?" Estevan asked as soon as he saw me.

I looked around the house, knowing we would be leaving immediately after the show. This time there was something in my chest that made me feel longing. This home was not something I looked forward to every year, but this time, there was something warm attached to this house.

"I'll be back for you later, boy," I said to Joker as I pet him.

"We have to go, Ofelia." Estevan motioned for the door. I took a deep breath and followed him. He had his black SUV parked right at the entrance, and that's when I noticed two cars were flanking it.

I pretended like this level of security was normal.

"What's wrong with Bane?" I opted to ask instead as he drove us downtown to the theater.

"Nothing major. He just took a bad fall, that's all."

"He fell?" I barked. "How? Nico said he was ill."

Estevan shrugged and gave me a small smile. He looked softer than Nico did. His features were golden, whereas Nico's were dark, but something sinister lurked behind those hazel eyes. You looked at them too long and you could see insanity staring back at you.

"Nico was busy with today's opening. He probably heard wrong to what I told him. Don't sweat it, little one."

I threw my head back against the cold leather and scoffed.

"I'm twenty-three. You can stop calling me 'little one,' you know? By our society standards, I've been a woman since fifteen."

"Not going to happen," he said. "I remember you— scrawny and scared; you used to hide behind Nico's leg, whenever I or any of the other men were around."

I smiled.

"I remember that," I said.

It wasn't vivid, more like fading fragments. There were a lot of things that I had forgotten over the years. They might be some of the most insignificant ones for some people, but to me, they had meant the world.

Like the first time, Nico gave me my room. Tears fell down my cheeks. It took a while before I could sleep on the bed and not in the closet because it reminded me of my time in the cage. Small, confined spaces gave me comfort. It's why all my beds had canopies on them. Something I never asked for, but Nico made sure I had.

"Estevan..." My voice trailed off, unsure if he was even the right person to ask.

"Yes?"

"Did Delia come by last night?"

"No one's allowed into the gates after sundown."

His voice was final, and I wasn't going to keep asking him anything more after that. Instead, I sat and waited patiently until we made it to the back of the theater.

"You have nothing to worry about, Ofelia. There is no one that does it better than you."

As soon as the doors opened, it was chaos, and I smiled. This was where I thrived. Before every show, I would feed off everyone's nervous energy and let it fuel me. I would relish in fear of others and conceded in knowing that I didn't fear being onstage when I was there; that's when I felt free.

Being onstage was where I didn't have to pretend like I didn't have it together. My madness was welcome there. My sins were expected. And even when I died a little every day, not one single person on the stage could tell, and it felt great deceiving them all.

"Ofelia!" someone shouted, and I spurred into action. I let the makeup artist get me ready and turn me into the beautiful angel everyone expected to see when I put on my costume and slid my hands down the black feathers.

We all lined up by the curtain.

"*Benvenuto nella danza dei morti.*"

Showtime.

The show always started the same. We all danced together in synced harmony. Then one by one, the dancers would start dropping.

Normally I didn't look for Nico, but today my eyes searched for him, except I couldn't see him anywhere. Not even the usual men he kept at his sides. We were nearing the second part of the dance when something or rather someone in one of the private boxes caught my eyes.

I could only see half of his face, but what I could see was beautiful. A sharp jaw and angular nose gave him a refined look. He was talking to Estevan or rather arguing. The moment that the lights started to go down, he looked up.

"Ofelia, let's go." Fernando pulled me by the arm.

His cold fingers on my warm skin was the trick to pull me out of the trance I had fallen in. Shaking my head, I followed after him. All the dancers were busy changing or taking bathroom breaks before getting to the last part of our show.

I needed air, but I knew no one would let me go anywhere. Instead, I settled for going to my dressing room. I was the prima ballerina, and with that came some perks.

When I opened my door, the first thing I noticed was the flowers on my dresser. There were at least three dozen of white roses.

I wasn't particularly fond of flowers. The only things that brought genuine joy to my life were my boys and dance. Everything else was just shallow things that brought fake joy. At least to me, they did.

Flowers died, but moments lasted forever, and I'd rather preserve those.

A note stuck out amidst the white roses. It was black with gold foil.

"Beautiful as ever, my pretty ballerina."

My head pounded at those words, striking a chord I couldn't ring.

"My pretty little ballerina."

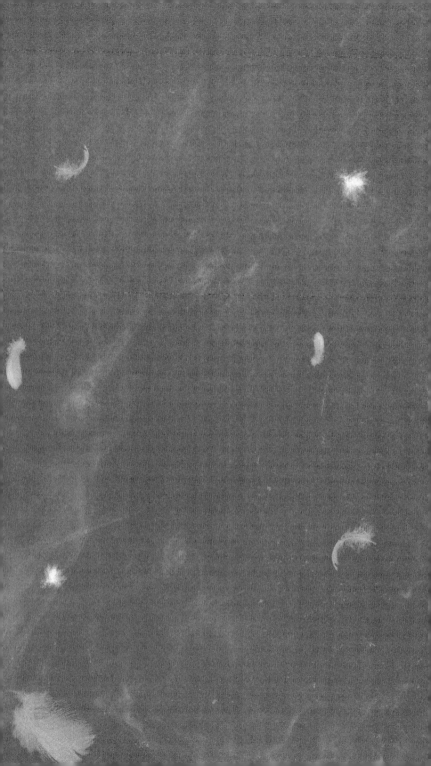

11

NICO

My money came from the rich. They needed someone to get their hands dirty for them, and here I was doing the job for them. If it meant I got what I wanted, I didn't mind getting my hands dirty.

Being in this line of work for as long as I had, you learned to detach your feelings from the things you saw or heard. Everyone had a sob story, and if you paid mind to all of them, you were bound to get lost in hate.

The world was a fucked-up place. It was a dog-eat-dog world, and the sooner you got that through your brain, the easier it became to mind your own business.

I learned to channel my anger early on. I realized that the ones that wronged me were still breathing, but doing the things I did would get me a little closer to them. Who cared if I lost my soul along the way? We were on borrowed time on this earth anyway. They could take my soul. After all, I wouldn't need it once I was dead.

Looking down at my watch, I knew the show was just about to begin. It was why I wanted this done tonight. Half of the elite would be here at the opening, which meant security and press would be at the front of the theatre, and it would leave our parking grounds completely free.

"Shipper," Geraldo said as soon as he saw me. I tried not to let my irritation show as I offered him a carefree smile. "I got what you wanted."

"Say it a little louder, why don't you?" I retorted snidely.

Geraldo rolled his eyes.

My men were stationed everywhere in the theater. This show was my masterpiece, and the little ballerina that brought the show to life was my grand prize. Although I needed to do something about her as well, for now, she was something I had to put in the back of my mind. If I started to analyze every little thing, then I might as well call the cops on myself.

My operations required all my attention. People liked to call me the Shipper, but I liked to think of myself as the perfectionist. I went over all the possibilities with fine precision. Estevan and I would oversee all the angles, and then we decided which one worked for our advantage.

"We will stay for the introduction, then I will meet you in the back."

Geraldo rolled his eyes but ultimately nodded.

I had fifteen minutes to mingle with the people and let them see my face. Show them that their grandmaster had come to celebrate with them.

As I mingled, one of the men in my box caught my attention. Everyone in Italy knew who he was. I wasn't scared of him because he owed me a favor. Sooner or later, everyone did.

"Estacado," I told the man.

"Dos Santos," he replied without looking at me.

"I didn't think you would come to the grand opening," I

said as I noticed he was not alone but with his wife. I knew why they were here. They had come to show the world that they were trying to move on despite their recent loss.

"Life does not stop when one loses a child. It nearly falters. We must pick up the pieces and keep on pushing back."

Wasn't that the fucking truth. You learned to pick up the broken shards and kept on going. I nodded at him, getting the message he was trying to tell me.

He wanted me to let him know if I had any information on the person who was responsible for kidnapping his daughter, but in this case, I was clueless.

"Enjoy the show," I said as I patted him on the back.

If I knew who was the one responsible for killing women like flies around here, then I wouldn't be here. My company would be nonexistent, and I would have already gotten my revenge.

Even though I didn't want to, my eyes wandered to the front of the stage. She stood there, standing out amongst the rest. Ofelia always stood out among her peers. She had a cloak of loneliness that clung to her. It was like a shield to stop people from getting too close to her. It was what intrigued me about her in the first place. She had been nothing but a child, dancing for predators, and the way she did it was poised, even if she was scared for her life.

Her eyes were vacant like she has seen the worst of the world and had no will left to live, but the moment she started to dance was like she breathed life into the room. Her movements were life, every twirl and spin was something to behold, and for just a fraction of a second, there was joy in her eyes. It was when I liked to look at her the most. When she was lost in her dance was when she and her madness would become one, and her eyes sparkled.

That was my first impression upon her seeing her in that room. I felt something in my gut twist and churn, but it was probably because it had reminded me of my sister. Ofelia, in that room, alone, dancing for all the men, made me swallow back the bile in my throat because I knew it could easily be Diana.

When I took the meet that day, I had no intention of playing dark knight, but fate had other plans. There was no way I could have left Ofelia alone in that room. I didn't regret bringing her with me.

Years later, I still couldn't do it, even if at this moment I hated myself for it.

My palms burned from how hard I was fisting my hands. I looked around the room, and it calmed me down. I had a full house tonight. Not that I had expected it any other way.

People loved to have front-row seats to tragedies, and that's why our show did so well. It was one fucking tragedy. No one other than Estevan knew where I had gotten my inspiration for it. It was a secret I was prepared to take to my grave.

My eyes traveled over Ofelia's features once more, before I walked out the doors. Once I was outside, some of my men were already there waiting for me.

The drive wasn't far. Geraldo had followed instructions to a T.

The trucks that drove our equipment to the airport were parked here. The people who worked here were loyal to me. The money I paid them was too good for them to narc on me.

"Where's your delivery?" I said, getting straight to business.

The little punk smirked at me. If I had the luxury of

doing what I wanted, I would make him beg for his life before I killed him.

He nodded, and two of his men pulled out a large crate from the back. The moment they threw it on the ground, I heard the muffled cries.

I didn't flinch, grit my teeth, or anything. That girl's pleas fell on deaf ears.

I wasn't in the business of saving broken girls. I had saved one, and I had gotten more than I had bargained for.

"I expect the payment is already in my account?" I asked as my men moved the crate to the truck.

"Yes." Geraldo smiled at me. "Glad that you took care of it so quickly. Now I can go back to enjoy the show. I gotta admit, Shipper, you have one fine-ass daugh—

Unfortunately for him, he didn't get to finish his sentence. My knuckles stung from where I punched him, but at least the fucker should be grateful I didn't use my entire force.

"What the fuck, Shipper." The little shit spat the blood that had pooled in his mouth toward me.

"Call me Shipper again, and I will cut your body into tiny little pieces and throw it in the sea. Unlike you, dipshit, I don't need daddy to do the dirty work for me. As for *my* Ofelia, I suggest you keep your eyes to yourself unless you want me to carve them out with a spoon and feed them to you."

My nostrils flared when I smelled the rancid smell of piss.

"Get him out of my fucking sight and take him back to his father," I told my men, who were laughing at him. "Preferably alive."

Punching Geraldo had only taken the edge off. Truth be told, I needed another type of release. And the only way I was going to be satiated was inside Ofelia's pussy, and I couldn't have that.

There was no doubt in my mind she was unraveling, but I just didn't know what to do about it.

Ofelia held the key to getting my revenge, but she didn't talk about the past, and I would never force her to tell me. She had already been through too much; it would kill me if I did that to her.

She clutched on to me since the moment I brought her to live with Estevan and me. We were barely growing our business, thinking of a way to move and grow so we could serve our revenge, when one day this little girl danced, and an idea sparked to life.

I owed her my wealth if I was honest.

She hated being away from me. She became obsessed with me, and now that she was older, it was insufferable. The one thing she wanted from me was one thing I could never give to her nor anyone. Monsters didn't have hearts. The constant beating was a hindrance to remind you of stupid moralities that I would rather stay forgotten.

Hearts made you soft, and in my line of work, being soft got you dead.

I made my way to the theater, knowing I would make it just in time for the curtain call. On the way there, I pulled out my cellphone and made a call.

"I said to only call here if it was an emergency," a groggy voice answered me.

"Roman, it's getting worse," I told him.

There was some cursing on the other line.

"I told you this would happen," he told me, but I stayed quiet. "I'll be there as soon as I can, but I won't be alone."

Then the line went dead.

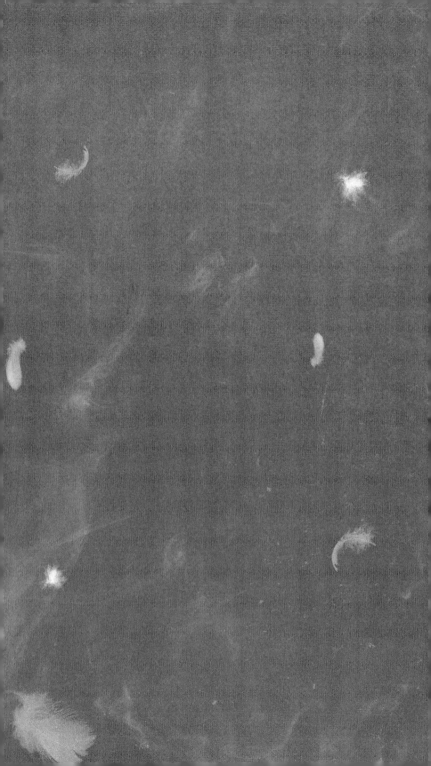

NAMES

It was easy to call her names.
To call her crazy and say she was insane, because her madness was sealed in darkness and her normality was not tamed.

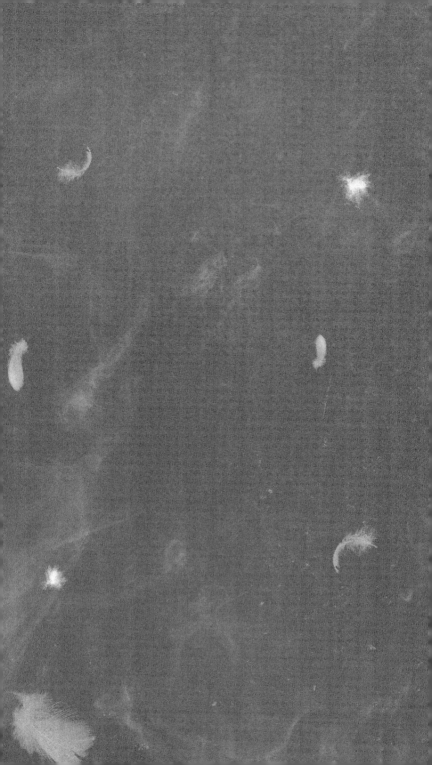

OFELIA

There was nothing like feeling cold blood on your skin. The way it stuck to you. The nectar of life just flowing around you. It was exhilarating. How it smelled, the texture, knowing that someone else needed that very liquid to live, and here you are just playing with it.

My eyes had adjusted to the dark from my cage. They no longer wandered aimlessly, trying to latch on to some light. The sooner you realized there was no one saving you, the faster you accepted your fate.

The girl in the cage next to me had not learned this lesson.

She cried at all hours, and I hated her for it. This was the only moment I had for myself. There was no dancing and no twirling—no eyes on me, no dancing for older men.

When I was in my cage, I just existed in blissful darkness.

"You need to stop," I told the girl. "Master doesn't like it when we cry."

Those were the first words I had spoken to her. She'd

been here for three days, and I had hoped I didn't have to be the bearer of bad news that once you made it down here, there was no going back. The devil didn't like to give back his toys. That's why when a soul was lost in sin, it didn't get to go to heaven.

"A-aren't y-you scared?" she asked me. Her voice was already broken.

"If you are down here with me, then you are safe. Master likes to keep his favorite ones wrapped in darkness. It's when you are up there that you should be scared."

The worst feeling in the world was losing time. You could cut your hair and it would grow back, lose money and you'd make some more, but time—once it was gone, there was no second chance to get it back.

When I woke up, I recognized the room I was in immediately. It was dark; the canopy here was a thicker black to help hide the city lights that could be seen from my window. Nico liked to keep all his houses different, and that's how I was able to tell apart my rooms instantly.

Turning to my right, I already knew what I would see outside of the window. Big Ben could be seen from afar. We had arrived in London, the second stop on our tour, and I had no recollection of it at all.

I brought my leg up to my chest, and the movement startled Bane, who was lying in bed next to me. It felt like I had not seen him in weeks. I brought him close to my chest and began to cry into his fur.

"I missed you so much, boy," I whispered into his neck.

He whined in glee as I petted his coat. My hands stopped petting him when I felt the bandage that adorned his paw. I vaguely remembered Estevan said he had fallen.

Why did this happen to me? I tried to recall something

but came up empty. I had so much sadness inside of me, and I couldn't understand where it came from.

Why couldn't I remember how I got here?

I had a show. I remember seeing that man and Estevan... my brain couldn't recall seeing Nico. I couldn't even remember the second half of the show.

When my tears hit Bane's fur, he began to bark. I held on tighter to him because I needed to feel the warmth of someone, even if it came from my dog.

The door to my room burst open and Nico walked in, with the light from the hallways illuminating him. He wore a white T-shirt with light gray sweatpants, and I couldn't even marvel at how well he looked because I couldn't keep it together.

He walked in like an imposing enigma, and taking one look at me, his whole stance changed. He went soft right before my eyes.

"Ofelia?" he questioned softly.

"Why does it feel like I'm going crazy?" I cried.

He made his way across the room until he was at my side. That's when I noticed Joker was trailing behind him.

Nico sat on the edge of the bed. He didn't allow himself to get close enough to me, not even now when I needed him the most.

"You passed out from exhaustion after the show. The doctor said you've overworked yourself. He gave you some sedatives so you could rest."

His answer calmed me a little bit. Not enough, but it eased me.

"I don't remember anything, Nico."

"You've been practicing from sunrise to sundown lately. It was too much for your malnourished body. You need to start taking better care of yourself."

He ended the last part much harsher than the rest of the sentence. I guess a part of him had a point. With all the stress, I was barely eating.

"How long have we been here?"

"We just arrived last night," he told me.

"Oh, okay," I said, feeling better about everything.

Joker jumped on the bed and cuddled me. I couldn't help but smile at my canine sandwich.

I felt Nico's eyes on me. When I looked up, he was looking at me with an intense look on his face. I looked down at myself, wondering if I had drooled all over my cheeks.

"What?" I asked.

"Nothing, just glad to have you back."

"You say that as if I had gone away or some shit."

He gave me a sad smile, and I wondered about the meaning behind it.

I wanted to soothe his wounds, to make him happy, because even though he never asked me, he had made my dreams come true. I had been a small girl, dreaming of fame and glory. I wanted to dance for the world. Travel country to country to play for sold-out tours.

The price I had paid to get here was steep, but I couldn't look back at that now. All I could do was move forward.

I rose to my knees, and Nico watched me with guarded eyes. In one blink, I could see him over me as he pumped inside of me. I knew it had been a dream from my tired delirium, but I wanted it to be real. I needed him in me so bad right now I throbbed.

As soon as I moved, the boys jumped out of bed.

"Ofelia," Nico warned.

"In my dream," I started to say as I got closer, "you climbed on top of me."

"Not this shit again," Nico said, annoyed.

I didn't stop.

"You fucked me and fingered me at the same time," I said, my voice sounding turned on by the second.

Nico's throat bobbed.

My knees hit the back of his chest, and he went still. He stopped breathing, and I smiled at the power I had over him.

"You are tense, Daddy," I whispered in his ear.

"Ofelia."

It was all he managed to say.

I didn't push him. At least not now. Instead, I started to massage his shoulders. My fingers dug into his muscle. And I wasn't just saying he was tense for the sake of touching him. A man like him carried the world on his shoulders. I forgot about my lust for a second as I tended to his needs. After a second, he started to relax the more I massaged him. My fingers roamed over his back, his neck. The moment I began to massage his scalp, he moaned.

"Fuck, that feels good," he said.

I pretended like I didn't hear it, even if his words had me feeling like I could fly. When love wasn't given to you freely, you took every scrap you could, and you hoarded it, saved it, and replayed it on a rainy day. It was those moments full of pure love that got you through the tough times.

"Lie on the bed," I told Nico, and he went still.

I couldn't help but laugh. It was somewhat funny how the man everyone seemed to respect and fear was scared of a little ballerina.

"Are you scared of me?" I teased him.

"It's not appropriate," he replied as he made a move to get up.

"Please," I pleaded with him. "I don't want to be alone right now."

He stood still for a second, and I wondered if he would end up leaving.

He turned around and faced me. I was raised on my knees, and I wasn't even up to his chest. Nico licked his lips, and my belly fluttered. I felt a rush of wetness in my pussy. If I didn't have him soon, I would combust. I knew it.

There were no words said as he came to my bed and lay down. Once he was there, I got up from mine and went to my vanity.

Our housekeepers kept our houses stocked whenever we came. I grabbed a bottle of my favorite lotion and brought it with me.

"Do you want me to take off your shirt, or do you want to do the honors?" I asked with amusement.

"The shirt stays on," Nico bit back.

"That's just silly. No good masseuse will give a massage with a shirt on," I replied.

"Good thing you aren't a masseuse."

"Nico!" I barked at him.

There was some silence, and after a few seconds, he got up enough to remove the shirt from his body.

I bit my lip to contain a moan.

This was not how I had envisioned Nico in my bed, but I wasn't about to ruin this gift by talking too much.

The bed creaked with my weight. My chest started to palpitate, and my palms began to sweat. This didn't matter since I was going to be putting lotion on them anyways.

I loved the lotion. I knew men did too because whenever I wore it, I got many compliments, from both men and women saying I smelled edible.

And I wanted Nico to eat me up.

"What are you doing?" Nico ground out the moment I straddled him.

I didn't reply. Instead, I got to work massaging him. It took a few seconds, but he relaxed.

As for me, well, the more I touched him, the wetter I got. I was lifted on my knees because if I let him feel my weight, he would tell just how soaked I was.

When he started to groan, I couldn't help it anymore. I let myself fall on him. Nico's whole body went rigid when he felt just how wet I was for him.

I still didn't say anything and continued to rub him as I moved my pussy back and forth. The friction felt good but not enough to make me come, and I needed to come. I needed to scream my release into the darkness to let the world know I was not broken.

"All done," I said breathlessly because I was no more turned on than I had been.

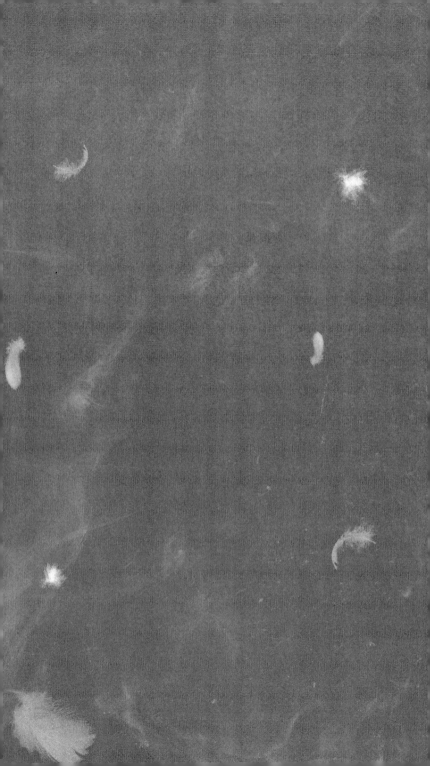

13

OFELIA

Nico was breathing heavily. I expected him to get up and leave, but instead, he turned around, lying on his back. His eyes were closed, and despite being cautious around me, he seemed at ease and content.

I wondered how much I could push him.

"Do you feel like returning the favor?"

His eyes sprang open, and at that moment, I hated the dark because it didn't do any justice to those blue eyes.

"I'll hire someone to come tomorrow," he said.

"But I want one now," I pouted at him.

"We don't always get what we want."

"That's not fair," I whined. And I already knew what he would say to me. He'd told me this whenever I said those words.

"Life's not fair, remember that."

I smirked at him.

What wasn't fair to him might be a dream for me.

I reached for his hand, and he cast me a look, trying to see what I was up to.

"I just need a little a massage," I said in a breathy voice.

"Not going to happen," he said in a final tone.

"Fine," I told him.

Instead of me insisting that he do it, I rested my head on his chest. He was lying horizontal on my bed, and I was vertical.

The mirror across the room was big enough that he was about to get the show of his life. I didn't act right away because I needed him to close his eyes for a second.

"Remember the first time you took me to get some ice cream?" I asked.

"What of it?"

I shrugged.

"You used to be so nice to me. You would buy me anything I wanted. You even let me sit on your lap when you would work."

"You were a scared child." He said it like that was all the answer in the world.

This time it was me who closed my eyes.

"I'm still scared," I whispered. As if closing my eyes would make the words any less true. A part of me felt trapped, and I didn't know how to untangle it.

I was about to get up and just give up for tonight when I felt Nico's hand on my cheek. His thumb stroked my chin. He was trying to soothe me.

"I'm sorry I can't do more for you, little swan."

I opened my eyes at the heartbreak in his voice. There was something that held him back, something that stopped this wonderful man from living.

When I twisted my head, I bit my lip when I saw that he had closed his eyes.

Don't do it, a part of me said.

You'll never know unless you try, another part whispered.

Adrenaline coursed through my veins as my fingers slipped into the waistband of my leggings. Nico still had his eyes closed, and with each of his breaths, my guilt intensified, but so did my need for him.

My skin hummed with electricity as my fingers glided down my hips, pulling down my leggings so I could give myself enough room to play.

I released the breath I was holding when my index finger glided over my folds. I was wet and aching.

"You have always done *enough*." The last part came out on a breathy moan.

My fingers dipped inside my pussy, and my back arched. My head dug into Nico's chest as I filled myself, thinking of him.

"Ofelia," he rasped out.

I didn't dare open my eyes or look at him. My fingers kept going in and out while my thumb started to circle my clit.

I felt him sit up.

With my other hand, I lifted myself back and scooted over so I was lying against him.

"Don't you want me to feel good?" I managed to ask.

He didn't say anything, and I took this as an invitation to roam his chest with my hands. I was getting so close. I just needed a bit more.

"I want you to do it," I moaned. "I want you to touch me."

I was lost in my pleasure with the way my fingers roamed over my folds. I didn't notice Nico moving until my back hit the bed.

When I opened my eyes, the first thing I saw was him unlike I had ever seen him before. I'd seen him mad, or so I thought, but that was nothing to the hell he had contained in his eyes. The blue burned like a storm about to unleash.

"You need to stop this foolishness, Ofelia," he spat out.

I didn't listen to him. I spread my legs a little more and inserted two fingers so deeply they caused me pain. My head thrashed back, and my hips bucked.

"Nico." I moaned his name breathlessly and without shame.

Pain radiated from my wrist. I looked down, and my heart rate sped as my impending orgasm only intensified when I saw that Nico was holding on to me. I didn't care that it was pain as long as the one giving it to me was him.

He yanked my hand out, pulling it in front of our faces. My fingers were coated in my wetness. Nico looked at me and then at our joined hands.

I could feel the anger that radiated from him. He was right there; I just had to push him.

"You do that to me," I said, trying to push the last of his buttons.

His nostrils flared, then slowly, he brought our hands to his chin. The tip of my fingers grazed over his stubble. The feeling between my legs intensified. It was embarrassing how close I was to coming undone.

"Is this what you want, Ofelia?" he asked through gritted teeth. He put one of his legs between mine, then rubbed his knee between my folds. It felt divine, but it was not enough.

"You want *Daddy's* dick?" his words were laced with venom.

I was humping his leg, and I didn't care. I didn't care

about what I was doing anymore; I just knew I needed him to break and claim me. I needed him to show me I was his, and I didn't care how low I stooped to make it happen.

"Yes."

Warmth engulfed my fingers as Nico brought them into his mouth. I watched in fascination as he tasted me, the way he closed his eyes, and I wondered if it was because he liked my taste.

His eyes opened as he pulled out my fingers slowly, and I watched him transfixed.

"Hmmm," he said against them.

The tip of his tongue glided down my index finger down to the curve of where my thumb conjoined.

"Your pussy is nothing special, Ofelia."

My brows scrunched in confusion. Before I could process what he did and what he meant, I howled in pain.

Nico had bitten the tender skin between my thumb and index finger. I gaped at him.

"You need to worry a little less about getting on my dick and more on your dance," he said as he threw my aching hand on the bed. "When I look at you, I still see a *child* —pathetic."

He climbed out of bed and left my room without another word.

───

WAS THERE AN EQUIVALENT OF BLUE BALLS FOR women? Purple clit? There had to be something because I was in pain. Both my pussy and my heart ached.

Nico's words kept replaying in my ear.

Pathetic.

And I had been pathetic. There were many signs, or so I thought, but apparently, none of them were pointing at me.

Our London show would be in two days, and then we had to fly over to the next stop on tour and get some practice in.

Bane was waiting on the bed. He watched me as I got ready.

"You like me, don't you, boy?"

He woofed his response.

Since I was going to practice later, I wore a black skater dress and some flats. The weather wasn't as nice here as it had been back home.

Once outside of my room, I made my way down to the kitchen. I needed food if I didn't want to pass out from exhaustion again. No way in hell was I giving Delia an opening. That bitch could rot in hell.

I had one hell of a poker face. If I could thank ballet for something other than grace, it would be my ability to stay stoic.

Nico was drinking coffee while he chatted with Estevan and two other of his men.

"Good afternoon," I greeted them as I made my way to where Nico was, since he had the pot of boiled water next to him.

"Feel better?" Estevan was the only one who greeted me. The other two men excused themselves.

"A bit achy, but I'll live." I shrugged it off. Nico still hadn't talked to me.

I purposely grazed his midsection as I reached for a mug.

"Sorry, Daddy," I mocked.

"Did you tell her?" Estevan asked Nico.

I turned around just as I started to stir my coffee.

"Tell me what?"

Nico moved away from me, and it bothered me that he could call me names but didn't have the decency to look at my face afterward.

"You are due for a physical, so I have a doctor coming to check you out," he replied with ease.

"Not that," Estevan said. "About the charity ball." He smirked in Nico's direction.

I cocked my head.

"A ball?" Excitement could be heard in my voice. "Am I allowed to come?"

I didn't do much other than practice, and our tours didn't exactly sound like I was living life. Being invited to events that had nothing to do with our company was rare, and if Nico went, he did it alone.

"Yes," Estevan said.

"No," Nico shouted.

"Then I need to find something to wear." I smiled at Estevan since Nico was making it a point to not look me in the face.

"I'm not going for pleasure. I have to attend to business; I can't be worried about what Ofelia is doing."

I didn't let Nico's words hurt me. His insults didn't faze me, not when everything else he did soothed me. Maybe I was crazy, a little naive, but if the man really wanted me gone, I would be nothing but a memory in this place.

He didn't like it, but I had a place in his house, amongst his men, and the part he hated the most was how much he had let me into his heart.

"Us children get bored sometimes," I mumbled into my cup. "Perhaps I need to go find a guy to have a playdate with."

Nico's head snapped up in that instant, and I kept the cup firmly in place so he couldn't see my smile.

Estevan chuckled.

"Maybe it's time I lived on my own," I said as I put my cup on the counter. "Experience life a little more."

"That's a great idea, Bambina," Estevan exclaimed.

Nico cut him with a glare. "Don't you have to go somewhere?"

Estevan raised his hands in mock surrender, then left me alone with Nico. This time I was the one who couldn't look him in the eyes.

"You said you didn't want to leave," Nico said.

I dumped the rest of the coffee in the sink and started to rinse my cup.

"I said I wanted to stay in the company, but I think space would be good for us," I told him, even though space was the last thing I wanted.

When I turned around this time, Nico's glare was directed at me. You couldn't hate someone without having feelings toward them.

"If you think I am paying for an apartment so you can entertain men, you are out of your fucking mind."

"You could always entertain me." I smirked at him. He swallowed. "But you don't want to."

If my master had taught me one thing in the years I was with him, it was that men did what they wanted. You couldn't make a man want you, love you, or keep you. I already had one of the three I could be patient with.

"Come on, boy, we have some shopping to do," I called out for Bane so he could follow me.

I was sidestepping Nico when he put an arm in front of me to stop me.

"You have no idea what you're getting into, my little ballerina. Don't go to the party."

I patted his chest and smiled.

"I've been dancing with bloodied feet for half of my life; pain does not scare me."

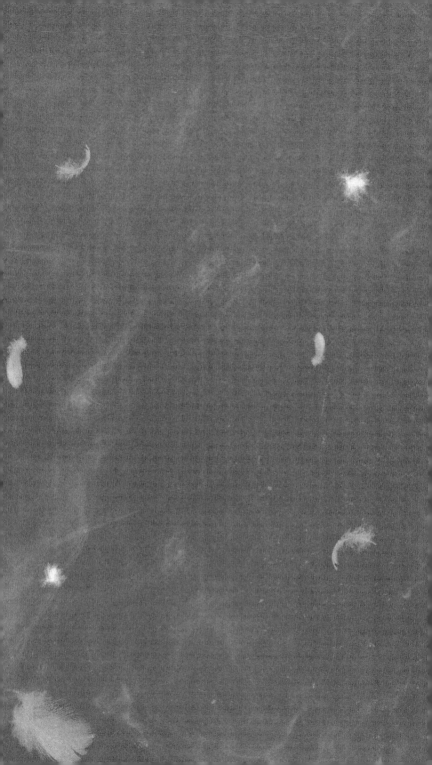

DANCE

If we could do nothing but dance, defy gravity, and defy time, I promise to give you everything I have in my life. I'd dance until my feet were scraped raw and my knees ached from standing up.
I'd give you everything I had so just for a moment, I could call you mine.

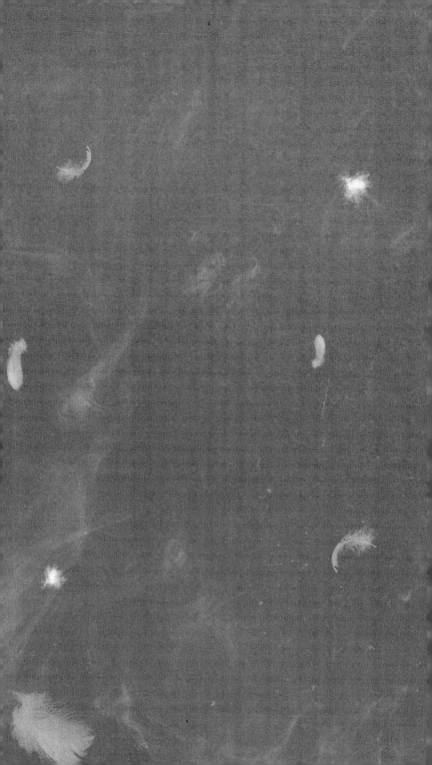

14

OFELIA

IT WAS WEIRD TO STARE INTO A MIRROR. TO BYPASS THE things that made us unique and beautiful and stare at all the imperfections we couldn't stand. To see all the ugly little things that were a fraction of who we were. It was sad to stare at something beautiful and not love what was reflected back.

For the life of me, I couldn't see what people saw in me when they watched me perform. I cocked my head and then did it again to the opposite side.

I supposed I looked good, but there was always someone out there that would look better. Maybe this inadequate feeling came from being rejected by Nico?

When I looked into my eyes, I saw unmistakable green eyes staring back at me.

Delia mocked me even when she wasn't near.

Ignoring that part, my eyes swept down to my dress. Red gown with a slit on the hip, my lips and shoes matched perfectly. My curls were coiled and untamed.

"If you don't hurry up, Ofelia, Nico will be leaving without you!" Estevan shouted from outside my room.

I doubted he would. I couldn't help but think I had him exactly where I wanted him at.

"I'm coming!" I yelled toward the stairs as I came out of my room.

Joker had been lying at my door and followed me as soon as I made my way toward the front of the house.

"What do you think, boy? I clean up good, right?"

He woofed his response.

When I came down the stairs, Nico was already waiting for me. He looked divine. He wore an all-black tuxedo, including black loafers.

I didn't say a word as I walked past him. Two could play his hot-and-cold game. Before I could open the door for the limo, he was already there opening it. I slid in without a word.

"Are you still mad?" he said cautiously.

"No," I replied.

He put his ankle over his knee as he watched out of the window.

"Is it because I didn't want you to come?"

"I'm not mad," I repeated.

He didn't answer right away. Instead, he put up the partition.

"Is this because I didn't fuck you?"

My head snapped his way.

"Or because I didn't let you come?"

My cheeks flamed, maybe more so by his carefree attitude.

I took a calming breath before I lashed out and blew away my new plan.

"Nope, like I said, it's time I find someone else to take care of my needs."

The asshole had the audacity to laugh.

"What's so funny?"

"Nothing," he said mockingly. "I'm just wondering how they will achieve that with broken fingers, no dick, nor a tongue."

"What are you saying? You won't have me, but no one else can either? That's bullshit."

Nico fixed his tie, and I watched him as he kept staring absently out of the window.

"I own you, little swan," he said in a cold tone.

Shivers went down my spine all the way to my toes. I knew he meant them as an insult, but the way my body responded to them was anything but repulsed.

"Caged birds don't last long in captivity," I told him.

I knew my words angered him because his fist clenched, but otherwise, he stayed perfectly composed.

We arrived shortly at a house. It was huge, three floors. There was a line of cars waiting to go inside through the gate.

I sat up when I saw how much security was out here.

"What kind of event is this one?"

"A private one," Nico replied, none too thrilled.

A guard came in and checked all of the guests. When he got to our limousine, Nico put the partition down.

"Nico Dos Santos and Ofelia Dos Santos," he told the guard.

His hand reached for mine and squeezed it. It was a warning so that I wouldn't open my smart mouth.

The guard checked his tablet, and we were let in.

"Security is tight," I joked.

"Xander had an incident a few years ago, and he doesn't want that to repeat," he told me, even though I had no idea what or who he was talking about.

We were going to be the next to be dropped off at the

entrance. Nico sat up a little straighter and turned to face me.

"There are many things I've kept you in the dark about. Because it's not your place to know and others to protect you."

I blinked and kept staring at him so he could keep going.

"Stay by my side at all times. If, for any reason, we do get separated, do not engage in conversation with anyone. Capiche?"

I saluted him. "Aye aye, Captain."

Nico glared. "This is not the time for your games, Ofelia."

The words I had at the tip of my tongue, I forced them back.

Our limo stopped, and one of the staff opened the door for Nico. He got out, then gave me his hand and helped me out. As soon as I was out, Nico wrapped one of his strong arms around my waist and led me inside.

My belly tingled. I'd sought his warmth since the moment I met him, and now he was freely giving it to me, but there was a catch. The thing was, I didn't care about it as long as I could stay in his arms.

I didn't take his warning, and maybe I should have. I smiled as we made our way to the house. It was nice, old money, and people were scattered everywhere.

If there was one thing that had always fascinated me, it was the art of dance. That's why my eyes immediately wandered to the performers that were in all corners of the room.

The first thing I noticed was the flexibility they had. They were in rings, aerial silks, poles, each looking more refined than the next. All of them wore white with a mask on their faces. I couldn't help to think they looked beautiful but sad that their expressions were tamed.

Now I could see why I had been invited. Here, I wasn't special; I was just another girl who could dance. I pressed into Nico a little more when the realization hit me.

"They're beautiful," I said in awe.

Nico's eyes went to the woman doing the aerial silks. She was a sight to see. The way she twirled in midair and then glided down, defying the laws of gravity.

"Jealousy—" He looked down at me. One of his hands wrapped around my cheek. "—doesn't suit you."

I sucked in a breath. He might not like to watch me at times, but there was no denying he knew me very well.

"I'm not jealous," I told him.

He didn't reply; instead, he kept us moving until we made it to the back of the house. The inside was beautiful, but the backyard looked magical. Fairy lights were placed around the gardens. A small orchestra played in one of the corners.

"Whatever you see, don't react," Nico whispered in my ear as he led me down the stairs.

At first, I didn't know what he was talking about. Everything seemed normal and classy, until I saw a small girl dancing on a podium by a pool. She was tiny and the only one wearing black out of the dancers. She twirled and spun, pretending like no one was here at the party.

My throat clogged.

I knew that feeling all too well.

"We are going to have company today, my little ballerina."

My master's voice thundered in the room. His words were not loud, but it was the first time I'd heard his voice in days. My cage was always dark; my meals got brought to me at night, so the light coming from his open door hurt, but it was something I welcomed. To see sunlight was beautiful. Even if I couldn't bask in its warmth, it felt nice to look upon it.

"Y-yes, Master." My voice was a little croaky from not speaking for a few days, but it was eager to please him.

He laughed, and joy spread through me.

"You keep it like this, and you will be let out more often."

A smile spread through my face, and even though I couldn't see in the dark, I looked down to my feet. The blood that coated them from last practice had dried out, but I could feel the scabs. This time I wouldn't complain about the pain or stop dancing if it meant I got to be outside.

"I'll be the best you've ever seen, Master."

I couldn't remember when was the last time I saw my family, but I knew it'd barely been a few months. The sad thing was I could barely remember their faces. Everything started to fade in this black hole.

"Ofelia!"

My body shook, and all I saw was twinkling lights moving.

"Ofelia!"

It took a few moments and a lot of blinking until the party came into focus again. This time I saw it with new eyes.

The people were transfixed on the dancers in a way that didn't sit right with me. Their gazes—my God, it reminded me of a time when I was spinning and men watched me. They wanted me.

"I'm going to be sick," I murmured.

Nico held on to my elbow and dragged me to the side. He didn't stop walking until we were hidden by the bushes.

At one point, the darkness scared me, and I was starting

to remember pieces of myself I had disregarded, but I was scared to discover the things my mind had forgotten. Not every memory was worth being remembered. Some things were better left for dead.

"Breathe," Nico said as he rubbed circles across my back.

How could I breathe when I was living my life in an in-between of present and past? How could I breathe when I was slowly losing my mind?

"I keep seeing him," I croaked.

Nico's arm stilled.

"Who?" His voice was low but lethal. It made the hairs on the back of my nape stand up, and a tingle ran down my spine.

"My old master."

"What did you remember?" Nico's question was demanding.

I could feel the energy that was coming off him, and I knew that I said something he didn't like, he would snap, this place be damned.

Before answering him, I stood up and took a deep breath. Then I turned around and faced him. "It's nothing I didn't have a blurry memory of already, but now I get these sudden memories, and they are vivid. I feel like he still has me."

Nico's thumb grazed the underside of my chin. He took a step forward, then tipped my chin so we were face-to-face.

"He's dead, Ofelia. He will never lay another hand on you."

I nodded, blinking back tears.

It was these moments when he protected me even from my own demons that I loved him the most, but even he had sins I could no longer overlook.

Nico's gaze was on my face. It burned. It took my breath away and let me feel like I was gasping for air.

Giving my head a slight tilt, I dared ask him a question I had been trying to avoid. I couldn't pretend when little things like some dancers triggered me.

"Is something on your mind, little swan?"

I licked my lips, and Nico's eyes followed the movement. The blue shone brighter, but for now, I wouldn't get caught in the web of his beauty. He was aware of my feelings for him, and he wielded that knowledge like a weapon.

"Why were you meeting with my master?"

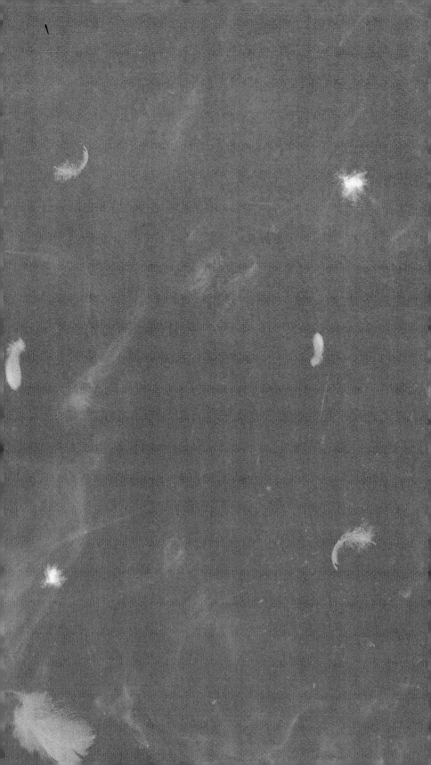

15

NICO

THE LAST THING I WANTED WAS TO BRING OFELIA WITH
me to one of Xander Yates's parties. They were always a
cover-up for his sick fetishes, if you could even call what he
liked a fetish. This one was a little different than the parties
he threw on the last Friday of every month. This one was
somewhat legit. It was a fundraiser of sorts, but everyone
came to see what kind of merchandise he had.

I got an invite because the cargo I brought with me from
Italy went to him. Xander used the opportunity to get me to
come to one of his parties, and when he told me about the
bidding, well, it was hard to resist.

I didn't count on bringing Ofelia. I didn't want her
mixed with filth like him, but I knew that I wouldn't be let
in without her. Estevan knew this and ultimately forced my
hand.

This was my fault for never taking Ofelia out anywhere
that didn't involve events for our company. Of course, she
would be eager to come.

"Why were you meeting with my master?"

Now I couldn't help but see the scared little girl I had

rescued. Fragments of young Ofelia kept resurfacing along with parts I didn't like, and some that were new. The older she got, the bolder she became.

"This is something we can discuss at a later time."

Ofelia glared at me.

"It's always the same bullshi—"

Her words died the moment my lips brushed against hers. I could feel her deep inhale with the palm that rested on her back.

I didn't allow myself any longer. The taste I had of her still lingered, and I hated that it wouldn't go away. It mocked me day in and day out.

"We will talk about this later," I pressed.

Ofelia looked up at me with doe eyes full of wonder and lust.

"Why did you k—"

"My my, aren't we a bit cozy?"

In an instant, I let go of Ofelia and turned around to see the house owner standing behind me. His eyes raked over Ofelia, and the only thing that kept me sane was that she was not to his liking.

"I was just having a word with my daughter. She doesn't do well in crowded spaces," I replied as I stood protectively in front of Ofelia.

Xander Yates smiled.

He was tall and pale with light brown hair. He had a cloak of arrogance that made you want to take him down a notch or two, but he was protected, so there wasn't much you could do.

"Thank you for getting my cargo here in perfect conditions." He looked at me slyly.

My blood boiled.

"I don't like to speak business in front of my daughter," I said coolly, despite all the ways I wanted to kill him.

He put a hand inside of his pockets and smiled. He was a charming son of a bitch, who used that to his advantage.

"Daughter." He chuckled, and then he shrugged. "To each their own."

It took all of me to not react after all. How could I when just seconds before I was kissing my so-called daughter?

"If you'll excuse me," I told him. "The bids are about to start."

He grinned like he was proud of the auction he had orchestrated. He took a deep breath, then gave a soft smile as he looked blankly at the bushes behind us.

"I, too, had a favorite once. There is something so thrilling about breaking someone over and over again and still have them cling to you. The worse you hurt them, the more they want to please you, and they live in this precious little cycle until their dying breath."

I didn't react because I knew that's what Xander wanted from me. Instead, I smiled at him, pretending I knew exactly what he was talking about. Ofelia had no clue how to play the game we were currently in. She pressed closer to me, and her hand gripped my arm, not fully understanding what was being talked about but subconsciously knowing it was despicable.

"Excuse me," I told him as I dragged Ofelia with me and made our way somewhere far away from him.

"You have a lovely home."

I closed my eyes when I heard Ofelia's sweet tone directed at Xander. There was nothing more I could do now than to just keep pulling her until she was far away, and then I could yell at her.

"You know what's the thing I've always loved about ballerinas?"

I stopped. My heart pounded, and my ears rang. My body felt hot, like I was ready to burst, but I didn't otherwise engage.

"Their bodies defy puberty."

Fuck this shit!

Sometimes, playing the devil's advocate had its limits, and I was at mine. Some kills were for revenge, others for mercy, and this would be a selfish one on my part, even if my revenge will make the world a better place.

My hand fisted in front of me, and I was already turning around, ready to punch today's host, knowing that as soon as he was on the ground, I would kill him before anyone could stop me.

"Long time, no see," a hoarse voice next to me said.

When I turned to my side, my eyes widened for a second when I saw Roman. He wasn't as tall as I was but broader. His black hair was tied in a low ponytail, and even in a suit, he made his gauges look classy.

His grip on my shoulder burned from where he was digging his thumb. He was aware of what I was about to do but still managed to look at ease.

"Roman," Xander said. "I wasn't aware you two knew each other."

"Ah, mate, now don't think you were the only one privy to this man's talents."

Another man appeared from behind Xander and patted him on the back. I blinked back, wondering how he got here; as for Xander, he jumped, not able to hide his surprised reaction.

The man was tall, and tattoos peeked from every part that was not covered by his tuxedo.

Xander schooled his expression. "If you two are here, I am guessing there's a reason."

The tattooed man patted Xander; his tone was light, but his eyes told a different story.

"You know Daddy doesn't like the attention, and we heard you are causing a stir."

I turned to look at Roman and found his gaze was on Ofelia, looking at her quizzically. Then he slightly turned his head, telling me to get out.

I still needed to stay for the auction, so I just pulled Ofelia next to me, and I took her to the other end of the pool to where the dancer was still doing twirls and spins.

Having Ofelia close eased me some. It soothed the beast I kept chained inside. I felt her warmth, which made it easier to look at all the people near me. Outbidding them would be hard, but this was a piece I needed if the information I had been told was correct.

She clung to my side; one of her arms was holding on to my chest, right below my heart. The way it thumped reminded me that I still felt, despite trying to pretend otherwise. Her other hand was gripping the jacket in the back.

My hand curved around her waist, and I bent to kiss the top of her head.

"We'll be going soon," I told her, and she nodded.

It wasn't long after when the lights all dimmed, and the performers who had been dancing all appeared behind the MC. Ofelia peeked her head up to look at all of them. I had no doubt that she could see pieces of herself in them.

"Welcome, everyone," the man greeted. "We are honored you could join us on this lovely evening."

Applause broke around the backyard. Men and women cheered. Pictures were taken for the society pages, but the real reason for today's auction wouldn't be revealed.

"While you walked around, there were different numbers displayed. This number corresponds with the item up for auction."

Ofelia gasped.

I pulled her in closer to me. All I could offer as comfort was a piece of myself.

"Not a word, right," she mumbled to herself.

I felt like a piece of shit, but so fucking proud of her.

The MC made jokes as he started to auction from the number one and so on. People raised their paddles and shouted numbers. The air was filled with excitement coming from all directions.

The higher the number, the more people seemed to lose the cloak of innocence they'd worn and started to show their true selves. I had brought a fragile swan to a room of monsters.

"Now for our final product," the MC announced.

Shouts went through the whole room. This next one was the prize everyone was after.

The little girl who had been dancing by the pool stepped forward. The mask was still on her face. All of the performers' faces were still covered. The privilege of seeing their faces went to their masters.

"Shall we start the bidding at 25?" the MC announced cheerily.

Last bids started between ten thousand and fifteen and sold at thirty or forty. The young ones tended to be sold for more.

"Thirty." I raised my paddle.

The moment I spoke, Ofelia let go of me and looked at me in disbelief. My hand, however, didn't waver despite how much she seemed to want to get away from me now. She seemed to think she wanted me, but she had never had an idea of who the real me was, and she was about to take a closer look and be terrified about what she saw.

More people kept shouting amounts, all of them eager to be the ones to destroy the innocence that was before us.

"Ninety!" I called out again, going twenty above the rest.

I waited to see if someone else would up my bet, but even though everyone here had pockets, they didn't think it was worth it to spend so much money on something that was meant to be disposable. After all, you could easily get it for cheaper somewhere else. It was rare when merchandise piqued my interest, and I was allowed to keep it, and all they had to do was pay a small price for their freedom.

"I won't go anywhere, but let me go." Ofelia tried to get away from my hold, but I couldn't let her roam free.

Yates didn't look happy about my winnings, but he couldn't do much unless he wanted to cause a scene, which would be bad for business.

"The last thing you want is for me to let go," I whispered in her ear, high from my winnings. It was the only reason I was acting delusional.

"Going once...going twice... S—"

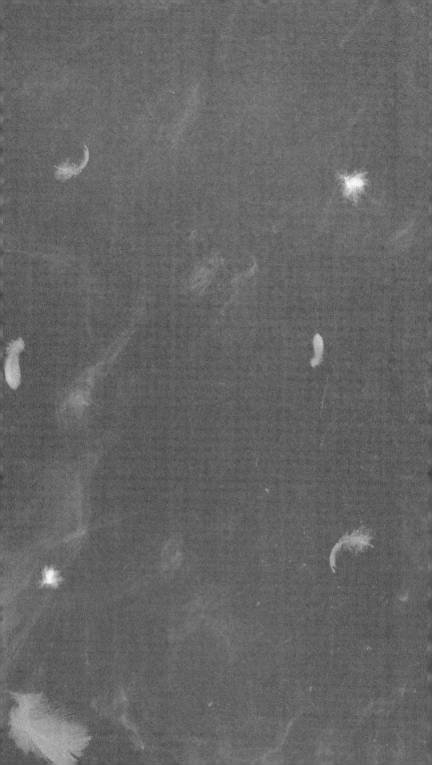

STARS

There are no longer any stars in my dark skies.
They were made of people who I believed shined bright. I
hooked my hopes and dreams into their light.
That's why I now appreciate the beauty in my night
because it no longer shines with deception and lies.

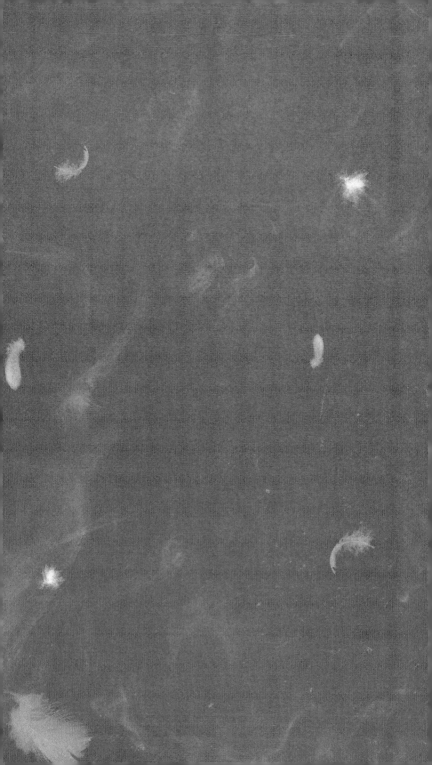

16

OFELIA

I was going to be sick.

Bile had been gathering in my throat since the moment I realized what was really going on in this party. My stomach had been churning and burning.

Since Nico started yelling numbers, I'd been trying to get away from him, but the arm he had around me became like steel. The only thing I knew I couldn't do was cause a scene. The men who had been talking to him earlier scared me. It wasn't anything about how they dressed or looked because, just like Nico, they were all beautiful in their own way. No, it wasn't that. It was something about their eyes; I supposed like called to like, and once you saw death reflected in your own eyes, it was hard not to see it in others.

"Ninety!" Nico yelled.

"I won't go anywhere, but let me go," I hissed.

There was a triumphant smile on Nico's face when no one else challenged his bid. He didn't let me go; his fingers spread across my abdomen. I could feel his nails tearing the thin material of my dress and clawing into my skin.

Nico bent his head, and his hot breath cloaked the tip of my ear, making me shiver.

"The last thing you want is for me to let go."

Have you ever looked at someone long enough and realized you were wrong about them all along? The person you had made up in your head was not the one in front of you? That you had built castles out of sand, and for that reason, they would not stand.

"Going once...going twice... S—" the host started to call out the end of the bid.

My Nico might be a lot of things, but at the end of the day, he was my protector, and this one in front of me was getting off on the idea of winning.

"One hundred and fifty!" a smooth voice called out from the other side of the room.

Nico's head spun that way along with mine and everyone's in the audience. I didn't know if I should have felt relieved that someone else won. For the life of me, I couldn't understand why handsome, refined men had to be sick and twisted and get off on things that should be illegal.

The voice belonged to a handsome man. He was tall and fair with dark eyes and hair. Our eyes met from across the room, and he winked at me.

A whimper escaped my lips. My head was starting to throb. I just wanted to go back to the house, get on my bed, and curl up to my dogs.

The man who had been giving me the creeps gave a smirk in our direction, and I got a feeling he didn't want Nico to win.

"Let's go," Nico said through gritted teeth as he dragged me with him.

I bit my lip, trying to contain all the curse words I wanted to say to him. I let him lead me out again, and my heart cracked for a second when I saw all the empty corners and there were no longer performers, knowing they went with someone else.

I let Nico drag me, and I couldn't help but feel numb. I felt like a kid who wished upon shooting stars to grow up and find out all those wishes landed on metal planes.

Nico must have texted ahead of time because our driver was waiting for us at the entrance. As soon as the doors to the limo closed, I lost it.

"Let go of me," I screeched as I pulled my arm, trying to yank it free from Nico's hold.

For someone who wanted me gone for most of my life, he didn't want to let me go. I kept thrashing, trying to get as far away as I could, but he held on to my other wrist and, with both, pulled me closer. I landed on his lap, except this time, I didn't want to be near him.

"This is what you wanted, isn't it?" Nico taunted.

I wiggled, trying to get away, and he seemed to pull me closer. It was like he needed me at this moment, and the second I let my weight fall on his, I knew just how much he needed me.

His chest rose and fell. His eyes were dark and intense. "Are you scared of me now, little swan?" Nico's voice was low and controlled, but I heard the self-loathing that dripped with every word.

"You are—"

"A monster?" he added as he pulled me forward until my face was inches from him. I sucked in a breath. My anger was slowly turning into confusion. I was angry, but there was also no denying I still wanted him to fuck me. My pussy was wet.

"What were you doing with my master?" I whispered as I moved my hips against his hard-on.

"Scared I'm like him?" he mocked me.

"Let me go." I squirmed over him.

One second I was still on top of him, and the next, he had me under him. He grabbed one of my legs and curled it against his hip, his hand sliding down my skin leisurely. Goose bumps spread all over my skin. I felt my nipples pucker.

His other hand was at my throat, squeezing hard enough that it made breathing difficult but not enough to cause any real damage.

It was like he had a point to prove, maybe not to me but to himself.

"Does it sicken you?" he asked through gritted teeth.

"Yes," I hissed.

His eyes widened for a second with disappointment, but his shoulders lost some of the tension, as if this was the reaction he had been expecting.

"Is this why you kept away from me?" I managed to choke out. "I outgrew your tastes?"

His nostrils flared.

"I'm too much of a woman for you now?" I spat.

Nico got closer, his face full of rage. I could feel his hot breath on my skin.

"It's because I still think of you as a child that you—"

His words died the moment that I moved and caught his lower lip between my teeth. He said the words, yet his body said otherwise. I bit his lip until his blood coated my tongue. The taste of copper invaded my taste buds. There was so much hate and rage, but none of it was for each other but at the circumstances we had found ourselves in.

His hold on me had loosened. I used the opportunity and ran my fingers through his hair, then pulled, and at the same time kissed him. Nico kissed me back with all his self-loathing. It was a bitter kiss full of hate and blood but over-powered with lust.

I felt the car stop moving and a door opening and closing. I knew Nico heard it too, and I knew he could be pulling away at any second. One of my hands moved down his back, curving to his waist.

Nico pulled back, both of us breathing heavily.

"This doesn't feel like you don't want me," I told him as my hand rubbed his hard-on. "Too bad you disgust me."

Nico smirked at me. With one hand, he held down to my waist while he brought his fingers to my pussy.

"Is that so, little swan?" he groaned.

Tingles spread through my whole body the second his fingertips touched the apex of my thighs. They were soft at first, teasing me like he was scared to go any further.

All my nerve endings were on high alert, and every single one of my cells was concentrated at my core. Nico chuckled when he inserted two fingers inside of me.

"This doesn't feel like you're disgusted," he said in a smoky tone upon feeling my wetness.

Before I could respond, he pushed his fingers deeper in me and moved them. My eyes closed and my back arched. He pulled them out and inserted them again. A whimper left my lips, and I cursed myself for being weak where he was concerned.

"That doesn't sound like you're disgusted by me," he groaned. "You're fucking soaked."

My hips started to move of their own accord. I'd been so frustrated by this man I couldn't take it anymore.

All you could hear in the car was our heavy breathing and the sound of my wet pussy as he fucked me with his fingers. I didn't care if it was wrong. If at this moment, all I felt for him was rage about the things he kept hidden from me. This was something I wanted for myself, to have his memory replace someone else.

"You're so fucking tight," he told me as his fingers moved faster.

"Don't stop," I moaned as my hips started to move against him.

Nico's response was to scissor his fingers inside of me. He leaned in closer to my mouth, going to my neck and leaving butterfly kisses along the arch of my neck.

"Too late for that now," he groaned more to himself than to me.

His fingers came in and out with more force than necessary, but I welcomed the pain. I thrived on it because perfection didn't happen overnight—it took blood, sweat, and tears to be achieved.

I turned my head to meet his lips, only for my gaze to collide with his. Those blue eyes were burning up, and the fire inside of them was caused by me. That information took me even higher than I already was.

"Is that what you wanted?" he said as he kissed my forehead, then the tip of my nose. "For Daddy to make you feel good."

I moaned, and he kissed me. My hands went to his hair, gripping it, and Nico cursed. I needed to feel more of him to cause him a little bit of pain, just a small dose of what he had caused me. My orgasm washed over me. This was a better high than being onstage. The burn of it made you soar and left you breathless afterward.

When I opened my eyes, Nico was still holding on to me. His gaze had gone soft. He ran a hand over my curls.

"You're so fucking beautiful. It hurts to look at you."

I sucked in a breath at his admission. All the times I

thought he wasn't paying attention, that he didn't see me, I was speechless.

Nico sat up and fixed his tie. I went up with him trying to kiss him again, but he pulled back.

My stomach sunk, my throat constricted, and my lips wobbled.

"Well, now that that's out of the way, you can leave me alone."

Nico didn't look back at me as he left the car, and that rage I felt earlier at the party came back tenfold, but this time it was followed by shame.

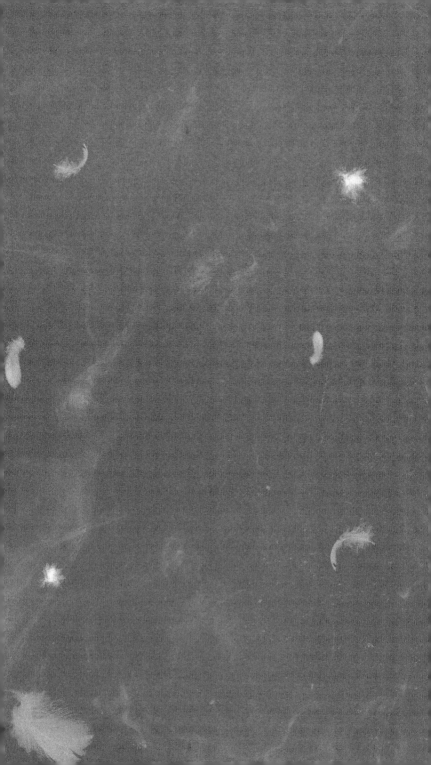

17

TIME STOOD STILL FOR NO ONE. IT SUNK ITS CLAWS into you, and all you could do was hope that you got everything out of life.

Steam covered my mirror. I wiped it off and looked at my reflection in the mirror, and I could see the years had caught up to me.

My hair was dripping wet, yet I could see some gray was starting to show. A towel draped around my middle. Years of disciplining my body kept me in better psychical shape than men half of my age. I gripped the counter at the sight of my dick tenting the towel. My cock was still fucking hard, no matter how many times I had jerked off. It should be fucking embarrassing, but my attraction to Ofelia wasn't fading; if anything, it kept getting stronger.

It went hand in hand with my need for revenge.

Last night, fuck, last night shouldn't have happened, but the moment I had her under me, I lost all my self-control. Her pleas, moans, the way she tasted and smelled—it was perfection.

But I needed to wipe away the fear and disgust I saw

reflected in Ofelia's eyes. She thought she knew what I was up to over at the auction, but in reality, she had no idea. No one did.

Fuck, the way she felt—I needed to stop this foolishness and get my head in the game. We would be leaving London tomorrow after the show, and I couldn't help the feeling that all the pieces had finally fallen into place.

I ignored my hard-on and made my way to my closet. Since Ofelia had already left for practice, both dogs roamed around my room. They might obey me, but they doted on her.

Even I could I admit she brought some light into my world. The day I lost my little girl was the last time I had ever felt at peace. It has been eleven years of agony and torture. Maybe that's why I saved Ofelia at first. She reminded me of my daughter. They were around the same age, and as a father, I felt for anyone who was put through such a horrible fate.

Then again, what kind of father was I if I couldn't keep my own family safe. How many times did Estevan warn me that my girlfriend was losing it. I'd carried so much guilt I was afraid to speak up, to demand anything from her.

We were both young when we had Diana. She had just turned sixteen, and I was barely seventeen. Still, we tried to become a family. Maybe it was old traditions that kept us together instead of love, but we tried. I busted my ass working two jobs, making sure that my girls didn't have to go without food.

At the time, Estevan and I had gone our different ways. I had become a family man, trying to make my money the right way, while he sunk himself deeper in the shadows, making easy money that came at a price.

He was the first to warn me about Hilda, but I had been

too stubborn to see it. I never believed that while I was out working hard and trying to keep us together, she was trying to live the youth she missed out on while trying to raise a family with me.

It wasn't even the cheating that got to me. I guess we fell out of love but stuck it out with one another because we got comfortable. What tore me up inside was the fact that she could be careless with my little girl. She was off chasing her high, letting men come into our house.

What killed me was that I let it happen.

There was no bigger failure than that of a father who couldn't protect his daughter. A piece of you died right along with them.

That was the thing, though, wasn't it? I wasn't deluded enough to think my child had survived, but being in the unknown was killing me. Ofelia eased that pain. At first, it was the humbling feeling of being able to save someone else's daughter, but when I found out she had been sold by her own parents, I couldn't let them have her.

I protected her, and I could never give her the love of a parent because I felt guilty that I couldn't give that to my own child. That guilt built a barrier between her and me, and now years later, the wedge was big enough to filter lust.

Through the years, Ofelia grew up to be a beauty. Even a blind man could see it. But that wasn't what attracted me. Beauty faded, but that fire someone had inside of them, that will to survive that shit, remained burning steadily through the years.

Once I was changed, I looked for Estevan, letting him know I wouldn't need him today. I looked around the house at the obvious sign of wealth it displayed, and I couldn't help but think it all came at the cost of my daughter's head.

Her disappearance turned me into a different man—it made me a monster.

The ruthlessness I displayed early on was why I took charge of this corrupted ship and not Estevan. I sometimes wondered if he resented me for it, but he never showed any signs of it.

"Where to, sir?" my driver asked as soon as I opened the door to the car.

"The theater," I told him.

Roman was probably already there, and I was afraid about what he would say. I was filled with dread at the thought of losing Ofelia.

Part of me wanted to believe it was because she was my moneymaker, and even though no one could ever replace the space, Diana left. Ofelia filled other parts of me. She made this world bearable. After I rescued her, everything was a wonder to her, and for a moment, it was nice to see the world through her eyes. To see beauty in life once more—too bad it didn't last. It never did. All I could do was chase temporary highs, and so far, Ofelia was starting to become my drug of choice, which wasn't fair to her.

When I got to the theater, I ignored the dancers and made my way to the top of the stage where I agreed to meet Roman, except he wasn't alone.

One thing I could count on was my poker face. I had perfected over the years, especially since I had Ofelia throwing herself at me since she was eighteen. For some, sexual abuse made them scared of sex, and for others, it made them hypersexual in a way to want to own what was done to them.

Either way, I hated thinking about it because whatever was done to Ofelia, I was sure was also done to my little girl.

To want Ofelia...well, that made me feel disgusted with myself.

Roman was watching Ofelia intently, his eyes following her movements. He had two companions, the tattooed man from last night, and—

"What the fuck is this?" I said through gritted teeth upon seeing the man who beat me at the auction.

"Howdy," the bastard said with a smile. He had light skin, with eyes so dark they looked black.

"Aw, mate, you miss your Texan roots, don't you?" The tattooed one patted the man's cheeks playfully.

"Do you two have to act like you're sucking each other's dicks all the time?" Roman asked in his hoarse voice.

"What the fuck is going on?" I asked once I was standing next to the aisle they were seated on.

"Nico." Roman waved a hand at me and then to his companions. "Gideon." He pointed to the tattooed one. "And Bas."

"He stole my girl," I told Roman through gritted teeth.

"You can have her," Bas said coldly. "Little girls aren't my style."

They weren't mine either, but part of why my show did so well was thanks to these sales. People often wondered how the show was filled with such raw energy. They could taste the fear and the hate, and the answer was horrifying all on its own.

I looked down at my dancers, and at the center was Ofelia, and surrounding her were the rest of the broken girls and boys I had managed to save.

"What's going on?"

"We didn't think it was wise for you to win, especially after that altercation with Xander," Roman told me.

"It's not like he doesn't know what I'm doing."

All three of them looked at me. The only one who looked like he took what I did seriously was Roman.

"Look, mate," Gideon said. "Sometimes it is best to play the card you are given and let that dish turn stone-cold until you can dish it out."

"Welcome to the dance of the dead," the MC spoke, and his voice vibrated through the speakers around the room.

Gideon rubbed his hands together. "Now that's my kind of dance."

"How many ballerinas you think I can fuck before we leave? If I do threesomes, I'm sure I can get all of them," Bas told him.

I was going to castrate him, make him eat his dick, and then kill him.

Roman put a hand on my arm to soothe me.

"They're dipshits, but if anything happens to them, the aftermath won't be pretty."

Gideon looked at me and grinned. "My girl doesn't like it when I get hurt."

Both of the men snorted.

"I'm sure Daphne would be thrilled if someone beats your ass," Bas answered.

Roman could tell I'd had enough and got up, walking down the hallway away from them.

"I've gone over all of your notes and those of Estevan's too."

"And…" I stopped to hold my breath, hoping he didn't give me bad news.

"She's getting stronger."

I let go of the breath I was holding.

"Either her mind can heal after the trauma, or it can finish shattering," he said, still looking at the stage.

"Her affliction is getting worse."

Roman nodded.

"Don't push her, Nico. I know you want answers, and I get that, but will you be happy if they come at the cost of her life?"

And there lay the million-dollar question. It was a double-edged sword. If I didn't get the answers I wanted, I wouldn't get my revenge, and I'd come to resent Ofelia. And if I did, and I got my answers, I would have finished breaking my little swan.

"Should I be concerned about Xander?"

Roman shook his head.

"No, he's been insufferable ever since someone stole from him, and the way he sees it, you keep stealing merchandise before it can be disposed of."

Some called me the Shipper, but to the most depraved, I was their grand master. It was the reason I was allowed to do what I did with no repercussions. My show was tragic and filled with pain, anguish, and death because all of my dancers were broken and had to be faced with their tormentors at one point during the tour. The anguish on their faces was heartbreaking, the fear so raw you could taste it.

And I was the sick bastard that exploited it.

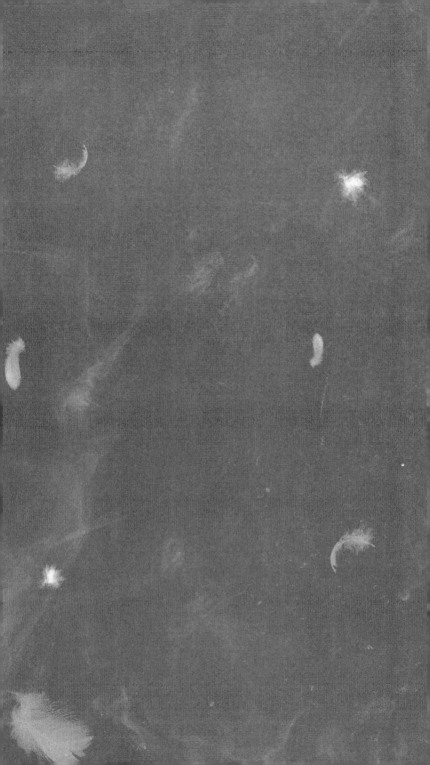

ANSWERS

She wanted answers, he asked more questions.
She wanted honesty, and he was deception.
She was tired of being treated with half-truths and some
lies.
When in reality, he was trying to protect her fragile mind.

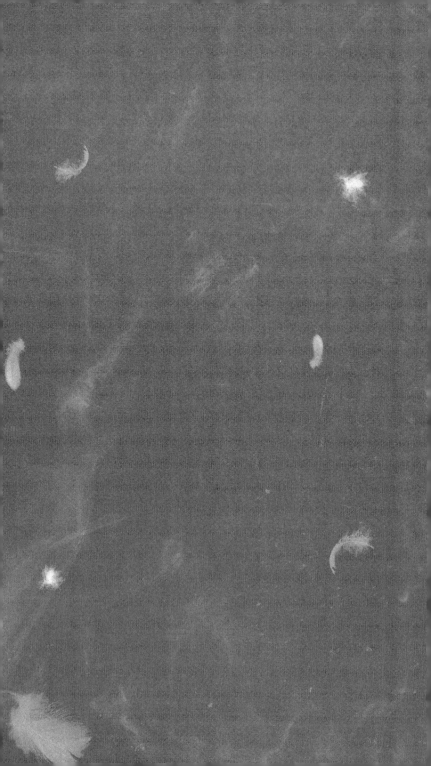

18

OFELIA

THE EYES OF MEN BURNED ON A WOMAN'S SKIN. THEY either warned you or excited you. I didn't know which one I felt right now. A part of me had always been open to Nico's gaze. It was like a warm blanket on my skin.

You're so beautiful it hurts to look at you.

It was all the validation I had been looking for, only to find out my warm blanket was actually a cloak from hell with a fire that scorched and burned away parts of your soul.

A part of me was now willing to see all the things I had blissfully been blind to all of these years.

I bent my waist and lifted my leg as I extended my arm. The sweet burn spread through my body. There was nothing like having a routine, especially to a girl like me. I didn't necessarily have money nor a family, and the only thing I could depend on was my discipline.

I felt more gazes on my skin, and I took a deep breath. It never went away, the unease of male eyes—the uncertainty of what was to happen.

"Dance, little swan."

The voice in my head startled me that I took a wrong step and crashed with the dancer next to me. She jumped back like her skin was on fire, fear etched into her eyes. I looked at her face, and for a second, saw my own.

"You've grown up to be a beauty." My master smiled at me. Part of me wanted to beam at him for his praise, as if being beautiful was something I had accomplished.

"Take her away," he told one of his men.

Fear crawled down my skin. It sunk its claws deep into my pores. I inhaled it and exhaled it all. You'd think living here, I would be desensitized to fear, but that was the thing about it; the manifestation of it kept changing—evolving. Just like we grow, so do our fears. As children, we feared monsters who hid in our closets and under our beds. But now we knew real monsters were people who walked out in plain daylight and used the shadows to play. I did not doubt that given a chance, the man escorting me to my room wanted nothing more than to play with me—except his type of play, I wouldn't survive.

He held on to my frail arm, his fingers digging into my skin, and he chuckled.

"He'll get tired of you soon enough," he said, and I knew that the day my master got tired of watching me, I would be fair game like the other girls.

When we got to the hallway to the room Master kept me in, I saw another of Master's men with the new girl. Now that we weren't confined in the darkness, I could see her better. She was slender and taller than me. I couldn't see her face, just her shiny black hair.

As we passed each other, her face turned my way. The only thing I could see was crystal-like tears as they fell onto the floor.

"Ofelia," a groggy voice woke me.

Followed by that, I could hear the thumping of my heart. It was beating wildly. When I opened my eyes, I blinked a couple of times, trying to clear the haze that my memories provided.

There was a man with me, and then I could feel someone else holding me. That's when I realized the heart that I kept hearing beating wildly was not my own.

The man in front of me gave me a kind smile. I recognized him instantly; he wasn't the type of man you forgot: tan skin, a neatly trimmed beard, and white teeth that gleamed. His voice sounded raw, like he couldn't breathe.

"Get away from me," I hissed when I realized he had also been at that party.

The man smiled at me.

"It's okay, Ofelia. He's a friend," Nico whispered in my ear.

His hands on me reminded me of what we did last night. The way he touched me, the fire I had lit in his eyes.

"I don't trust you or your friends," I told him, trying to get out of his grasp.

Those blue eyes I loved so much flashed with pain, and guilt settled in my gut.

"Your little swan is growing up," the other man croaked.

Nico glared at him and then turned his attention to me.

"What happened?"

"Nothing, I'm fine," I lied.

I looked at portraits on the wall. My memories were coming back to me more vividly, and each time I remembered something new, I would be crippled with fear. Something about it all didn't sit right with me.

"Ofelia," Nico warned.

I turned to look at him, and that's when it sunk in that

he was holding me on his lap. I licked my lips, and he sucked in a breath.

A throat cleared. "Since we are all here, I'd like to get Ofelia checked out."

My cheeks warmed with embarrassment.

"You are not checking me for anything," I spat. "You were there last night."

He didn't let that faze him. "If it makes you feel better, Nico can stay."

It didn't make me feel better.

"Nico tells me you have been having a lot of fatigue lately."

I tried to move again and get away from Nico and the false sense of security he provided. I never had rose-colored glasses, and I didn't know when I decided to put them on.

"He is a doctor," Nico said, as if that would make me feel better. When he saw that I was still tense, he explained further. "I can count on one hand the number of people I trust with your life...and he's one of them."

"Is that supposed to mean something?" I bit back because I was angry with him—most of all frustrated.

"Stop being an annoying brat," Nico said as he rearranged me, probably so my bony ass would stop digging into him.

I looked down at our joined feet. He was in nice pants, and I was still wearing my tutu with sheer tights.

"I'm Roman," the man said. He pulled a stethoscope from the pocket of his jacket, and from another, a pressure cuff. "Do you always get dizzy when you remember things?"

My body froze.

I didn't like talking about my past, not even with Nico.

Roman laughed. "It's okay. Nico has told me a little about you. I have some experience in the department."

"I bet." I scoffed. "Tell me, Doctor, do you make sure all those girls are in good condition to be sold? Is that your role?"

He smiled sadly at me.

"I'm the one who analyzes the ones who make it out alive."

Girls like me. The ones who defy all odds, but even if you make it out alive, a part of you is still stuck in the past.

Nico started to rub circles up and down my arms. That fake warmth that he provided needed to go. He might not be like my master, but I couldn't be blind anymore to the things he did, especially if it involved girls like I had been.

Roman finished checking on me all while I sat on Nico's lap. I wanted to wiggle on him and maybe grind myself too, at the same time run away from him. I couldn't get the image of the other dancers out of my head. They swirled in my mind mixing with memories of the past.

Nico and Roman started to talk, and I tuned them out. That girl, I got the feeling she was important. My whole life with my master had been darkness until she came along.

"Ofelia," Nico whispered in my ear, and I got shivers running from my spine down to my core.

"I'm going crazy, aren't I?" I whispered, still staring at the wall.

Nico became still beneath me. But it was Roman who gave me words that I found strength in. He looked rough, but there was an air of kindness to him.

He bent and tapped my head.

"When shit starts to go crazy in here."

Then he tapped the left side of my chest.

"It means you are stronger than your trauma."

I sucked in a breath.

"Till next time," Roman said as he walked out of the room without a backward glance, leaving me alone with Nico.

Strength was something I thought I possessed. I walked through hell, and here I was living now in paradise, but it turns out all I have been doing is calling the flames that surrounded me warm peace. How strong was I if I couldn't look past what Nico was guilty of?

It tore me up inside, and the love I felt for him was slowly morphing into hate.

A few minutes passed, and neither of us moved. We were at a stalemate. I didn't know if I could continue to love him blindly, and he still held himself back by the imposed chains he gave himself.

Nico was the first to make a move. His arms wrapped around my waist, and his chin rested on my shoulder. I heard his deep inhale, then felt the exhale like lava on my skin.

"Let me go," I said in a monotone voice.

I waited for him to do just as I asked, but his response shocked me.

"No," he said as he pulled me back toward him.

He was hard beneath me. I felt tingles between my legs.

"What did you remember, little swan?" he asked cautiously, and that had the hairs on the back of my neck rise.

"Why do you care?" I replied.

The truth was, I didn't want to share this with him. He already knew about the other stuff; this memory was one I wanted to guard close to myself.

"Don't play that game, Ofelia," he pressed on.

"It was nothing," I lied.

Nico's response was to manhandle me until I was straddling his lap and we were face-to-face.

"Do not lie to me," he warned.

His blue eyes were intense, but I didn't know if it was lust or rage that I saw reflected back in them.

"It was nothing of importance," I told him, trying to get away but failing when his hold on me became stronger.

"You are wrong," he said, his face getting closer, his lips hovering over mine. Every cell of my body became alive at that moment. "Everything you do is of importance to me."

The honesty in his voice had me confiding to him; maybe if I did that, he would also confide in me.

"I keep seeing a girl," I said, and Nico's eyes flashed, but everything else was calm. His body language did not change. Instead, he cupped my cheek tenderly.

"How do you know it's the same girl?" he asked as he began to stroke my hair.

"I don't know; I just know it. It was around the time that I met you," I said, and Nico froze. The hand that was on my hair dropped to my shoulders.

"Tell me more," he demanded in a lethal voice.

"No," I breathed. "What's so special about her? Was she the reason you were there that day? Was she going to be the person you were going to buy? Are you really as sick and perverted as the rest of them?"

Nico was heaving.

The hand that was playing with my loose strands was now wrapped around my throat.

"I'm fucking tired of your games. I don't care what you think about me, but tell me everything you know."

I could not believe this was the same man who I had thought cared about me.

"Ofelia." He squeezed my throat a little tighter. I

squirmed in his lap, my hands going to his shoulder to try and push him away, but he wouldn't budge.

"Why do you think it was around the time we met?" This time, Nico's voice wasn't demanding but was more like a plea.

"B-be-cause..."

His hold on me loosened.

"Master was starting to...prepare me."

Nico closed his eyes and dropped his head. I didn't need to look at his gaze to know he was in pain.

"No one ever touched me, but that didn't mean I didn't hear my master and the perverse things he did while I danced. It's not like I didn't know that he was waiting for me to get a little older. He would bring men, and they gathered in a room..." I stopped to take a breath, my throat clogged with emotion.

"You were there that day," I told him, and his face snapped back, his stare penetrating me. "You saw the way men looked at me. I had to dance in far worse conditions with my eyes closed tightly, praying to God that I didn't hit something or touch anyone. Somehow with my eyes closed, tears still managed to spill down."

"Poor little swan," Nico bit out. His hands come to grip my wrist. "You aren't with him. Stop calling him your master." His words were harsh. They made me flinch, and my stomach recoiled. "I don't want to hear more about your sob story."

Pain sliced through my chest, and it split me wide open.

"Now tell me about the girl," Nico roared as he pulled on my wrist, treating me no better than a rag doll.

That pain I felt, I let consume me and give me strength. I turned it into power. My wrist burned from where he didn't let go of me, but I pulled free.

"Why? Was she one of your favorites? Are you trying to find her and fuck her?" I screeched the words in his face.

My rage was nothing compared to the one Nico unleashed. His body vibrated. He stopped looking at me altogether.

"Get. The. Fuck. Off. Me," he hissed.

This was fear like I had not felt in a long time.

"Is that it? Was I right?" I pressed on.

My bony ass landed on the floor. I could feel the pain on my tailbone from where Nico threw me off. I looked up at Nico, who looked like death himself, and I wanted to recoil and worship him at the same time.

Nico started to walk out of the room, but before he opened the door, he spoke, and his words turned my world upside down.

"I was there that day, hoping I could find a lead on my daughter."

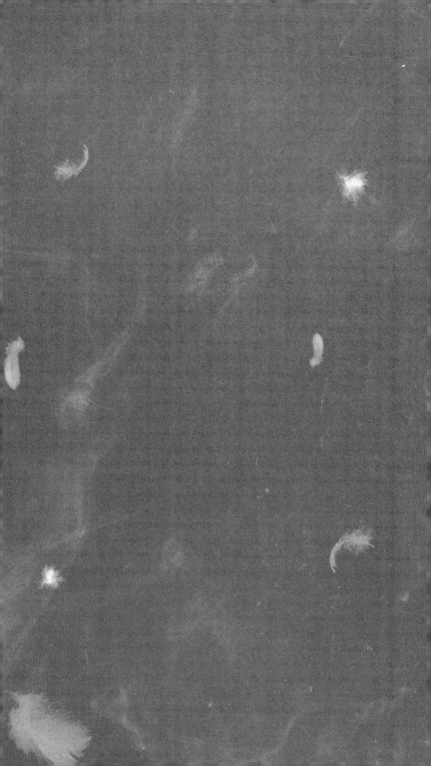

HELL

Her body was on fire.
Her soul was ripped and shredded.
Everything she thought she knew was crumbling
around her.
Her life was hanging in the precarious thread between life
and death. For she had lived in Hell and was forged in fire.
Instead of incinerating, she burned brighter.
She was a master of many faces, shedding her old skin like a
snake.
One thing was for certain. Hell cannot burn away what it
helped create.

SLEEP DID NOT COME EASY TONIGHT. I KNEW I SHOULD
be resting for tomorrow's show, but I couldn't get the image
of Nico out of my mind. The way he looked before he
walked out of the door was a sight I wouldn't be getting out
of my mind anytime soon.

The tall, imposing man I knew was one beat away from
crumbling. I felt like the world's biggest bitch. I had goaded
him, taunted him, and I had fucked up massively.

There was no way that I was going to be able to sleep
like this. I turned on my side, and Bane pressed his face into
my chest and gave a soft wine. I kissed the top of his furry
little head, then grabbed his paw.

"How's the leg feeling?"

He woofed his response, and I took that as a sign that he
was getting better.

"*I was there that day, hoping I could find a lead on my
daughter.*"

Nico had a daughter. It explained so much about him. It
explained why he was closed off, complex, and guarded.

Why in the last seven years had he made no mention of his family?

He had a daughter, someone he cared so much about he surrounded himself with men like my master in hopes of finding her. I wondered if he had a wife or a girlfriend—and why was a sick part of me jealous?

I guess I had seen Nico as mine for all of these years, but he had been someone else's first. I made him my whole world, and I merely existed in his.

"Were there other girls?"

Back then, I had been shocked and too young to recognize the hope in his voice as he asked me that question. I took a deep breath, and pain sliced down my chest, and a tear fell down my cheek when I realized why he had kept me around all of these years.

He did tell me, didn't he? I wouldn't be any use to him dead.

I went to my nightstand and found a pack of cigarettes. My hand shook as I pulled one out. It was a mix of rage and disappointment.

"Fuck," I screeched when I couldn't find a lighter.

Bane stood up, looking alert. I was having an anxiety attack, and I needed to calm down before I had a complete meltdown. I felt like throwing up as I made my way out of my room. Joker came out running from the other side of the hall.

I knew that Nico was in his office. Instead of continuing to the kitchen, I made my way over to him. It wasn't wise, not in the state I was in, but I couldn't help it.

By the time I made it to the threshold, I had noticed one of the doors was open. He probably left it that way so Joker could alert him when I made it out of my room. Bane made his way inside now that he had caught up to me. I felt terrible that I made him chase after me.

Before walking inside Nico's office, I took a breath, trying to calm myself.

Nico was sitting behind his desk. He was leaned back on his chair. He wore a plain white shirt that clung to his chest; his hair was not messy but styled, still fresh from having showered. My stupid heart skipped a beat at the sight of him.

"You didn't keep me because you cared about me," I stated, and he didn't say a word. "You kept me in hopes of finding a lead on your dau—"

"Don't," he growled.

"I was just a means to an end," I whispered, and more tears spilled.

The silence was deafening. A part of me had hoped he would deny it, but sadly that wasn't the case. I saw the way his throat constricted as I called him out.

"All this time, I pretended we were a family, but now I see why you had me at arm's length."

"You don't know anything," he said in a grave tone.

I took a step toward his desk and another until I was right in front of him.

"You should have been honest with me," I whispered.

"I don't owe you any explanations."

"I'm sorry..." I rasped out. "I'm sorry saving me was a waste."

"Enough!" Nico growled at the same time he got up and slammed his fist into the desk. "Don't play the victim. It doesn't suit you."

I flinched at his words.

"You're a good man, Nico," I said with all honesty so he would know what I had told him the other day was not true.

I guess part of me knew that there had to be another reason why he was hanging out with scum.

His laughter broke through the silence, followed by the loud thud of his weight landing on the chair.

"I'm not a good man, Ofelia," he said.

The rawness of his voice had me walking around the desk until I was standing in front of him.

"You saved me. You didn't have to," I told him. Tentatively, I reached for his head and ran my fingers through his hair.

He raised his head, and I could see the agony in his eyes. He didn't say a word as he took the cigarette I still held in my other hand and, without a word, threw it on the floor.

"I'm the reason my daughter is dead," he flatly stated.

My God, the burden this man carried on his shoulders was surreal.

"You want to know how I know you are a good man?" I asked, even though I didn't expect an answer.

"You at least tried to look for your daughter."

This time it was me who held his chin in my hand and forced him to look at me.

"You didn't give her away freely," I said, knowing that Nico would not have done what my parents had.

He scoffed.

"I was a coward," he said as he pulled away from my touch. "I was in a marriage that was going down in flames, and instead of being home and trying to fix it, I spent my days working myself to the bone. I didn't have to spend much time with my family, and no one could say a thing because I was just providing for them..." His chest was rising and falling, and I stood there, letting him give some of his burden to me.

I never had the opportunity to do much for him, but this

I could do. I'd gladly carry some of his pain. After all, I'd been carrying my own, and his would be a welcome distraction.

"I didn't count on the fact that my wife was trying to do the same, except she didn't have a work to escape to, so she started to use drugs." He laughed cynically.

"She couldn't blow our savings without arousing suspicion, so she started to fuck men in our bed for her supply." Nico made a disgusted face.

"By this point, Estevan had heard the rumors, but I didn't have the evidence needed. She didn't look like a coked-out junkie. A part of me was in denial that the sweet girl I knocked up at seventeen was capable of doing disgusting things to get her fix."

"Oh, Nico." I breathed his name like a prayer.

He dropped his shoulders and bowed his head.

"My daughter would be in the house when she would bring men... She was using more than she could pay, so eventually they just took my daughter as payment."

I sucked in a breath and closed my eyes for a second. I fuzzily remember my parents handing me off, but this girl, fuck, she must have been out of her mind.

Nico raised his head again, and our eyes met. We were two halves of the same fucked-up coin. I was the side that lived with the trauma of what had been done, and he was the side that lived with the aftermath of a loss.

"I still think you are a good man," I repeated.

"Yeah," he said in a low voice that hit me straight to my core.

Nico was no longer feeling sorry for himself. The air in the room changed. It scared and turned me on at the same time. Now that I understood him a little more, the boundaries he kept were starting to disappear.

Nico stood up, and I could see the imprint of his half-erect dick through his sweatpants. I was no longer looking down at him but up. He towered over me. He put a hand to my hips, guiding me to the edge of his desk. I felt his hands grip my bony hips through the silky satin material of my nightgown.

"I wasn't a violent person before the incident," he said. "I didn't get into fights. I wasn't like Estevan, working as hired muscle for street gangs. I did right by the law."

The edge of the desk was digging into my ass. My chest was rising and falling with anticipation of what he would do next. Nico bent his head and put the messy curls out of the way so he could whisper in my ear, "I had no problem killing my wife."

If he was trying to scare me, it wasn't working. All I felt was the urge to console him. I needed him to feel how much I cared about him.

"You don't scare me." I turned my face so I could look at him.

"Losing our daughter seemed to have knocked some sense into her. That was her rock bottom, but she didn't deserve to get over her addiction, not after it was her fault my world was torn to shreds. Through the whole investigation, she had been sober, and the more I found out about her and what might have happened to my little girl, the more I wanted her dead."

Nico's fingers were digging into my skin. I believed I was the only thing keeping him sane and tethered while he took a trip down memory lane. I bit my lip so I wouldn't whimper. I could be his anchor.

"I made her relapse, and as she overdosed on the bad merch I had given her, I took a cigar and waited for her to die as she begged me to save her life."

I was now lying on Nico's desk with him hovering over me. One of his hands was next to my hips, supporting him while he grazed his thumb over my throat with the other. Between my legs, I ached. My nipples were hard and pebbled, and I could feel Nico's arousal on my thigh.

"She wasn't dying quick enough, and I had to embark on my journey with the devil." Nico's hand wrapped around my throat lightly. "So I choked her. Had her body shake under mine; her scratches on my arms lasted for days." He then moved his other hand and put it between my legs, sliding it up until he cupped my pussy. "And when it was all done, I felt at peace."

His thumb moved, sliding under the barrier of my underwear, and I moaned when he stroked my wet pussy. His eyes flashed, and his nostrils flared.

"It was justice," I choked out.

Nico was breathing heavily. "Don't you get it, little swan? I will massacre anyone and anything that stands in my way of my revenge."

"Is it because I'm the same age as your daugh—"

The words died on my lips as my eyes rolled back the moment Nico inserted two fingers deep inside of me.

"You get so fucking wet for me," he murmured in awe.

Since he stopped moving, I did it for him, rolling my hips against his hand. I got the feeling his daughter was a touchy subject, so I would leave it alone for now.

"You forget I'm not innocent, nor am I pure," I told him as I wrapped my legs around his hips and brought him closer to me.

When I moved to sit up, I was surprised he let me. My hand went to the waistband of his pants. Nico held his breath, waiting for my next move. Without breaking eye contact with him, I pulled his pants down and was pleasantly surprised someone as polished and refined as him had gone commando.

"Did you forget how you found me?" I whispered as I took his dick into my hand. He was long, hard, and thick, and I couldn't wait to have him inside of me. He was going to destroy me, and I was going to let him. "I was covered in blood, and you saved me."

I lay back on the desk, and then I started to guide him into my entrance. When I felt the tip begin to penetrate, I spoke again.

"Everything you are feeling right now..." I said in a breathy voice since he was slowly thrusting into me. "Take it out on me. Make me beg for it."

"Goddammit, Ofelia," Nico cursed as he sunk deep inside of me. He had his hands on either side of my head while he tried to catch his breath.

"Are you fucking happy now?" he groaned as he pulled out only to slam back in, causing my back to arch with pleasure. "Is this what you wanted?"

"Yes," I moaned as I wrapped my legs around his hips tighter.

At this moment, I felt like I could finally spread my wings and fly. There were no barriers, and nothing was impossible anymore—Nico was my peace.

He took hold of my cheeks with one hand and then brought his head down so he could kiss me. This kiss didn't compare to the one I had forced him into. No, this kiss was full of passion and rage. The type of kiss that carried poison, and even if it was killing you, it had you begging for more.

Nico moved his lips in a firm position, making me feel full of him to the point that I kept moaning into his mouth.

He chuckled. "Is that all you can handle?"

My brows knotted in confusion as he pulled back. Nico

pulled his shirt off with one hand, and my mouth watered. He was all male. The way his tan skin was sculpted with muscles. Just the right amount of chest hair and a light happy trail. The indents on his side would make any woman want to get on her knees for him and worship him.

Without a word, he flipped me, so now I lay on my stomach. He then proceeded to remove my nightgown, leaving me naked.

I shivered when I felt his lips on my bony spine. He kissed and licked his way up my torso until he got to my nape.

"Nico," I whimpered when he took my earlobe into his teeth.

"In the next few minutes, you're about to start begging, brat, and depending on how well you fuck me back, I might let you come," he growled in my ear.

I moaned when he took hold of my hair, wrapped it around his fist, and pulled it. He then wrapped his other hand around my waist, protecting me from the edge of the desk. I raised on my tiptoes, knowing this was the performance of my life—glad I could endure hours of dancing on my toes just so I could please Nico.

"Why do you always feel so fucking good," he moaned as he slammed in and out of me. My legs shook. I didn't let up and stayed on my toes for him.

"More," I begged him.

His answer was to tug my hair back.

"Is this what you wanted, Ofelia?"

I couldn't answer him. I could barely form a coherent thought as he filled my pussy that even now, I knew no one would ever compare.

All you could hear were my moans and the slapping of our skin.

"Nico..." I whined, desperate for a release.

"Beg me," he demanded as he pulled out only to come back at me and making me see stars.

All I could do was whine and moan as he fucked me mercilessly. My nipples rubbed against the wooden desk, and I knew they were chafing, but I couldn't find it in me to care.

I was so close I was vibrating with need.

"*Daddy, please!*" I screeched the words, and they ricocheted through his office walls.

Nico let out a string of curse words. He then brought his mouth to my shoulder.

"You're such a fucking brat," he said before he bit my shoulder.

Cum started to coat my walls as I finally exploded.

PART 2

REVELATIONS

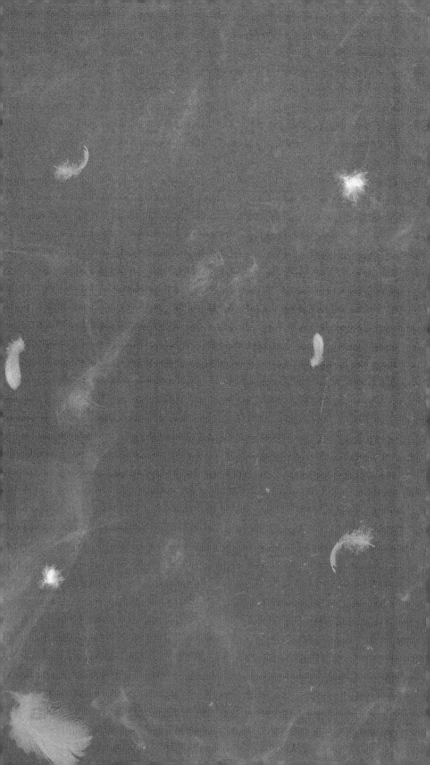

JUDGMENT

And who are you to call her crazy?
Who are you to call her insane?
Have you lived through her madness and basked in her sins?
How easy you judge things you've never seen.

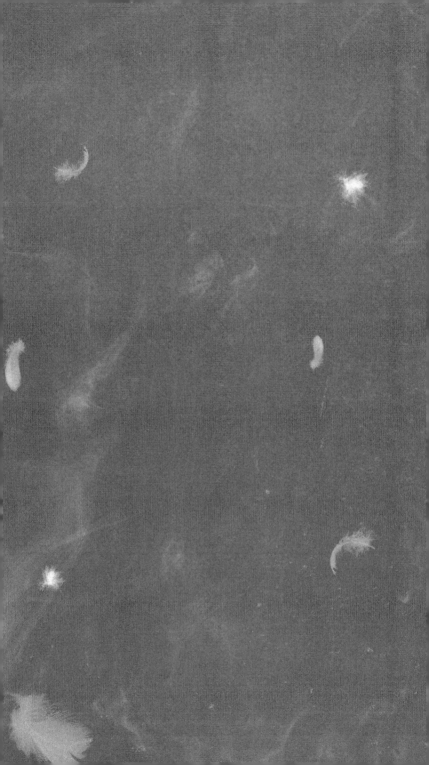

THERE WERE ALWAYS THOSE FEW SECONDS WHEN YOU woke up that you felt immense peace. Your mind had yet to overwhelm you with reality, and for those few seconds each day, you had no worries and no pain.

It was blissful.

This time I expected that feeling to go away, but it didn't. The first thing I noticed was the dark curtains that adorned Nico's balcony door. I bit my lip to suppress my smile when I felt my legs tangled with his. My head rested on his chest, and I felt his hand playing with my hair.

I knew I'd had happy moments in my life, but up until today, I didn't think I had felt as alive and burden-free as I did at this moment. Everything was perfect. The way his legs were entwined with mine, the contact between the smoothness of my legs and his scruffy ones. The smell of his skin and how it was all I could inhale.

You'd think lying on his sculpted chest would be uncomfortable, but there was nowhere else I would rather be.

"Morning, Ofelia," he said in a smoky tone.

For the first time, I knew the real meaning of what people meant when they said they got butterflies. It was tingles all over your skin, a tense feeling between your legs, and the urge to want to smile and please.

I pressed my lips against his pec and smiled as I kissed his skin. Last night had not been a dream. My imagination wasn't playing tricks on me.

After Nico fucked me on his desk, he carried me to his room, where we continued embracing and kissing. Last night had been perfect.

"Morning," I told him as I sat up.

Nico looked at me with guarded eyes. He was lying back on the bedframe. Either it was still early, or he'd decided to sleep in today.

Being with him made me brave. I moved so I could straddle him. His eyes traveled from my face, down my exposed breast, to where the juncture of my thighs met his waist. I cupped his face and bent to kiss him.

"This is how you should greet me in the morning from now on," I told him, and his lips twitched.

"Is that so?" he said with amusement.

His hands reached for my waist, his fingers digging into my skin like he was trying to make sure I was also real. Then they moved slowly up my stomach until he cupped my breast. I let out a soft moan, and my head thrashed back when he put his lips on my nipple and tugged it into his mouth. Then, when I was wiggling on his lap and panting, he pulled back and started to laugh.

"You're so fucking needy," he noted.

I leaned forward as his hands roamed over my torso. "Afraid you can't keep up with me, old man?"

One second I was still on top of him, the next, he was

already over me. Nico grabbed my hands and pinned them over my head.

"Are you being a brat just so you can get fucked again?" he murmured alongside my jaw.

It was the truth. I was trying to get fucked again. I had this insatiable need that didn't seem to go away. If anything, it only got worse.

"Please," I begged him.

He chuckled.

"You have a show tonight, swan, and you're already sore as it is," he told me a little too smugly.

It was true I was sore. I felt it every time I moved my legs. I saw bruises on my hips, marks on my skin, yet they weren't enough. Of course, as someone whose bones had defied their natural shape, this did not disgust me. Quite the contrary. But then, I guess his smugness probably came from the fact that there was some blood on him when he pulled out.

"What will you do today?" I asked as I played with his hair. I was going to use every excuse I could to touch him. There was still too much to talk about, but if I kept things light, he wouldn't be running away from me—from us.

"I have to get some things ready for tonight's show."

"Can I come with you?"

"No." His tone startled me.

Gone was the content Nico, and in his place was the unshakable man he had always been.

"Look, Ofelia," he said, those blue eyes boring into mine. "The men I deal with, they aren't the people I want around you."

I took a second to gather my thoughts. As painful as it was going to be, I was determined to help Nico find any lead on his daughter. He saved me, and it was my turn to save him.

"Will you tell me a bit more about what you do?" I bit my lip as I asked the question. "I know you aren't like my master, and I know why you are on this journey, but..."

Nico's eyes clouded with agony for a second. Then, he took a deep breath and used one of his hands to play with my curls.

"You want to know why I still keep associating myself with those men when my daughter is most likely dead?"

I closed my eyes. It had been seven years since he rescued me, and no one ever lived that long, not in those conditions. Girls like me had a life expectancy, and once we reached it, we weren't of any use anymore. Had Nico not saved me, I would have been dead.

"If it's too painful to talk about it, you do not have to tell me a thing."

Nico looked at me for a few seconds, then kissed the top of my forehead.

"I started this mission with a vengeance on my mind and hate in my heart. I was desensitized to everything that was going on in this world."

"What changed?" I whispered, too scared that he would stop sharing things with me if I spoke any louder.

Nico flipped us again to our earlier position.

"You happened," he told me. "Seeing you..." His jaw got hard, and his eyes went cold. "Seeing you covered in blood, it did something to me. For the first time, I realized the position I was in. I could continue being a selfish prick and ignore all the children who could use my help just because I couldn't find my own, or I could do something about it."

"That's why you took Delia and me," I said.

"Saving you was a sort of atonement for me. I made it

my mission to heal all the broken parts of you, and once you were whole..." He trailed off.

"You were going to let me go?" I said accusingly, even though that was now irrelevant.

"That was the plan. I wanted to make you better, then give you back to your parents."

"But my parents didn't want me," I finished for him.

Nico brought me down for a kiss. His lips crushed against mine. My arms wrapped around his shoulders, and I devoured him with the same intensity he did me. This feeling was why age and gender or anything that labeled us didn't matter. Not when emotions like this were tied to another person's soul. They sucked you in and, in return, gave you so much more than they robbed of you.

"You were so scared at first. You latched on to my every word, looked up at me like I was a god," he said. "All while it hurt to look at you because you became a reminder of what I had lost and what I could not save."

"I'm so—"

He cut off my apology with another kiss.

"I kept you at arm's length because that was my problem and not yours...then you started to dance again, and everything shifted. The dead look in your eyes was lifting, and you started to live again."

"And you started your own company?"

He started to play with my hair once more, and I think he did that when he was nervous.

"You wanted to know what I was doing at the party the other day?"

Before yesterday, his answer might have scared me but not today. There was nothing this man could do that would ever make me hate him. So I nodded and waited for him to continue.

"All of the dancers in our company are somewhat like you."

I sucked in a breath, and my eyebrows scrunched in confusion.

"When you give someone a lifeline, they would do whatever it takes to hold on to it. And that's what the company is to many of them. The ones who make it with us were rescued from perverse owners, much like the one who owned you. They enjoyed the fine arts and made the children they bought their toys."

My heart started to beat wildly at the information he was giving me. "The ones who dance or are young enough to be taught are bought by me."

"You're saving them," I breathed.

"It's not easy to get other people's toys. Unfortunately, there's a price to pay for that."

The hold he had on my waist became stronger.

"What's the price?" I asked.

"They get to be free, but they know that sometime during the tour, they will get to see their old masters on the stage, smiling down at them. They will relish the fact that they have broken them while my dancers suffer silently during their dance."

My mind raced back to the other day when I bumped with the other dancer, how she flinched at the contact. Then I kept seeing their faces. I thought they'd kept a distance from me all this time because I was under Nico's protection when in reality, we all were. There was no distance at the end of the day. We were all minding our own business, just trying to survive.

"I profit from their agony," Nico told me, disgusted with himself.

"Is there any other way to free them without their old masters coming to see them?"

Nico cupped my cheeks. "It's the company or it's death. There's no other option for them. I'm the last resort."

I leaned into his touch. "I think you are a great man, Nico."

He shook his head. "I still use them in hopes of getting a shred of information."

"Can I ask you one more question?"

"Make it fast. I have to get going," he told me.

I pouted because I wanted to spend more time with him like this. I was going to become very selfish when it came to him and his time. I couldn't wait for tonight when he got ready to leave again. I loved every minute of being by his side, but if he was going to fuck me from now on, I would love it even more.

"Ofelia," Nico said as he gripped my hips.

"Oh, yes," I said, a bit flustered. "Why did you only keep me here with you and not Delia? I mean, she obviously didn't have a family to go back to either."

Nico sighed.

"Because you were your master's favorite, the one he kept at all times, so I figured if anyone knew anything, it would be you."

I guess that made sense, but Delia, being on the outside, might have seen more than me. I opened my mouth, but before I could say anything, Nico kissed me. He rolled us over so he was hovering on top of me.

"Have you ever wondered what it would be like for me to eat your pussy?" he said in a husky tone.

I bit my lip and nodded. I imagined everything sexual with him. Then, whenever I would start to remember that night, I would shut it off right away and replaced those unwanted memories with fantasies of Nico. Maybe that's why I always threw myself at him? Because he made me feel safe and was the only man I knew I could fully trust, not just with my soul but with my body as well.

"To have me kiss your body?"

Nico kissed all the way down to my navel, then spread my legs and bent them. He looked up at me through hooded eyes, and I don't think he had ever looked hotter.

He put his lips on my mound and spoke. "To lick past your slit, then fuck you with my tongue until you started to pull my hair, begging me for more."

I felt two of his fingers teasing me. Rubbing me up and down with feather-like strokes. He parted my pussy lips with his two fingers. Nico looked at me as he brought his mouth to my pussy and licked my clit.

Correction: now that was the hottest thing I had ever seen.

"It sounds like you have given some thought to this," I said on a moan.

"You have no idea," he groaned as he continued to lick my folds. My hips started to move of their own accord from the feelings he was awakening inside of me. His lips brushed over my clit, and then he swirled it with the tip of his tongue.

"Fuck," I whined as I pulled at his hair.

Nico's chuckle vibrated at my core. Then, when he inserted two fingers inside of me, my hips raised off the bed, only to have him slam me back down.

"I'm so close," I moaned as I moved my hips to grind against his tongue.

Nico chose that moment to hold my clit with his lips and suck. The pulsating sensation was too much and not enough. My skin felt numb and hot. I was coming undone.

His fingers started to move faster.

"I want you to come all over my face," he commanded.

My vision went black for a second, and then I did as he asked. I felt my pussy constrict around his fingers as he ate me a little slower.

I was a panting mess when Nico pulled back with a satisfied grin on his face.

"Now I have something pleasant to get me through the day."

If I could have come back with a sassy comeback, I would have. But, instead, my eyes zeroed in on the scabs he had on his thighs; however, before I could ask how he got them, he retreated to the bathroom.

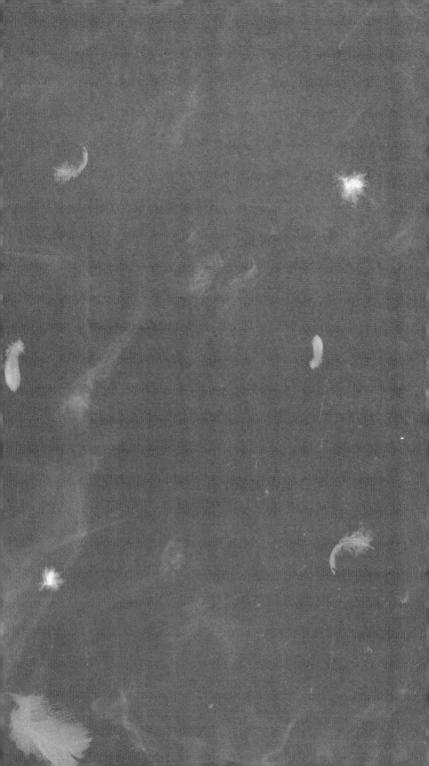

Estevan was waiting for me outside when I finally made it downstairs. I never slept in late, especially not on days we had a show. I could still feel Ofelia all around me, I had the taste of her in my mouth, and I didn't regret it.

How could I when she made me feel alive again, like living this life was actually worth it? I wasn't young and naïve anymore. I'd fucked my way through my mourning, through my rage, and not once had I felt like I did last night.

Ofelia might be content for now, thinking she knew everything. Still, I kept the other part of my business a secret. So she didn't know I would deliver just about anything if the price was right. It was a necessary evil if I wanted to keep providing for everyone. The show did well on its own but not enough to afford us the life we all lived.

In a sense, we were all gypsies, wandering our way through the world. None of us had a place we called home. No one liked going to their motherland because it held bad memories for them.

"You look like you're in a good mood." Estevan smirked at me.

I regarded him with a look that said not to try me.

"You don't usually wake up this late," he continued, utterly ignoring me. "But hey, if I had pussy as young as Of—"

I turned back to look at him. My hand was gripping his shoulder. "Do not finish that sentence."

Estevan's jaw went hard. We were business partners, and I knew it probably got on his nerves when I acted like I was superior to him, even though I was. He might have been the one to introduce me to this life, but I had been the one who kept us here.

"So that's how it's going to be?" he said. "I've been with you since the start, and now I can't make one simple joke?"

"Ofelia is off-limits to you and everyone else."

My words were harsh, and his eyes got colder.

"Since your office door was wide open when you were nailing her, I didn't think you would mind," he replied back casually.

My hands were tightly fisted.

"If you ever look again, I'll kill you." The words left my lips before I could process them.

"Don't forget who does all the dirty work while you sit on the throne," he spat as he got inside the car.

I held on to the bridge of my nose and took a deep breath. When I opened the car door, Estevan didn't acknowledge me.

"My hands are as dirty as yours," I told him.

Estevan turned to look at me. "Look, I just don't want you to get hurt. Sure, Ofelia is young and beautiful, but don't lose sight of what's important."

My jaw hurt from clenching it. I didn't say anything

more until we got to the docks, where we would be picking up firearms that I would be smuggling to our following location.

Estevan was wrong. It wasn't even Ofelia's age or beauty. Our bond went much deeper than that. It started with a broken soul covered in blood. Sure, when I saw her lying there on the floor semi-dead, I felt something tapping in the heart that was already dead. Our eyes met, and it was like I could read her mind. She was done, she was ready to let down and die, and for the first time since I had embarked on my fucked-up journey, I wanted to save someone else. It was all fine, keeping her at arm's length until she started to dance again.

The first time I saw her talent and passion was about one year after I saved her. It was past midnight, and she wasn't in her room. She tended to sleepwalk, and I got worried she had hurt herself. I found her in the gym playing the same song on repeat. She had no ballet flats on, but she kept doing the same dance over and over again on bare feet. I saw her fall again and again, and each time she looked at herself, her eyes burned brighter with determination, and she got up stronger. Her feet started to bleed when I finally called out to her, but she ignored me. It wasn't until she was satisfied with herself that she stopped. At that point, she was panting, and I could tell she was exhausted and sleep-deprived, yet she smiled at me. It was the second time she'd made my dead heart skip a beat.

"*I nailed it.*"

I couldn't help but return her smile. "So you did."

My eyes went to her feet and looked at the blood. "I'll get one of the guys to get you some shoes tomorrow."

She stopped smiling for a second, and then she beamed at

me. I wasn't prepared for her to embrace me. "Thank you, Daddy."

I cringed.

"Listen, little swan," I lashed out right away, and this time she looked like I'd slapped her. "I'm not here to play house with you."

I already had the family, and I fucked it up. I wasn't looking to get back what I had lost.

Ofelia was a cute girl, but when she matured, she was stunning, and yet I didn't set out to fall for her. I was fine biding my time until she was useful to me.

It was on the eve of her eighteen birthday. The staff got her a birthday cake since I'd forgotten. She had her hair in tamed curls that cascaded down her back. She wore a simple black dress with just a hint of makeup. Ofelia looked at me, and she fucking thanked me, as if the life I gave her was something to be thankful for. From that day on, she would join me for meals. She would talk about anything and nothing, just trying to keep me some company. Then, at night before going to bed, she started to bring me a drink or a coffee.

It wasn't until we started the company that shit changed. By this point, our relationship had already changed to something somewhat platonic.

We were in the theater where the first performance would take place that she kneeled for me with an almost frenzied look in her eyes.

"Please, let me please you."

With those five words, Ofelia ruined everything. From that day forward, she had kept me on my toes. There were two sides to her, and I fell for the side that pushed me out of my comfort zone. As she got a little older, I think she teased me more than anything to get a reaction from me. But even when she didn't say anything, I wasn't blind to the way she looked at me.

Part of me felt like a dick because it was fucked-up. Not only was I older, but I also held financial power over her. So I tried to fight it. But when she looked at me the same way she looked at the crowds who go to watch her dance, it left me speechless.

The intensity in her stare, the way she lived to try and please whoever watched her, it was beauty all on its own.

"We're here," Estevan said, interrupting my thoughts.

I looked at the docks and saw Alejandro there, and I wondered why he had gone to the opening preview in the first place if he was planning to meet us in London.

"Let's get this shit over with," I told him, eager to get this done as soon as possible.

Once at the docks, Alejandro made his way over to us as soon as he saw us.

"Nico." He nodded at me and then looked at Estevan. "Estevan, thank you for taking this cargo."

"You didn't mention this at the opening," I added right away.

Alejandro shrugged. "I don't like talking business when the old man is around."

Fair enough. Not that Emilio hadn't done any dealings with us either, but I could understand the animosity on Alejandro's part. I needed to stop being paranoid.

"I was surprised you had contacted us," I told him.

Estevan chuckled. "Nico doesn't let his guard down for a second."

Alejandro gave us an easy smile.

"Nico is very well recommended. He seemed like the person to go to, and hey, I get to stay in town and watch the show. So it seemed like a win-win situation."

My stomach felt uneasy as I remembered the way he looked at Ofelia—my Ofelia. Now that I had let myself have her, I wondered how much this would change all the aspects of our lives.

"So, how did you get in the business?" I asked, trying to get as much information as I could.

Alejandro shrugged it off. "After my godfather passed away, my brother and I inherited his business. Some more lucrative than others."

I was about to ask more, but his phone rang, and he stepped away.

"You need to cool it," Estevan warned. "I know he has a hard-on for Ofelia, but this is business."

I've been doing unsavory shit since I started doing this, so working with Alejandro shouldn't be any different.

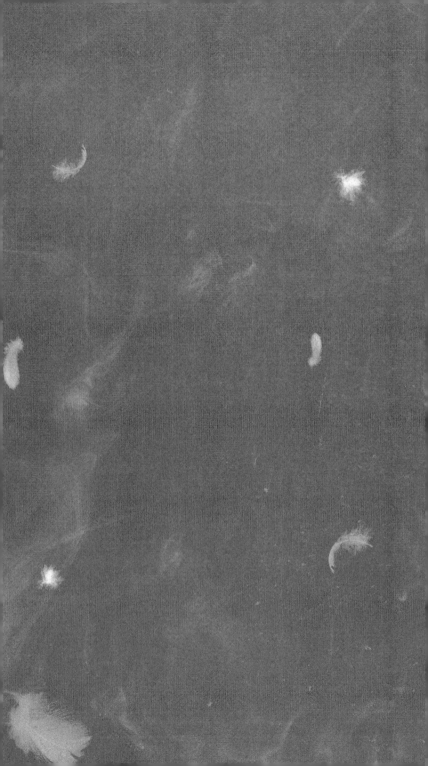

SAVING

You didn't need to save her.
You just needed to love her.

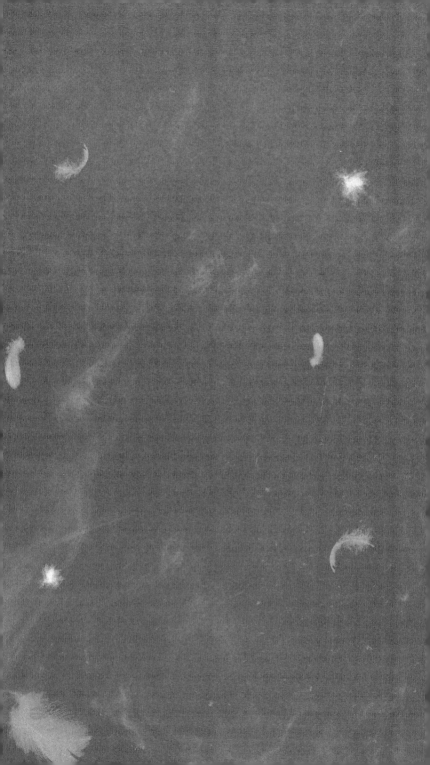

22

OFELIA

I WALKED INTO THE THEATER WITH NEW EYES THAT night, now that I knew exactly what was going on with all the dancers. Funny how we can be selfish and oblivious when things don't relate to us. How we can forget the rest of the world is in pain just so we don't take that burden on as our own.

The practice was going on, and the first person I saw was the girl from the other day. Her face was no longer in agony, but she was still cautious about the world around her.

This time as I joined them, I smiled at all of them. Again, I felt a sense of pride in what Nico was doing. How he was helping everyone here, and I wanted to take part in their healing process.

Everyone looked at me weirdly, and no one smiled back at me. I sighed, but I didn't let this discourage me. Instead, I made my way to the room that was reserved for the prima ballerina.

As soon as I walked into the room, I halted when I saw all the white roses in my room. Every inch of it was covered in white roses. I looked at my reflection in the mirror, and I couldn't help but notice the change in me as well. For the first time, I saw beauty staring back at me.

I was so caught up looking at my reflection that I didn't notice Delia was in the room. She glided effortlessly through the flowers, her hands touching every single petal. When our eyes met, I could see the envy in them.

In her hands, she held on to a gold-and-black card. It was the same card as before, and for a second, my stomach felt queasy.

"Give me that," I said, trying to reach for it.

Delia smiled and sprinted away quickly. "What do we have here? A fan? You should meet with him. We both know you are not woman enough for Nico."

I needed that note.

I forgot to ask Nico if it had been him who had sent the note with everything going on. I mean, it made sense. The first time I received flowers was after that kiss, and last night.

"To my little ballerina, can't wait to have you again."

Delia's smile fell the moment she realized who had been the one to send the note.

"So he chose you in the end?" she spat at me. "How long do you think you'll hold his attention?"

When I looked at Delia, some of the hate I harbored against her was starting to fade. She had drawn the short end of the stick, and in the end, I had won. Not only did I get the home, but Nico was now mine too.

"I'm sorry," I told her with kindness and sincerity I hadn't shown her in ages.

She glared at me.

"Do not pity me," she spat, and then a smile curved at her lips. "I know something you don't know."

With that, she threw some of the flower vases on the floor and walked away. I ran to the vases, trying to clean up some of the damage she had made.

Amidst the water and thorny roses, I found the note. Blood stained the inside of the note, and I wondered when I had cut myself?

"I think it's time for her to join the others, don't you think so, Uncle?" the guard that usually accompanied me said.

I closed my eyes tighter as I did a pirouette, pretending like I didn't care that they were talking about me.

"Not yet, my boy. She still entertains me. Meanwhile, you can use her companion."

I dared peek at my usual guard. His shoulders sagged, and he scrunched his nose. "She bores me now. She used to get frightened at every little thing I did, and I loved watching those blue eyes get filled with terror, but now they are just blank—like I said, boring."

Part of me was so repulsed I wanted to throw up while the other was terrified with fear I had to pray I wouldn't piss myself.

"I want to be the one who breaks her," the guard said.

My master started to laugh. It scared me at how joyful he sounded.

"There is more than one way to break a person," my master told him. "Now take her away, and bring the other one."

The relief I felt made me feel sick. I was safe, but the girl that would be coming out was not, and I couldn't bring it in me to try and take her place. I was not strong enough for that. I was a coward.

My usual guard sighed, but he took hold of my bony arm and dragged me back to my black pit. "You will be mine, little ballerina," he said in a docile voice as his eyes promised pain.

Unlike the other times, my guard left me by the entrance to my hellhole while he went to get the other girl.

How sad was it that I had been trained well that they knew I wouldn't make a run for it. Anyways, it wasn't like there was anywhere to hide. My fate had been sealed off a long time ago.

I stood there waiting patiently. The longer I waited for the door to open, the more the unease inside of me grew. There was havoc inside of me, and I didn't know how to control it. But I knew that if I made one wrong move, that was it for me.

The door opened, and my stomach stirred. The girl came out, and she was no longer crying nor whining. She looked like a zombie. She was beautiful. Thin, dark hair, tan skin; then our eyes met, and my breath caught at the way her blue eyes sparkled.

I was going to be sick. I barely made it to the bathroom when I was already heaving. There was no doubt in my mind and my heart that the girl who had been with me was Nico's daughter.

As soon as I got it together, I ran out of my room and searched for Nico through the theater. He had to be somewhere in here, right?

I was out of breath, running back to my room, not noticing where I was going, and coming to a halt when I hit a man. His face was turned, but there was something familiar about him.

"I'm sorry," I apologized, and he seemed to turn his profile even more so I wouldn't look at him. My stomach was in all kinds of knots already; I didn't think much of it.

WHAT THE FUCK?

The play had already started, and every single seat was filled. As I pirouetted my way across the stage, my eyes wandered over to the spot Nico usually took as he watched, but I couldn't see him anywhere.

Estevan was standing near one of the exits with two other men. One of them—I really couldn't see his face, and the other smiled and waved at me as our gazes collided. I believed his name was Alejandro.

I went about my way, dancing until the first half finished. The need to tell Nico what I had found out was intense, but I began to get a little calmer as I started dancing.

Once I was back in my room getting ready for the second part, the flowers held my attention again. I could marvel at them now that I was alone. Even though Nico wasn't here, he made sure I would be thinking about it.

I would try one more time to find him before the show, but then a small smile spread over my lips as I realized I was now sharing his bed.

As I wandered around the back hallways, I came to a halt for a second time that night. But, unlike the other man who didn't dare acknowledge me, this one had a different reaction. He grinned at me and held on to my abdomen as if he had a right to touch me.

"Ofelia, it's been a long time," Alejandro said.

"Are you enjoying the play?" I asked as I smoothed the ruffles on my tutu. I tried my best to look calm.

Something in me was yelling at me to run. Call it a gut feeling, but I ignored it. We were in a building full of people; here, I was the star, and no one would dare do anything to me. That would be foolish, right?

As soon as the bell for the audience to go back to their seats rang, I sighed in relief.

"Duty calls," I told him.

He smiled again, but it was still off, like something so sweet but sticky that he wanted to lure you in and catch you with.

"May I go through?"

"Of course," he said as he stepped aside, and I felt relief.

Once in my room, I changed my white tutu for the black one. Then, it was time to play death. It's why people came from all over the world to watch me. They wanted to see the naïve, pure ballerina lose control.

As I took my place behind the curtains, the lights started to dim. Then, as the curtains began to rise, I craned my neck to look upon the stage once again when a lone figure caught my eye.

The theater was dark, but I still saw the man standing in the middle of a row. He was in a black suit, with one hand inside his pants' pocket, while the other hung with ease.

He was looking right at me.

Even through the darkness, I could still see him. Even more vividly than I did before. My nose scrunched, and suddenly I could smell burned flesh.

The violins started to play, and I took my position. It was now time for the second act and my grand finale. My leg shook a bit as I put one in front of the other and got ready to go on my tippy-toes.

I turned my head, and I was met with Delia's cold stare. She looked pale, as if she'd seen a ghost. I didn't question it because I didn't care much for her, and a bad day for Delia meant a good day for me. Ignoring the look she gave me, I raised my hand, ready to dance my way across the stage like the angel of death—pirouetting havoc in my wake.

The orchestra started to play, and as soon as the cellos got louder, it was like I was no longer in this theater but another.

Suddenly I was dancing; I was no longer twenty-three, but I was sixteen. My white tutu was not stained but soaked in blood. I looked like a newborn devil rather than the white swan.

My body shivered uncontrollably, goose bumps covering my arms. I looked around, but I was alone. I couldn't remember who was here with me anymore.

When I twirled, I was back in the present. My heart thumped with the beat of the drums that now echoed in the auditorium. My face was a calm mask because death had many faces, but a scared one wasn't one of them.

One of the male dancers came, and he put his arms on my waist. I whimpered because I was sore from last night's events. I couldn't call it lovemaking because Nico and I weren't in love, were we? What we did last night was not making love. If I had a word for it, I'd call it an awakening.

As soon as we stopped dancing, the male dancer dropped to the floor as he pretended to die, another innocent victim left in my wake. At first, I started as another innocent dancer alongside them, just as clean and pure as them, but then I would betray them one by one.

I let go of all my worries about the fact that I had finally gotten what I wanted last night. I put on my brave face and smiled at the crowd. They ate it all up—the innocence on my face, the smile that was worthy of a toothpaste commercial. They didn't know I was only soft on the outside, but on the inside, I was made of scales and claws. Something beautiful to be guarded but was already shredded to pieces.

I twirled again and glided my way across the floor until I made it to the other end and did an arabesque. My hand was stretched with my chin straight, my left arm and leg behind me as I supported all my weight on my right leg.

The man in all black was back and watched me, and next to him was none other than my daddy, Nico.

It was like time ceased to exist as past and present merged together. I ignored the fact that Nico was not even looking at me. He always made me feel like I wasn't in the room. He would look at everyone except for me, but he said it was too painful to stare upon my face. Still, you'd think that after fucking me and waking up with me this morning, things would have been different.

Bile rose up my throat because he had no trouble looking at Delia—even after him swearing up and down that she did not exist for him. When I put my foot flat again, I immediately went into a fouetté. As I finished spinning, only then did I see the face of the man who was next to my father. He was the man from earlier in the hallway.

His face was burned, the scarred flesh spread across his cheek down to his mouth. I knew I wasn't close enough to see, but I brought it from memory. I turned again, and Delia was right there with the same look on her face.

For the first time in my life, I fell—death succumbing to the demands of life.

I didn't turn to look at Delia, for I knew she would be triumphant. Instead, I lay on the floor, and I remembered.

The sins of our past always catch up to us.

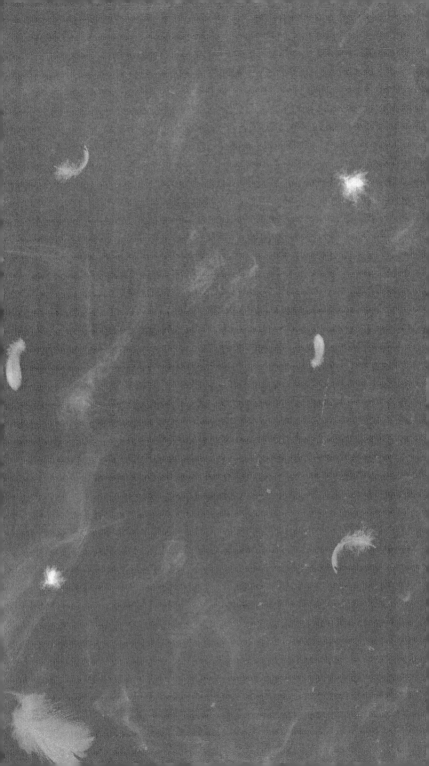

SINS

You can't cover up the sun with just one finger, just like you cannot cover up your lies with half-truths. You can bathe in holy water, but your sins will still remain. No amount of water will wash away the damage you have made.

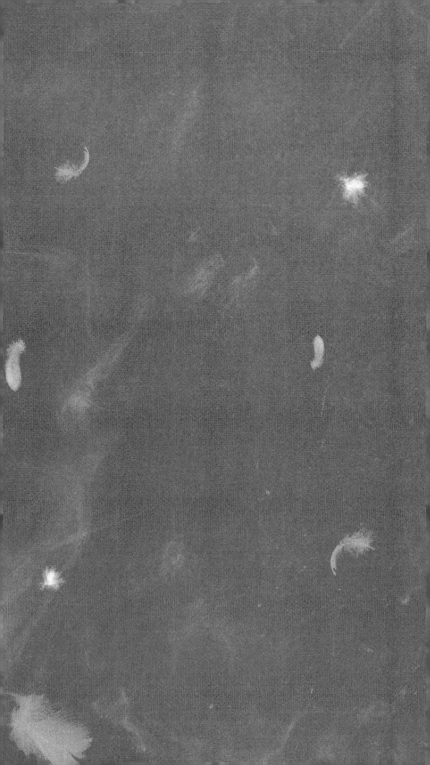

WHEN I WOKE UP, MY HEAD WAS THROBBING. I WAS alone in my room with hundreds of roses giving me comfort. I sat up and hugged my knees to my chest and buried my head between them. How many times did I wish to know the extent of what was done to me, but now that the memories seem to be rushing at me, I would have rather stayed in the dark.

I never thought I would be running away. It always seemed like an impossible thing to do since Master was always guarded, and at least when I was with him, I knew I was safe from all the other men. I was okay if their eyes lingered on me as long as they never touched me. I knew I had it easier than all the other girls. I could hear the girl who shared a cell with me cry. Her pleas were full of desperation, and for the first time, I understood where she was coming from.

The smoke made it harder to know where I was going or running to, but I knew that I would make it outside as long as I kept going up. To feel sunlight for the first time in years would be my reward for making it out of this hellhole. The smell of fresh air was what kept me going, despite the shouts and footsteps I heard behind me.

I made it to a set of stairs, my heart pounding as I took that first step toward freedom when the pain spread through my scalp all the way to my nape, and fear overtook my body.

"I got you, little ballerina."

I pulled against the pain in my neck as soon as I recognized the voice of the bodyguard that was always near me.

"We need to get out of here before it collapses, brother," another voice called out to him.

"In a second," my guard replied as he pulled me by my hair. We made it to the top of the stairs, and tears finally fell as I realized I was so close to getting free. He opened the door to the auditorium and threw me by the hair. I landed on my hands and knees, my fingers digging into the cold floor. How many times did I dream of being a renowned ballerina performing for the world?

The air was too thick that I started to cough and wheeze. My scalp still burned like a bitch.

"I told you, you were going to be mine," my guard said right before he raped me.

I begged and pleaded, and none of it seemed to work, but then again, my fate had been sealed since the moment I left my home. I was not the same girl I had been years ago. There was no way I would sit still this time. I had no idea why my old guard was here and why he was with Nico, but there was no way I would stick around to find out.

I went to turn the doorknob and was pleasantly surprised when it turned. At least I could move around.

When I made it through the door, the rest of the dancers were still there.

"How long was I out for?" I asked no one in particular.

The girl I had bumped into before turned to me, and

she was the one who answered me in a timid voice. One of these days, I would get to know them; I would know their stories and carry all of their burdens with my own.

"You passed out right as the show ended. The audience was in a frenzy, excited about how it all turned out. Master Nicolas brought you back here, then left in a hurry."

"Master Nicolas?" I questioned in a harsh voice.

The girl looked down. "He doesn't like it when we call him that either."

As long as they didn't call him daddy, I didn't care what they called him, but calling him master—he didn't need the burden of that title.

It seemed like I wasn't out for long. I wondered where Nico went. I needed answers, so I was going to go after him.

Delia was outside the main hallway doors, and it looked like she was waiting for me.

"You remember him, don't you?"

Delia had been found with me in that theater before it burned down. Did he get her before he got me? I needed to take time to think and breathe so I could concentrate on Nico's daughter.

"There used to be a time when I hated myself for not knowing everything, for living blissfully blind, but now I see why it was blocked."

When I turned to look at Delia, she was gone. I shook my head and made my way toward the front. I should have changed, but people loved me and more when I was in my stage outfit.

"Twice in one night," Alejandro's voice rang next to me as soon as I stepped foot past the threshold.

I jumped back.

"Oh no, I'm just looking for Ni—my dad."

He seemed amused at my choice of words.

"I saw him with Estevan earlier. I'll take you."

In all honesty, I didn't want him to take me. Instead, I wanted to talk to Nico, to tell him the man he had been talking to earlier had been the man who raped me on the day he found me.

What had happened afterward? Why was I alone?

Pain—there was so much pain. It was in every cell of my body, sweeping its way down my system. There was blood on my tongue, coating down my chin. I bit the tendon in his neck. Pulled at his hair and scratched it until someone else restrained me.

"The fire is almost here; finish up and go." The other person who said this sounded a lot younger and maybe a little scared.

"Ofelia."

"Ofelia."

"Ofelia." Alejandro grabbed my arm and shook it a bit.

I blinked back, perplexed.

Nico complained that I liked to live a lot in my head but failed to see the shit that went out in the real world. He called it childish, and I thought it was to shield myself.

If you stayed inside your own mind, it was harder for anyone to harm you because you never gave them the time to go through your walls.

There was nothing to be afraid of anymore, not when the monsters I feared the most had already hurt me.

"Lead the way," I told him.

Alejandro smiled at me. He went across the room, opening another door that led to a back stairwell.

I hesitated for a second.

"After you," Alejandro said as he stepped aside and opened the door for me.

I really needed to find Nico. I wanted to know why he was with the man with the burned flesh.

I took a step forward and smiled at him as I passed by him, and we made our way up to some stairs. The higher we climbed, the less I could hear the people who were in the auditorium. We were across from where the performers had their rooms. Now I knew why Nico kept us isolated and the face of the company was just me. I was the only one strong enough for such a job.

The last flight of stairs had an opening, and it was darker. Unease went through me.

One step, and it was game over.

My foot made contact with the last step, but my head was gripped back. The strands of my hair were pulled savagely against my scalp. The burn of it... fuck, it was like boiling water.

I whimpered, but before I could say more, a hand covered my mouth.

His thumb dug into one of my cheeks while his other fingers felt like they were carving into my skin. My jaw ached, and his hold made it impossible to try and bite him.

At that moment, all I wanted was for my teeth to tear into his skin. To bite it off like paper.

"It's been a long time, little ballerina," he said, and I felt cold. Hives covered my skin. Memories of the past tried to make their way back, but my mind was on overload. It just wasn't possible right now.

That didn't matter, not when my back hit the wall and something dug into my spine. It wasn't sharp, but it fucking hurt.

"I've waited a long time for this," he said, sounding lunatic.

There was no way for me to speak, I couldn't see since it

was all dark, but all I could do was feel. The way his hand roamed over my black pantyhose, the way his nails would scrape them and were ready to tear over them any second.

Or how his breath was scalding like flames of fire licking your skin. The way it went up and down my neck and how his breathing was worse than nails to a chalkboard.

"Do you remember me?" he mocked before he tore my pantyhose and ripped my panties. I screeched into his hand. It was no use, but I couldn't help it. My eyes watered, and my pussy burned. The sting was something familiar yet foreign enough.

The way it pulled your soul out of your body, then pushed it back after it was missing a few key pieces.

I screamed into his hand. The muffled sounds did nothing but cause saliva to cover my face and bile to rise up my throat because I couldn't believe I was once again down this road.

After a while there was some peace—it was falling all over my face in wild cascades.

Finally, there was an ache between my legs that spread to my hips.

Perhaps the one that should have been the most obvious of all, was the blood. It coated my hands from my fingers down to my arms, like willowy veins that ran on the outside. There was more between my legs, but the puddle that lay by my feet had me scared.

That's also when I noticed a pair of strong legs running adjacent to me. They had me caged in so I wouldn't move. Tan solid arms wrapped around my middle, and a voice kept calling my name over and over again, trying to beckon me into normality.

That's the thing about reality; once the veil is removed,

there's no going back. The rose-colored glasses stopped working, and darkness swept through all the fucking cracks.

"Ofelia...cara mia."

It took a second to come back into the madness that existed in my head. Nico's words wrapped around me like warm velvet. Soft enough to soothe me but thick enough to protect me.

"Calmati sei al sicuro."

Calm down? Because I was safe? How could he say that to me when I could feel pain between my legs. I could feel my arms still gripping my waist. My mouth was dry from the screams that failed to leave my lips.

How can someone be safe only after they had not been?

I looked down to where Nico held me.

My body jolted when I saw that his white sleeves were now red. The blood had stained all over them.

"Can you get up?" he asked of me in a low tone.

When I didn't reply, he nodded, and that's when I saw Estevan was in the hallway with us.

"Este benne, mia dolceza," Nico reassured me.

He told me everything was fine, but I knew it wasn't, and it would never be.

After all, this wasn't the first time it had happened to me.

Unfortunately, rape wasn't a thing you ever got used to.

Estevan slowly got down and then reached for me simultaneously as Nico pushed me toward him.

Estevan carried me in his arms as Nico rose to his feet. Once he was up, I got transferred over to him.

Years later and we were back from square one. Back to the place we started.

Orphaned little girl who had been a victim to the urges

of men, and her dark savior who wished he could turn back time to stop it from happening.

"*La mia ballerina*," he whispered in my ear. It wasn't sarcastic or to throw a dig at me. On the contrary, it was said with something that sounded a lot like affection, except I didn't want it. Not now, not after he had to find me once again at the mercy of a cruel man.

I burrowed my face in his chest as he walked us down a set of stairs. When we passed the main auditorium, it was bare. No more people lingered.

Nico kept talking to me, but I kept ignoring him. The time to speak had passed. He didn't get to try to be my hero only after he felt guilty once again.

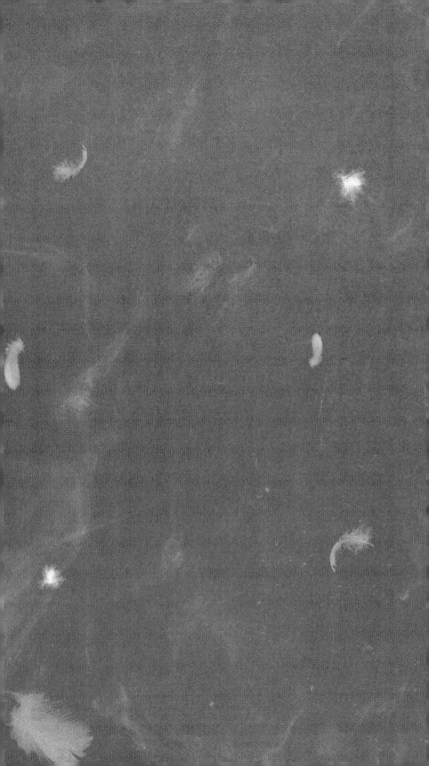

ALL MORNING I HAD BEEN KEPT AWAY FROM OFELIA, I was counting down the minutes until I could be with her again. I wanted her over me and under me. I wasn't really picky. Now that we had passed those gates, I didn't think I could go back to how things were before.

I closed my eyes and felt her nails digging into my skin. I had the taste of her pussy on my lips. I wanted this day to be fucking over so that I could be between her legs again.

London was always one of our busiest stops since from here we went to the United States. So most of my money usually came from this one trip.

The play had begun, and I didn't mind being a little late since reporters were usually trying to hound me for an interview, and the animosity was also great for sales on my part. A lot of people also came to the show to make some connections of their own. When you knew the right people, you could find a pipeline to just about anything sitting in the audience of my show.

"Are you going to keep seeing Ofelia? What did the doctor say?" Estevan asked on our way back.

He was against Roman doing any work on Ofelia, claiming that it was inhumane making a tortured child like Ofelia remember things she had kept hidden.

"You are the one who told me to move on and be happy," I said without looking at him.

Was he jealous? Did he have a thing for her too? The thought made my blood boil. Or was he repulsed by my actions as I once had been?

"I just meant that there's a lot of secrets that girl carries in that mind of hers. What if you don't like them when they come to light?"

"What she is, is a survivor," I said in a final tone. The rest of the way back to the theater was quiet.

I was a lot of things, but foolish was not one of them. I wasn't deluded enough to think Diana was still alive. There was always an expiration point in this business, and she was way past it. I just needed someone to pay for what was done. I needed their blood, their pleas and screams, so my job as a father would be fulfilled.

Estevan went right ahead as we got to the theater. Meanwhile, I had to greet some of the most important guests while all I wanted was to look at Ofelia.

"Master," a docile voice stopped me.

I flinched whenever I heard my dancers call me that, but I knew that telling them to call me anything at this point was useless. Calling me master gave them a sense of tranquility. They had one foot in this world and one in the past so that if I ever betrayed them, they could say they knew I would do it all along.

"Yes, Paola?" I asked one of the extras. I had gotten her out when she was around Ofelia's age. She didn't suffer as much as my other girls, but she was one of the ones who had probably seen the most and worst of the world.

"You said that if we ever saw someone delivering flowers to Miss Ofelia to let you know."

I kept my face impassive. I knew everything that happened in my company. Every single person who came to my events was vetted by my men. I knew all of their sins and was ready to use it against them if they fucked me over.

Even more so, I knew everything that happened with Ofelia. No one got near her without my permission, so I was aware of the flowers she got sent last time but didn't think much of it because someone as beautiful and talented as her was bound to have fans.

"Where?"

Paola looked nervous before answering me. That wasn't a good sign. My dancers were twitchy on a good day; them being extra nervous made me cautious.

"Her dressing room, Master."

She left before I could thank her. So before seeing the show, I made my way to Ofelia's dressing room. It was better I checked this out while she wasn't there, or else the urge to fuck her would probably win out.

I denied myself the taste of her, and now that I had all of her, it was going to be a feat on its own to control my urges.

The moment I saw the inside of her room, my body locked up. I prided myself in controlling my emotions, but seeing all the flowers had me wanting to kill the person who sent them. I didn't like it—not one bit.

Sure, people sent a dozen roses to someone they admired, but what I was looking at seemed more like an obsession. I needed to get to the bottom of this. The roses were white, just like they had been last time. That meant it came from the same person. Usually, this wouldn't be a big deal except for the fact that our tour was international, and we weren't in the same country.

I slammed Ofelia's door when I went out and searched for Estevan. He was the head of security, and I needed an explanation before making him eat his meals through a straw.

When I finally found him, the second act was about to start. He was at the top with Alejandro and another man.

"Enjoying the show?" I asked as I let my presence be known.

All three men turned to look at me. Alejandro was the one who responded.

"Ah, Nico, this is my older brother, Giorgio."

Estevan didn't seem surprised by this news, even though they were new to me. But, of course, this was the kind of stuff I prided myself in knowing.

Alejandro's brother didn't have much of a choice but to look up at me, and when he did, I could see why he kept his face hidden; half of it had been burned off. That must have burned like a bitch.

"Is this your first time seeing the show?"

He looked at the stage before answering, "It has been a long time since I have seen her dance."

Applause broke through the theater, and all of our heads turned toward the stage. My heart dropped as I looked at Ofelia lying unconscious on the floor while the audience ate it up. I didn't know why I expected anyone to realize she was no longer acting when we were in a room full of monsters who fed off others' demise.

I left without another word, trying not to run out. If I did so, I would be giving everyone a show they wouldn't forget and exposing a weakness. Until now, people weren't sure of the nature of our relationship, and it was better to stay away.

I managed to rescue Ofelia out of hell once; I wasn't sure if I could do it a second time.

The curtain had barely closed when I made my way to pick up Ofelia from the stage.

"What happened?" I growled to the rest of the dancers, making them jump and take a wide berth from me.

Fuck, this was not the time to lose my cool.

"We didn't know, Master Nico. She was fine, then she just collapsed."

Goddammit.

How many times had I told her she needed to take care of herself? It was going to be up to me to make sure this kind of shit didn't happen again, even if I had to tie her to my bed and feed her my fucking self.

As soon as I walked into her room, the smell of roses repulsed me. I needed to get to the bottom of this and deal with Ofelia later.

Two things I was sure of at the moment. The person who was sending the flowers had to be here, and two, if Ofelia wanted to keep jumping on my dick, she needed to take better care of herself since she could barely handle getting fucked.

"I'll deal with you later, swan," I whispered against her cheek.

I left the room, not thinking much of it. This side of the theater was closed to everyone, even most of my men. I didn't like to make my dancers twitchy, and they didn't do well with people. So they were hidden, but they knew not to let anyone go through those doors. Ofelia should be fine.

What I needed now more than ever was words with

Estevan and trying to figure out who was sending the damn flowers.

Everyone had a breaking point, and I was reaching mine. Many bloodsheds need to happen to get to the top, and I had paid my dues, but I didn't mind reminding people how I got this bloody empire.

It was foolish of me to think that it would be easy to get by without attracting attention. Everyone loved to fucking praise me, try to buy off one of my dancers, or get me to do business with them right then and there.

When I finally spotted Estevan, I noticed he was still with Alejandro and his brother.

"Is everything okay?" he asked, knowing full well Ofelia lying on the stage was no act at all.

"Yes," I told him, annoyed that I had to come in search of him. "Can we talk?"

"I was going in search of you; Giorgio has some information for us."

I gritted my teeth. I wanted to find out the culprit behind the flowers and get Ofelia the fuck home.

"Perhaps another time."

Then they told me the one thing that was sure to get me to forget about everything that was going wrong tonight.

"He has information on Diana."

My whole world fucking stopped at the moment. My knees buckled with the impact of the news, and I felt like I would throw up or cry in relief.

I nodded for both men to follow me and took them to one of the empty rooms.

"Talk," I barked as soon as the doors closed.

No one said anything, so I grabbed Giorgio by the collar of his shirt and pushed him against the wall.

"Speak or I'll kill you."

He smiled at me as he raised his hands. My eyes went to the exposed skin in his neck and noticed what looked to be bite marks.

"You said you had information on my daughter. Now speak, you bastard."

"I, too, was a captive," he said, and my hold on him lessened. That was my weakness; I couldn't bring it in me to hurt those who had already been scarred by the men who thrived in that kind of life. "I have all the scars to prove it."

"Get to the point?"

He looked me straight in the eye as he answered me, "She was in Vito's possession for two years and used to share a cage with Ofelia."

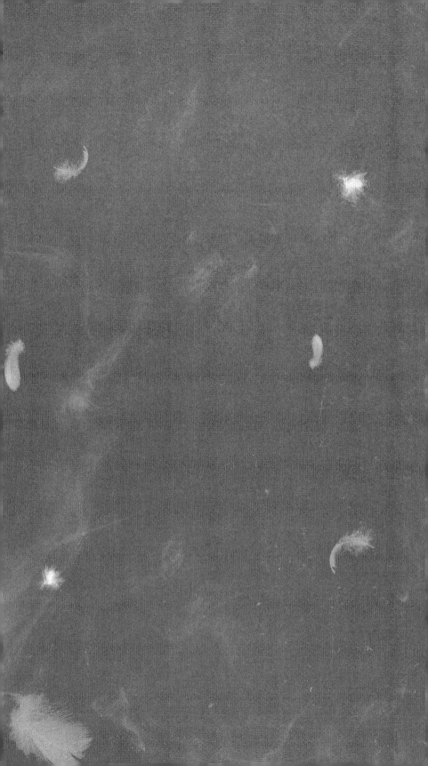

ALL ALONG, I KNEW OFELIA WAS A CRUCIAL PLAYER IN this mess, but until recently, I didn't think she had any direct contact with my daughter, just seeing her in passing, but to share a cell...

Giorgio smiled, pleased with himself. "Your little dancer is not who she appears to be."

"That's enough," Estevan said.

I took a step back and let go of Giorgio, thinking about how to proceed with this new information. But I couldn't rush in with it because all I would do was cause damage and pain to Ofelia, and I didn't wish to hurt her in the process of retribution.

"What do you want?" I asked, knowing that everything came at a price, and Giorgio sharing that little bit was the thing he needed to get me hooked.

"How much is the information worth to you?" The fucker gave me a slimy smile.

"What. Do. You. Want?" I repeated through gritted teeth.

"I want your company."

He had to be kidding, didn't he? I looked at him, and when I saw the look on his dumb-fuck face, I knew he was not.

I began to laugh.

Giorgio and Estevan looked at me like I had lost my mind.

"Now, tell me why I shouldn't torture the information out of you?" I asked him. "I'll have you crying out all you know right before I kill you."

Giorgio lost the triumphant smile he had.

"Do not mistake me for a weak man."

Before I could say anything else, the door opened, and one of the guards I had standing guard rushed in.

"We lost Miss Ofelia," he said after catching his breath.

I felt my blood drain down my body. This was not fucking happening.

"What do you mean you lost her?"

Giorgio made a move.

"I can see your hands are full. I'll be back, Shipper."

Ignoring him, I went after my men with Estevan hot on my heels. When my men started to tell me what had happened, it was clear I should have given them orders to keep Ofelia away from the rest of the guests.

"I want everyone out. Cover every exit. No one leaves without us knowing."

For a second, I forgot about the damn flowers and Ofelia fainting. How could she be so foolish? She would pay for this, and the only way I thought she would listen to me was when I was fucking her.

"Everyone is out, but no sign of Ofelia."

I punched the wall.

"You need to calm down, Nico." Estevan came behind

me and put his hand to my shoulder, trying to calm me down.

Before I could bite his head off for telling me something so idiotic, another of my men came running.

"Sir, one of the guests said they saw Ofelia go through those doors with a man."

He barely finished talking when I started to run the hallway myself. It was secluded and across from where I kept my dancers hidden, meaning my men didn't pay much attention to this since no one in the company ever ventured out after a show.

How could I be so careless?

As soon as I opened the hallway door, I heard the noises echoing from the top all the way down to my bone marrow. They vibrated in my soul, adding more flames to my ever-lasting fire. It was fueled with rage and vengeance. This was just adding to it.

I took the stairs two at a time. My heart was pounding wildly. I didn't know if it was from exhaustion or because I was getting consumed in my hate.

Screams could be heard, and I ran faster. When I made it to the top, I came to a halt. The scene before me would be branded in my brain for eternity.

It was a fucking bloody mess. Ofelia lay on the floor, unconscious. I could see her tutu ripped and feathers on the floor everywhere. The moment I saw blood between her thighs, I bit my jaw. I was so enraged I blocked all the other noise.

My eyes traveled to the rest of her before I dealt with the man crying like a little bitch beside her.

Her hands were bloody and it was in her mouth too. That's when I noticed the severed finger, and then I realized that it was Alejandro who was screaming bloody murder. But, even as mad as I was, there was no denying I was damn proud of her.

"I want Giorgio, *now!*" I shouted at no one in particular. Then I made my way to where Alejandro kept sobbing and noticed all the scratch marks on his face.

I kneeled to be at eye level with him. Then I gripped his chin, forcing him to look up at me.

"Fuck," I hissed when I noticed the blood that oozed from one of his eyes. My gaze traveled down to where he was holding the damn eyeball in the other hand.

"What the fuck happened here?" Estevan said, part in shock, the other in awe.

"Take him to one of my safe houses. I want a doctor to stabilize him. I need to ask him questions before I kill him."

As soon as they took him away, I lay on the floor and took Ofelia in my arms, waiting for her to regain consciousness.

"*La mia ballerina,*" I whispered with so much hate, all of it directed toward myself. For as long as I lived, I would never forgive myself for this.

Ofelia was fucking mine, and it was time to show the world that you didn't mess with me, nor my woman.

Leaving Ofelia's side had been hard, but I reminded myself that my men had been ordered to shoot on sight. Joker and Bane were as enraged as I was. Both beasts had been restless the moment I laid Ofelia on my bed.

"You didn't have to do this, you know," Estevan said, sounding impatient.

My knee kept bouncing up and down, and my body felt

hot and cold. I had been waiting in the car for the last thirty minutes while waiting for my men to set up the safe house.

Alejandro was already in there, but I knew that if I were to walk in there before everything was prepared, I would end up killing him, and there wouldn't be any answers.

"Any word on Giorgio?" I ignored his statement and instead was more interested to know where had the fucker gone. He and Alejandro had been working together since the beginning. Back when the tour had taken off, they had their plan in motion, and I had been an idiot not to notice.

"No, we have searched everywhere as well as reached out to our connections, but we cannot find him. All I could gather is that since they were very young, they were raised by Vito."

No wonder they were all fucked-up being raised by Ofelia's old master.

"How do you think she's going to cope with this?" Estevan asked, and I refrained myself from killing him right there and then.

She barely coped with it last time. I had no idea if this would finish driving her crazy or be the catalyst she needed to set her straight.

"Don't ask questions that will get you killed," I told Estevan as I got out of the car.

One thing I could say was that my men followed directions well. The room had been set up the way I had asked for.

The floor was covered in a clear tarp, a set of tools all neatly lined up, and a chair with a light hanging over it.

Alejandro was sitting on the chair. His head was tipped over. The doctor had checked him and then sedated him. There was an eye patch on his face, and the hand with the finger that had been severed had been covered up. There was no way in hell I was reattaching the damn finger. Nevertheless, I was tempted enough to have it pushed up his ass.

"Wake him," I told no one in particular.

I half expected Estevan to be the one to do it, but he was hanging by the door, just watching me with keen eyes.

Alejandro jolted awake the instant the chloroform made it to his respiratory system. He started to cough, then gasp. I stood patiently while he got his shit together and raised his head to look up at me.

The moment our gaze met, I smiled when his eyes widened in shock and at the fact that he knew he was fucked now.

"Have a good nap?" I asked as I took a step forward.

I removed my jacket, and everyone's eyes went to my bloody white shirt. I had not changed it since dropping Ofelia at the house. I snorted when I heard the sound of his piss against the clear plastic.

"It was for the blood, but I guess that works too," I said sarcastically as I reached for one of the tools.

"You..." Alejandro started to whisper. "Might as well kill...me now."

The metal pipe in my hand was cold and heavy; my hand itched with the need to break Alejandro's knees.

"Now that's not fun," I murmured.

I didn't get to where I was without acquiring some persuasive skills. I circled him, scrunching my nose with the smell of piss. My men had tied him, so for shits and giggles, I rested the pipe on his lap.

"You must be in pain," I told him, even though I didn't care for his answer. "Let's add to it."

The breaking of his finger echoed in the quiet room, followed by Alejandro's howl.

"Two hundred and six bones in the human body..." I said. "That's one—two, if you count the one Ofelia bit off. So that leaves two hundred and four bones to go."

Alejandro started to thrash in his chair, and it was like music to my ears. Dying wasn't as easy as people believed, not when the human body fought to survive.

I broke another finger and pulled a tooth. Alejandro was crying like a little bitch now. The sedatives the doctor had given him must be wearing off now, which worked in my favor.

"Was it you who sent her the flowers?"

He didn't answer me, not that I expected him to do it right away. So instead, I took a step closer and pressed my thumb to his other eye.

"Why Ofelia?" I said the words in a lethal voice as I added more pressure.

"M-m-my b-b-rother i-i-s g-o—"

My hand went to his throat. "He's going to kill me, isn't he?"

I dug my fingers to his sides just enough to cause pain and discomfort but not to make him pass out on me.

"Fine, needles it is," I murmured as I pulled out a small pack of sewing needles.

He held strong with the first one. By the second one, he was starting to cry, and by the third one, he was already begging.

"Stop," he begged, right before the fourth needle went in.

"Tell me and I'll remove them," I said, removing the pressure from the fourth one but not taking it out completely.

"I know you all were prisoners of Vito," I said.

Alejandro laughed, coughing blood on the floor in the process. "H-he...w-was our godfa...ther."

They fucking played me.

"Why Ofelia? What do you know about my daughter?'

Estevan walked closer to me.

"Can you trust what he says in this state? Kill him, and let's go. We are already running behind as it is."

Alejandro started to bark again, and there was a pain in his eyes but something else also. The asshole had an ace up his sleeve. It was the only card a dead man like him could play.

"V-V-Vito...taught us h-his w-ways when we...came to l-I-Ive with hi-i-m," Alejandro said in an exhausted voice. He was close to passing out and then dying on me. "M-my b-b-brother...was ob-ob-obsessed with O—ofe..."

He couldn't finish saying her name.

"I-I'll... a-a-admit...I didn't get w-why n-not until I saw her f-f-for the first time."

"Is that why you raped her? She got away from you once, and it was time to have her again?"

Alejandro looked up and smiled at me. His teeth gleamed with blood.

"I didn't get my turn last time."

I fucking lost it. I grabbed the pipe that had fallen to his feet and smashed it over one of his knees. My ears rang with the way his knee socket broke inside of his body.

Alejandro screamed, and his body lifted off the chair.

"K-k-kill   me...but...b-b-befo-re...y-y-you...do..."   The words died on his lips, but he just looked at me, inviting me over with his eyes.

I took that as a sign to get closer to him.

He whispered the words of a dying man. He said them

with malice and laughter, knowing damn well they were going to haunt me once he was gone.

"*Ofelia killed your daughter.*"

I completely lost it. I slammed the pipe over his other knee. Then I took hold of his chin, adding pressure to his cheeks, forcing them open. Slowly, I slid the pipe inside his mouth, pushing past the resistance.

Alejandro choked around it, his body convulsing with the pressure I added. Then, finally, our eyes met, and I saw the moment he died, and the only thing I regretted was that the pipe going through his throat wasn't what killed him.

And I hated him for it because, in the end, he was the one who fucked me over.

"You didn't look surprised by his news," I told Estevan. I was watching him with my peripheral vision all night since he was acting cagey.

"Giorgio said the same."

I didn't think it was possible to feel like you had died twice in your life.

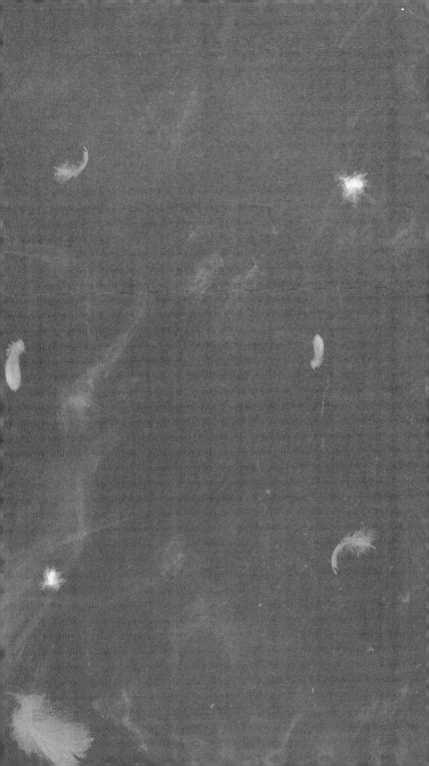

PEACE

She accepted that she had a raging war in her mind. She admitted that she was not like the other girls, pure and whole. She knew there were demons, and she took them in whole—for there was nothing like the peace that came with loving the blackness that resided in your soul.

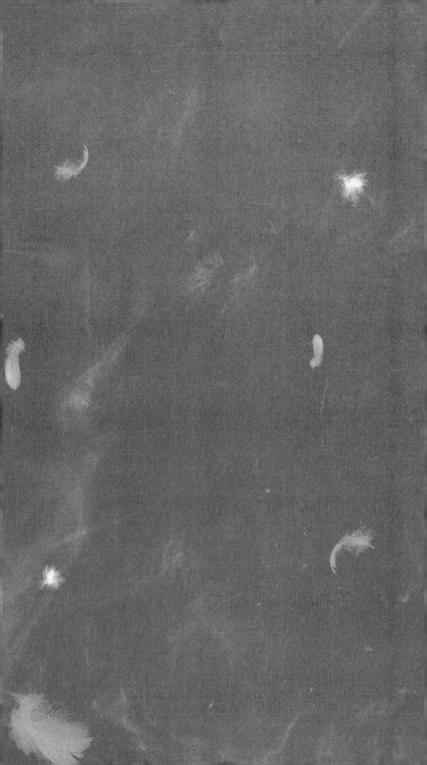

26

OFELIA

THERE WAS SOMETHING SO BEAUTIFUL ABOUT A DARK sky with no stars. A reminder that something beautiful didn't need to ask for attention. It was an abyss of darkness, pain, and despair. Yet, as you tried to find eyes in that pit of darkness, you couldn't help but think of how it was beautiful in all of its maddening glory.

I wished I could say the same thing about the darkness that currently surrounded me. But, unfortunately, it wasn't a cloak of warmth; mine was retribution. Sometimes, life was too good to be true, and sooner or later, you had to pay your dues.

How many times did I just go about my day sitting outside with the warm sunrays on my face, dancing in the rain, and smiling at how I had been saved. I called Nico my fate, my dark angel. I thought he was my salvation, but all along, he was just put on my side of the earth so he could prepare me.

It's never fun to play with a broken toy, and I had been broken, but Nico put me back together piece by piece. He took all my broken pieces and gave them a home.

I looked down to where my hands rested on my legs, and even though I couldn't see them, I could feel them. Even in the darkness, I saw red. How many lives did I take? How many people begged and pleaded for me to stop? These two hands had hurt one too many people.

"Dance, little swan." My master's voice still rang in my ear.

Now that I knew the meaning of those words, they mocked me. They slithered down my spine and crawled under my skin.

When I woke up after being assaulted, I was scared and reached out for Nico, only to find the bed empty. The only consolation I got was from my furry boys. They let me hide my face in their fur and cry.

I couldn't recall the moment Alejandro said the words to me, but I could hear them clearly now.

"What do you think Nico is going to do once he finds out you killed his precious daughter?"

My mind was still a mess, with all sorts of memories resurfacing. When I tried to think about the raven-haired girl, I remembered useless stuff more than I had before, but not the incident Alejandro was talking about.

I needed to talk to Nico and tell him my side of things, but it had been too late. He had already gone to get retribution on my behalf. When he came back, I knew that nothing would bode well for me as soon as I saw that lethal look in his blue eyes.

Those eyes I loved so much that reminded me of heaven now looked like hell had frozen over on them.

"Is everything okay?" I asked as I made a move to sit up on the bed, despite my body aching.

Nico didn't answer me. Instead, he went to his closet,

brought out a duffle, and gathered the things he would be bringing to the next stop of the tour.

"Nico, talk to me," I pleaded, already knowing he had found out the worst about me.

"You are dead to me, swan," he said as he came out. "From now on, I will make sure you know what hell is. Your sole existence is for my benefit only. I am the master of your life."

My throat constricted, and I wanted to cry. Then I looked to the door where Estevan lurked and passed out.

When I woke up, I was cloaked in darkness. It wasn't even a room where he had thrown me in. I knew it the moment we had taken off that Nico had asked his men to put me in the cargo area of the plane. I was in a huge crate that contained a bottle of water and a blanket.

Funny how the tables had turned from me. Maybe this was my karma for fucking Nico. Maybe my subconscious was obsessed with him, but it knew what I had done to his daughter and needed him to show me mercy when the truth came to light.

Based on everything I remembered, I still had one trump card, and I would play it when the time came. So it was safe to say this would be my swan song. I didn't see myself coming out of this alive.

I lay down on the crate, closing my eyes tightly when everything shook because of the turbulence. Then, when the plane finally calmed down, I smiled to myself.

Even if it had been one-sided, I experienced love. More-over, I had a family that, up until now, cared for me, so I had a good life defying my master's wishes.

I would never forget the way Nico touched me. How he felt inside of me. Even though he intended to kill me, I was okay with it because if I died by his hands, it meant that he would finally find the peace he was searching for.

"YOU LIKE LIVING HERE, DON'T YOU, SWAN?"

My body started to shake. This always happened when my master made me stand next to him so he could ask me questions. I already knew where this conversation was headed. Two times before this, it had happened, and I had been sleepless for days afterward. I didn't like to sleep right away because terrors would creep up on me, and it was a lot of screaming and begging.

"Yes, Master," I replied and bowed my head before him.

"Everyone pays their dues around here, you know."

My head was still bowed, and I nodded as a tear slid down my cheek. I hated myself for showing such weakness, but it couldn't be helped. It wasn't like I could split myself in two. One half of me carried the purity that still lingered in my heart, while the other half was the darkness I was forced to take on.

"I understand, Master."

My master clapped. He was a lunatic, getting happy for all the wrong reasons.

"Good, good, because you will dance for me once again."

I raised my head once more and tipped it to acknowledge what he meant.

"Giorgio, take her away," he said, dismissing me.

That's when the one who was always my guard stepped forward.

"Should I leave the light on this time?"

"Do as you please, my boy, just remember that swan over here is off-limits."

Swan—that's what my master called me when he stripped me of my name. It was the only thing I had that was still mine. Names held power, but mine didn't have any. It was just a reminder of where I came from. The only thing that was mine, because I was sure I was never leaving this place alive.

No one would ever know my name.

My guard stepped forward. He had on that cruel smile he always had reserved for me and held on to my arm as he opened the door for my room.

I guided myself through sheer memory to the place I called my bed. A few hours after being left alone, the room became bright. I had to close my eyes because it hurt my eyes.

The place I called home was nothing more than a massive cage with a bed. I looked at the tall bars; the top of the cage was all metal. This has been my home for many years. Even though I could feel them, it was a different thing to look at it. It was always a bitch when your situation slapped you in the face.

Although I didn't want to, I sat up and saw the other girl. She used to cry all the time, but was quieter now and withdrawn.

She was sitting down with her back to the bars. She turned her head, and our gazes locked.

There was no denying she was beautiful, but she looked like a corpse. There were no tears anymore; her eyes were blank. I could make out the blue more clearly now, but it was dulled over.

"Close your eyes when he comes," she said to me and then lay down, away from my view.

"What do you mean?" I asked.

She didn't answer me, even when I repeated the question minutes later.

It wasn't until a few hours later that I understood what she meant. But then, the door opened without the light in the room having turned off.

My guard stepped in. The moment our eyes met, he smiled at me. Chills went down my body.

"You might want to watch, little ballerina. You're next."

My lips trembled, and the temperature in the room dropped.

The girl told me not to watch, but human nature went against what we were told, right? I peeked through the cell bars, and I wished I hadn't. My guard was on top of the other girl. He was pulling down his pants. I stopped breathing for a second.

Then he bent, and I heard her gasp. That sound broke my fucking heart. That's when he turned to me, and I could see he liked that I was watching. So, I scooted all the way back and did as the girl had told me and closed my eyes.

Except, closing your eyes didn't mean you could no longer hear. I didn't know if that was worse, not after seeing how he was with her. I thought I knew why she no longer cried anymore, not when no one heard her pleas when she needed them the most.

I buried my face between my knees, trying to block out the sound with my thighs—it was useless. The noises seemed to go on forever. With every lasting second, something inside of me died. It forced me to realize just how much privilege I had. I thought what I had to do was hard, but it didn't compare. I would gladly take dancing on bloodied and whipped feet over being subjected to the mercy of men like my guard.

My guard was panting when the sounds finally subsided. I heard the sound of his zipper going up, and my legs trembled with fear that I would be next.

I was disgusted with myself when I heard him walk toward the door and I felt relief. He opened the door and reached outside to turn off the lights. Then, just as we were engulfed in darkness, he spoke to me.

"She's the next one," he said with glee.

A choked sob escaped my lips as the door finally closed.

The roles had reversed. The girl in the cell next to me had always been the one to cry, but this time it was me. With the two girls before me, I had not seen them until it happened. It was a fight-or-die situation. We were capable of anything when we tried to survive.

"It's okay," the girl spoke, causing me to stop crying and listen to her. "He told me what you have to do."

This time my chest shook. Again, I tried to hold back my sob, but I couldn't.

"I'm not going to do it," I hissed after a while. It was time for me to stop being a coward and take responsibility for the sins I had willingly committed.

"Come here," she whispered in a tired tone.

I had never ventured outside of my cage. The outside door was locked, but our cages were open. We never went outside since they had become our safe place.

I was nervous about going toward her, but I wasn't scared if she tried to kill me; in all honesty, I welcomed it.

The cage door creaked when I opened it. I held my breath as I made my way over to the other cage. My hands were in front of me to guide me for when I made contact with her cage. Her door had been left open. All I had to do was make my way inside.

I whimpered when my knees made contact with the floor. There was no blanket.

It was hard to try and not hurt her in the dark, but I

managed. She didn't give me further instruction, so I lay down next to her, hoping it was okay.

"I'm not going to do it," I said.

The girl reached for my hand, and I tensed. Her hands were cold and bigger than mine, and she crossed her fingers and tightened her hold on me.

"Please," she begged me in a hoarse voice. "You have to kill me tomorrow. I can't take this pain anymore."

I started to cry.

How fucked-up was it that she started to console me.

"It's what I want—you'll be giving me mercy. Please do it, I beg of you."

I cried harder.

"Please take away my pain."

Who would have thought making that promise would have come back to bite me in the ass. So the next day when I woke, she was already gone.

When Giorgio came to get me, the room was full of men and women, and Nico's daughter was on the floor. I couldn't see her bruising in the darkness, nor the smeared blood all over her raggedy dress; now I wished I had never seen it.

"Dance la mia ballerina," *my master had said.*

As I had done with two girls before me, I took the knife they gave me, and I killed her. I could swear relief shone in her eyes.

I cried as her warm blood coated my hands, and as her body shook, I sobbed. Then, for the first time, I looked up at my master, and I swore I would kill him.

"You will pay for this!"

A loud screech left my lips, and it felt like I was torn in two, and then I passed out.

So I guess it was poetic for Nico to give me peace in the same fucked-up way I gave his daughter.

As the plane went through turbulence again, I smiled in the dark. "Dance of the dead, indeed."

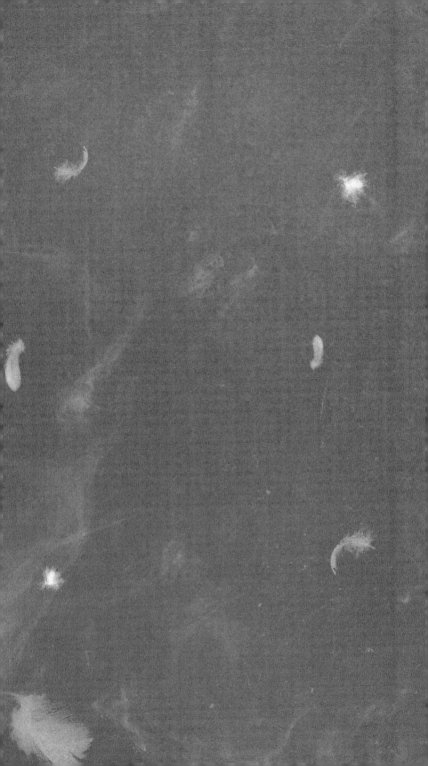

27

NICO

It had been one week since the last time I laid eyes on Ofelia, and I still couldn't bring myself to fully look at her.

I could still see Alejandro's face and his mocking smile. The way his smirk oozed with blood as he confessed that the woman I had taken under my roof and into my bed had killed my daughter.

There were still questions I needed to be answered, but so far, it all pointed to be true. Ofelia had been Vito's favorite girl, the one he didn't touch, but the fucker had always said there were many ways to break a person, and Ofelia was indeed broken.

The fact that Estevan had suspected already not only made me feel betrayed but made me wonder how the hell had I been so blind? He didn't share it with me but made it real.

I wanted to kill Ofelia right there and then with my bare hands. Choke her as she begged me for mercy, but there was a small part of me that wouldn't be able to do it—a small piece that would hesitate.

When I walked into her room, it was pitch-black. She always said it gave her a fucked-up sense of comfort because that's how her master kept her locked up. Well, I was the asshole who was going to make her life miserable.

She had no idea what was going on, just that I had berated her. Good, we were even now. An eye for a fucking eye. We both now lived with invisible knives stuck to our hearts.

Except she was the one to wield it first.

"N-N-Nico," she mumbled.

I laughed at the hopefulness in her voice.

"It's okay, swan. *Daddy's* here," I mocked.

She whimpered, and my cock grew hard, even though I wanted to make her pay for all the pain she caused me.

Scratching could be heard on the door. The dogs were trying to come in; they still felt loyalty toward Ofelia.

When I made it to the front of the bed, I stood there, just looking at her. Wondering how she had been capable of taking away the one thing I loved the most with her bare hands.

"Are you scared, Ofelia?"

She didn't answer me, but again, I didn't expect her to do so.

The bed dipped with my weight, and I heard Ofelia's intake of breath.

I reached for her, grabbing her ankles and dragging her down to meet me. She yelped, and my heart raced.

"This is what you wanted, little swan?" My voice came out like venom sticking to her skin. "To get *Daddy's* attention."

I hated my reaction to her, but most of all, I hated that despite her being scared, she was still excited, and that information terrified me. How far was I willing to go in the name of revenge?

"Now you decide to stay quiet?" I growled as my hand traveled up her shapely leg and the apex of her thighs.

"What is there to say?" she said breathlessly.

Her reply angered me. A pathetic part of me had hoped she would deny it. To demand to know why I had her locked up, but her silence spoke volumes.

"Nothing, I guess."

My finger slipped inside her pussy, and I cursed her for being wet for me.

"How much do you hate me?" she asked me breathlessly.

I pulled my finger out and spread her legs wider. Then with one hand, I pulled down my pants and lined up my dick to her entrance.

"Enough," I said, thrusting inside of her. "That I don't ever—" I pulled out. "—want—" I slammed back in. "—to see." I grabbed a bunch of her hair and pulled it until she whimpered. "—your fucking face again."

Ofelia was moaning, getting off on the pain I inflicted upon her.

"Are you going to come inside me, Daddy?" she mocked in a breathy voice, and I barely pulled out when I shot my release onto her abdomen.

"I will never forgive you for this." I spat the words into the dark room.

I pulled back, and Ofelia turned to her side.

"I know," she said, and it killed me even more.

I was almost out of the room when she spoke my name. "Nico..."

She waited for my reply, but it never came.

"Do what you have to do," she said, her tone sounding sad. "I forgive you."

My hands were tightly fisted. I slammed her door on my way out. Bane and Joker could be heard barking down the hall, desperately trying to come to her aid.

I slammed my fist into the wall in front of me.

She forgave me? I wanted to laugh at the fucking irony. When I rounded the corner, Estevan was there. He didn't look surprised to know I had been to Ofelia's room.

"What?" I spat at him.

He raised his hands. "Nothing. If you want to hate-fuck Ofelia every night, that's fine, but then again, what would Diana say about it all?"

I gripped him by the collar and pushed him against the wall. Estevan glared at me.

"Don't you ever mention her again," I told him in a low tone.

Estevan pushed me away.

"Yeah? You're the one fucking her killer instead of killing her."

"What is it to you how I decide to get my revenge?"

He snorted.

"Seems to me like you're thinking with your dick. What good does it do to drag her along?"

"You seem eager for me to get rid of her."

Estevan was breathing heavily. I was probably losing it.

"Don't be an idiot. Who has been with you since the beginning? Me!"

He was right. I needed to calm down.

"What information do you have on Giorgio? Anything new?"

Estevan seemed to lose the anger he had toward me earlier and smiled.

"That's why I came to find you," he said as he opened the door to my office. "Vito's old opera house has been restored."

That held my interest.

"No one really knows who did it."

"But you think it was Giorgio?" I asked with hope. I couldn't kill Vito anymore, but Giorgio was the next best thing.

"I don't know, but if you have a show there, he won't resist coming to get Ofelia."

"She would be bait." The idea didn't sit right with me.

"And do you care?" Estevan asked me.

"When she dies, it will be by my hands," I told him, and this pleased him.

"We will finish our US tour, then announce a special show for our fifth anniversary," I told Estevan, already planning everything in my head.

"I'll get on that right away," he said as he eagerly made his way out.

I stayed in my office until the early hours of the morning. It was right before dawn that another of my men made his way in. He didn't say anything but dropped a folder on my desk.

"Thank you," I told him as I reached for the information.

"Boss," he said.

I looked up at him, and he looked enraged.

"Whatever you need, we are on your side."

He didn't have to say more, for his words confirmed my suspicions.

It was funny how you could miss so many things in the heat of the moment. But, when looking back at it, the signs were all there, ready to slap you in the face.

"Thank you," I told him.

I had one more month to play a role, and then I would finally get vengeance on everyone who had caused me pain.

My days involved preparations, and my nights would involve Ofelia. The more my hate grew, the harder I would fuck her. It was almost an addiction that I wasn't sure why I had started anymore.

Sometimes, she was quiet and docile. Other times, she was as angry as I was and called me names. Maybe I did get off on her calling me daddy. After all, I had been a failure at being a father.

But no matter what version of her I would get, I knew she was always going to be wet and ready for me.

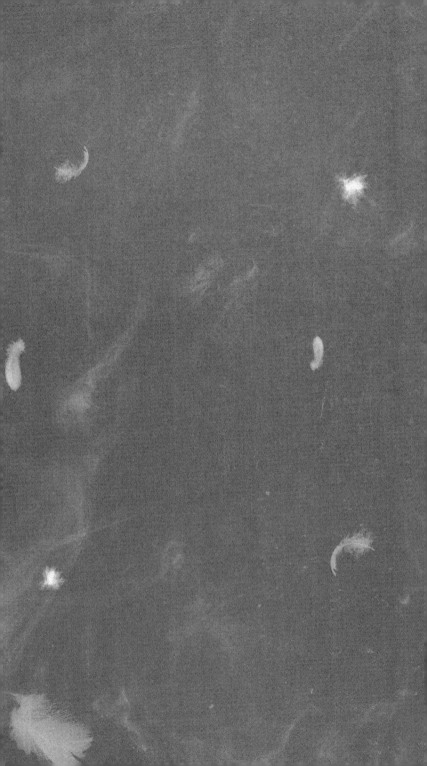

REBIRTH

Her life was not perfect; it was lonely and sad.
But when she met him, she felt alive for the first time.

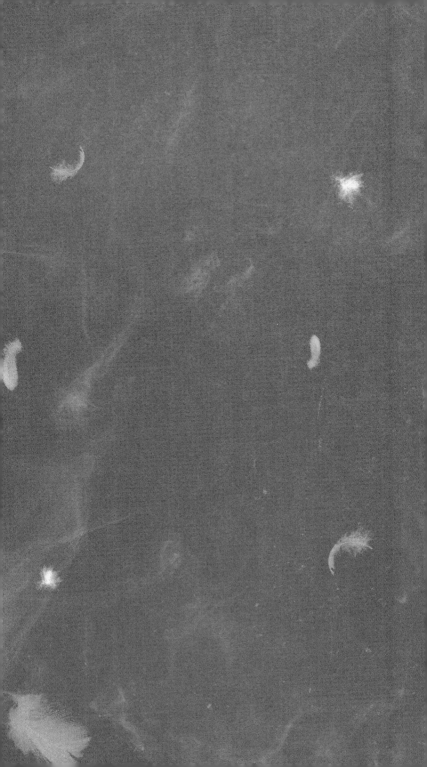

28

OFELIA

My life was back to the moment I remembered it to begin. My days were spent rehearsing, and my nights were in a black cage. Except, my cell wasn't an actual cage anymore, and Nico would come and fuck me with all his hate.

I waited for him each night. It was sick of me to get off on his cruelty and the way he taunted me, but I couldn't help it. As soon as my door opened each night, my pussy got wet. At first, he wouldn't let me come, but it was happening more often now.

The first time I came, he left the room right away, and I knew he hated himself for allowing me to find pleasure. So, I never mentioned it. I didn't say any of it. Not in the day when I would sometimes catch him watching me rehearse.

He was taking his revenge out on my body, and I was okay with it. I didn't know what that said about me, but my life was still different than it had been seven years ago.

I had a roof over my head. I had food to fill my belly, and the man who was fucking me was someone I loved. So, if this was how the rest of my life turned out, I was content with it.

Our US tour was going well. Nico usually got us penthouses so I could see the city lights, and if I missed one thing, I guess it would be that. He hadn't killed me, but as the door to the studio opened, I knew he would.

"Hi, Clarissa," I smiled at the girl who walked in.

She looked much better than when had I first laid eyes on her. She was still wary and shy, but her talent would surpass mine.

When I first saw her walk into practice, I had been confused because I thought Nico had lost at the auction. Who would have thought I had been there the day Nico got my replacement.

It was better than Delia, I thought to myself.

Since the day that everything changed, I had not seen her, but then again, I hadn't seen much of anyone.

Nico wasn't stupid. He couldn't just kill me. Not when he had made me a star. You couldn't have a show without its lead star. And now, Clarissa was training to one day take my place. It was cruel to have me train my own replacement, but it was deserved.

Nothing would ever compare to what I'd taken away from Nico.

"Hello," the girl answered me back.

"Let's start," I told her.

She gave me a small smile, and then her eyes landed on my feet.

"You got new shoes again?"

My throat constricted, and I blinked back tears, but I still smiled at her.

"Let's not worry about that," I hissed, trying not to cry.

At every new stop, I got handed a new pair of slippers.

Then, just as I was breaking them in, they got taken away. The only time I got my favorite pair back was on a show night.

Nico was just as creative as my master. The old bastard would whip the soles of my feet, then make me dance for hours, relishing the pain he caused me.

By the time we finished practice, my feet felt like they were on fire. I tried to walk, but I fell.

"You did well, Clarissa." I faked a smile at the girl who would one day take my place. It was not her fault, so I wouldn't burden her with my problems.

She twiddled her fingers, contemplating if she should help me or not.

"Go, rest now. We have a big day tomorrow."

She nodded.

"We are flying to Italy next," she told me, and my head snapped her way.

My brows scrunched in confusion. That made no sense at all to open our show there. We usually went to Latin America after the United States tour.

"Why?"

Clarissa shrugged. "Something about a fifth anniversary."

My heart started to race, trying to think about why or how this was even possible. Unfortunately, I wasn't privy to any information anymore.

"Yes, tickets are supposed to be super exclusive, and it will be held at a restored opera house that was popular in the fifties."

I was going to throw up.

"Are you okay?" Clarissa asked, but before I could reply, a cold voice did it for me.

"She's fine," Nico said.

My heart started to palpitate upon seeing him. The sunlight illuminated him, making him seem like a dark angel. Ever since that day, those blue eyes didn't sparkle anymore.

Clarissa bowed her head and scurried out of the room. Her reaction angered me.

"I get that you hate me, but don't take it out on other dancers." I glared at him.

He looked surprised that I had talked back to him.

"Does it kill you, little swan, to know you are training the girl who is going to replace you as my star?"

Yes, it did, but I would never tell him that.

"Are you going to let her call you *Daddy* when you fuck her too?" I spat at him.

I could see the vein in his neck pop out. He took a seat on the chair closest to me and pulled out a cigar, but otherwise ignored my question.

It almost reminded me of the old times when he would watch me rehearse to make sure I didn't overexhaust myself.

One thing I was glad of was that I had not fainted. Finally, no one would watch over me anymore. I didn't realize how much I counted on Nico being my security blanket.

I winced as the shoes came off, and blood coated my toes and soles. I wiggled my toes, trying to remove the stiffness from them.

Nico looked terrified as his gaze was fixed on my feet.

"I told you dancing with bloodied feet didn't scare me." I repeated the words I had told him a long time ago.

"My old master—"

"Vito," Nico growled.

I looked at him, confused.

"His name was Vito, not master."

I pretended like he had not corrected me and kept going. "My old master would whip my soles until the skin would tear, then once blood started to drip everywhere, he would make me dance."

"Why are you telling me this? To gain my sympathy?" I snorted.

"If I wanted your sympathy, I would tell you about every single thing I remembered."

Twice in one day, I managed to catch him off guard.

"You remember everything? Why haven't you said anything about it?"

My gaze met his, unflinching and unwavering.

"Because at this point, you'll just think I'm after your sympathy or your forgiveness."

He took a drag of his cigar but didn't prove me wrong.

"Did you enjoy killing her?" he asked after a while.

I got up and made my way over to him.

"Don't ask questions you don't want answers to," I said between gritted teeth.

Nico blew the smoke in my face. He leaned back and spread his legs.

Chills went down my spine.

"On your knees, swan," he said in a hoarse voice.

Our gazes were locked as I kneeled for him. He put the cigar between his lips, then proceeded to pull down his pants.

My mouth was watering. I wanted him in my mouth— no, I needed him.

"How long?" I asked, and for the first time in a month, I saw an emotion pass through those blue eyes. "And do you want me to deep-throat?"

Nico was breathing heavily now. I didn't wait for his reply as I took him in my mouth. He worked the elastic on my bun until my hair cascaded down my face, and then he proceeded to hold on to it.

"Suck me, little ballerina," he demanded.

He looked at me until he couldn't take it anymore, and his head fell back. He was godlike at that moment. Even though I was giving him pleasure, I knew that if he wanted, he could snap my neck in an instant.

The thought turned me on even more. It was a power trip to know I still had some sway over this man.

Nico came into my mouth without warning, fucking my face, almost choking me in the process, and I loved every minute of it.

The loud popping noise of my mouth releasing his dick echoed through the studio.

We looked at each other for a few seconds, neither of us saying anything but wishing that things could have been different.

It was finally me who spoke.

"Will I go full circle in the next show?"

He sucked in a breath and finally broke his gaze from mine. He didn't answer me as he pulled his pants back up.

"It's okay if I do," I told him with all sincerity, even though tears started to spill.

Nico didn't say anything as he walked away.

This was probably the last time I would see him, and I tried to memorize all of his features so I could take them with me to the afterlife.

"Thank you for the life you gave me," I hissed, trying to contain my tears.

He stopped.

"Don't talk anymore," he begged of me in a tortured tone.

I silently cried as I watched him walk away. Then, I waited for someone to come to get me. My tears had dried when the door opened again.

Estevan walked in. I couldn't believe at one point I thought he was my friend. He smiled at me, but it wasn't sincere.

"Come on, little swan. Time to go back to your cage." His tone was cheery, and I knew why.

I didn't engage with him in any conversation, not until we were near my room. "You must be happy that he's getting rid of me, aren't you?"

Estevan looked at me carefully.

"All we ever wanted was revenge for the person who killed his daughter, and that person is you, so yes, it makes me happy that Nico will get his revenge."

If I could kill one more person before I died, I would gladly kill him.

"Then why were you in that room that day, Estevan?"

I wanted to laugh at the shock on his face.

"You knew all along what I had done."

The triumphant smile he had sported all day morphed into a scowl.

"He will never believe you," Estevan spat. "You are the little whore who killed his daughter, and I'm his best friend."

I didn't get to say more because he shoved me inside the room. He was right. Nico wouldn't believe me. Estevan only pretended to like me so he could keep a close eye on me. I was not a threat, because I couldn't remember anything.

Sadness spread through me when I realized Nico would

be all alone once he found out Estevan had betrayed him. It was not a matter of if but when.

I wiped the tears from my eyes. At least he still had Joker and Bane. Then I cried some more because I missed them, and I would never get to see them again.

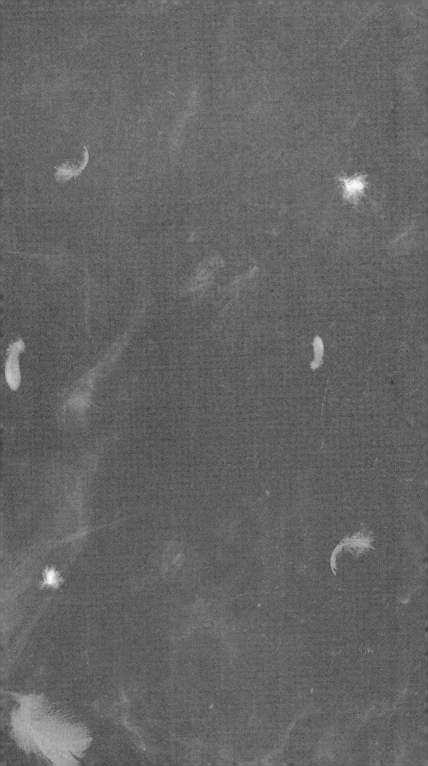

GRAND FINALE

It was the moment she had been waiting for.
The war she had tirelessly trained for.
She was ready for one more round.
This was her grand moment, her grand finale.
It was time for her final round.

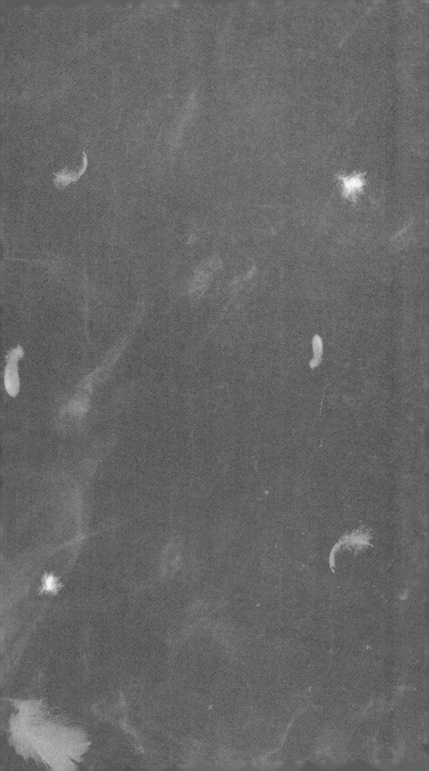

Isn't it funny how the more you try to grasp on to time, the faster it seems to go by? It's like it's done on purpose because who are we to try to be the masters of time?

Everyone was in a frenzy today. There was a wild current in the air. All the other dancers were running around the dressing rooms. I smiled as I looked at all of them.

How much I missed out by being selfish and lost in my own mind. I never really enjoyed the entire atmosphere of a show—the way all the dancers fed off each other.

Since I was no longer in Nico's good graces, I didn't get a room to myself. Instead, I was sitting on an old couch, my white tutu sparkling new. I sighed, then blinked back the bad memories.

There was something peaceful about knowing that your end was near. It made you feel invincible; if you knew death was coming, what else was there to fear?

I hadn't seen Nico since the last rehearsal I had in the

US; he stopped coming to me at night, and I wanted to hate myself for oversharing with him, but it was for the best.

Had he kept coming, I would probably have begged him to let me live. The old opera house had been remodeled, forgoing its original structure, and that's probably why I was able to look around and not see a ghost haunting me.

Then again, I was always kept in the lower levels, and I had yet to be on the stage. So I suppose it was only fair since my fellow dancers had relieved their nightmares, it was now my turn to do the same.

I ran to the bathroom as I heard the warning bell that the show was about to start. I looked everywhere, but I could not find Delia. A part of me wanted to verbally spar with her one last time. Then, as I washed my hands, it sunk in why I wanted to talk to her.

It was stupid and not my place, but I wanted her to watch over Nico. He didn't deserve the loneliness that was coming his way, and oddly, I trusted Delia.

"Ofelia, it's time!" someone shouted.

I dried my hands and hurried outside, running down to my spot at the front of the line.

"*Benvenuto nella danza dei morti.*"

The MC spoke those words that for so long felt like home. A smile graced my lips as the curtains went up.

There wasn't an empty seat in the house, and I smiled brighter. At least I would go out with a bang.

The first thing I saw as I stepped into the light was a young Delia lying on the floor. I twirled, and when I looked again, she was gone.

I raised my leg in the air while slowly going on my toes. The same happened again. This time it was the young version of me, but it was no longer bloody. The tutu was white, and I could imagine my old self smiling back at me.

When I spun, I did it with a smile.

The crowd ate it up, and little by little, I was finally letting go of all my demons. I guess they didn't want to follow me to hell.

It was slow, the buildup to the second act. How I would descend into madness. Then, when the first ballerina dropped, a loud boom of claps thundered in the opera house.

As always, before the curtains closed, I looked up at the stage to look for Nico. My smile fell when I didn't find him.

I rushed back to the dressing rooms and changed into my black tutu. It was time for madness to overtake me.

This time when the curtain closed, I felt the impending doom. This was it, my last show. As soon as the music began to play, I gave it my all. I didn't search for Nico anymore. I didn't look at the stage. It was me and the music.

I closed my eyes for what felt like a second, and I could see a vivid red. That's when I opened my eyes and realized it was chaos.

People were running everywhere. The red I had seen was a fire that had been started. I took a deep breath, and I could recall this smell from memory.

So this was how Nico wanted me to die.

I stood alone in the middle of the stage as people ran for their lives. My fellow dancers had deserted me, and the music had stopped playing.

"Well, the show must go on," I whispered to myself as I started to do the rest of the act all by myself.

It was hard to dance when you could barely breathe, but I managed. When my eyes started to burn from the smoke, I closed them. I knew this dance by memory, and I had the stage to myself, so I kept on performing.

I knew the fire was close to swallowing me whole

because I could feel the heat of the flames wanting to lick my skin.

Just a few more minutes, and then it would all be over.

I stopped for a second and decided that if I was going to go out, I might as well go out with a bang. I took a deep breath, then started to cough uncontrollably. I had one more jump to do, and I intended to jump straight into my fate.

I took a step forward and was ready to launch myself, when an arm wrapped around my waist.

Nico

As I had expected, the fifth-anniversary show sold out in minutes. Every pervert knew what the old opera house had been used for and wanted a front-row seat to whatever fucked-up shit I might have planned.

I didn't let myself see Ofelia anymore. Not after what she told me in the studio that last time. It gave me doubts, and I hated myself for it. I believed she came into my life for a reason. Destiny had woven its strings into both of us since the beginning. Now, it was time to tear them away.

"Are you ready?" Estevan asked me, en route to the theater.

"Sure," I told him, less than enthusiastic.

He grasped my shoulder.

"Cheer the fuck up, man. You are finally going to get some peace."

Yeah, too bad it came at a fucking price.

"You're right," I told him. "I just wished it didn't come with betrayal."

"I know, man, I know," he told me empathetically.

My driver went through the back. Before he parked, he moved the rearview mirror and gave me a slight nod.

I ignored it and instead turned to Estevan.

"Do you know if he's here already?"

"Just got confirmation a few minutes ago."

Estevan waited for the driver to open his door. I shook my head as I opened my own. I never forgot where I came from. He did it to show them they were beneath him, and I wished I had seen that sooner.

"Well, it's showtime," I said as another of my men opened the door for us.

I resisted the urge to go to the changing rooms and get a glimpse of Ofelia. It felt like an eternity since I had seen her face, but it was better this way.

"There are more men here tonight," Estevan stated.

"Double the security for the dancers," I told him.

The risk for them was higher than ever. I didn't want any of them to pay for the repercussions of my revenge.

Estevan shrugged.

"The show is about to start," he said with excitement.

I waited in the shadows as the MC announced the start of the show. Then, the curtains started to move, and I saw Ofelia's feet first.

I felt like such a dick for what I had done to her.

Just before I could look at her face, Estevan finally spoke. "We have him."

I turned around without a backward glance to the stage. I followed Estevan as he took me down a familiar set of stairs.

The lights dimmed the lower we went. It was no wonder Vito loved this place so much. One could get lost trying to find their way out.

We were back in the room where I had first met Ofelia.

I was gambling with my life at this point, but it was the only way I would get what I wanted.

I walked in ahead of Estevan, hoping he didn't shoot me right away.

"So where is he?" I turned around, playing dumb. Ofelia wasn't the only one performing tonight.

"Right here, motherfucker," Giorgio said right before he cocked the side of my head with a gun.

My head started to throb before I even hit the ground.

When I came to my senses again, I had been tied to a chair.

I began to laugh when I saw Estevan with Giorgio.

"Are you going to kill me like I killed your brother?" I directed my question toward Giorgio. I would deal with Estevan later.

He glared at me while I focused on the ruggedness of his burned skin. I needed to keep my cool.

"Aren't you wondering why Estevan betrayed you?" he mocked.

"Not really," I said nonchalantly.

I turned my gaze toward Estevan, and I knew my answer made him mad.

"I figured it out a month ago. I was just curious about what he was planning, so I played along."

Estevan was now glaring at me.

"Everyone knew out of the two of us, he was the idiot. That's why they preferred to do business with me."

Estevan started to laugh.

"I was the idiot? You're the one who couldn't see what was right in your face."

He was right. I had been an idiot, but now was not the time to dwell on it.

"Who do you think Hilda went to when she couldn't afford her supplier anymore?"

I had guessed as much. I was disgusted with myself for not connecting the dots sooner.

"She took more than what you could afford, so it was your ass on the line," I said, guessing what had happened. "You've always been a pussy, Estevan, so you figured you could sell my kid to get you out of your fucking problem."

Estevan was always the weaker of the two. Trying to prove to the world he was someone. So he started dealing to pretend he was tough.

"Fucking Hilda was always strung out; she didn't give a shit about it, not if it meant she could have another hit."

I was glad I had killed that bitch.

"This is all touching, but can we hurry this up," Giorgio said. "I'm trying to get my ballerina and dip with my share of the money."

As soon as he mentioned Ofelia, I came out of my skin. He was not going to get her.

"So this is what it is all about," I said, disgusted, but I couldn't say I was surprised.

Giorgio smiled at me triumphantly. My stomach was a pit of anger that was threatening to come loose. Giorgio opened his mouth, but words never came. It happened fast. Giorgio didn't have a chance to react as Estevan shot him. I braced myself in case I was next.

"Tying up loose ends?" I said, looking at my so-called best friend.

Estevan shrugged. "He served his purpose. Just the mention of your little swan had him ready to do anything if it meant he got to keep her."

"If you wanted my money, you should have just asked me for it," I told him with all honesty.

Estevan laughed maniacally. "It was supposed to be our money, then you started spending most of it, trying to save those broken bitches."

We made more than enough, but I guess the hunger for more blinded you at some point.

Estevan left me tied to a chair as he grabbed a canister of gasoline and made his way up the stairs. I prayed to God my men got my dancers out alive.

Maybe it was the fact that I could die, or just being in this hellhole, but I now realized that Ofelia had never been responsible for my daughter's death. She wouldn't willingly do it, of that I was sure. But, if I cast the blame on her, I also had to look myself in the mirror because I was the first person to blame. I was the first who failed at protecting her. Hilda and Estevan were the ones responsible.

When Estevan came back, he was whistling.

"You were always so high-and-mighty, trying to act like you were better than everyone else."

I didn't, but he wouldn't listen to reason.

"I'll let you in on a little secret now that you are going to die."

I held my breath.

"I was there that day your daughter was killed," he said.

"You fucking bastard!"

I seethed. I didn't know you could feel immense rage, then feel like dying all at once.

"She begged Ofelia to kill her because she knew it would end her suffering," he told me.

I closed my eyes. My body vibrated. I was coming undone.

"It broke her when she did that—what a sight it had been." Estevan came and patted my cheek. "I'll admit, I was always scared she would remember me, but she never did."

He then turned and walked away.

I needed to make sure everyone was out and made it to safety. Now that I had finally learned the truth, I could stop this fucking act. Estevan was so power hungry he didn't see what was right in front of him.

"We need to get going now," I said aloud, giving my men the signal that the coast was clear. I heard him run behind me instantly and undo my ties.

As soon as I'd suspected Estevan was involved, I planned this to a T. I had all the exits guarded, my most trusted men hiding in every fucking nook and cranny. There was no way I would leave this place without answers. It was poetic that this is where it all started and it was where it would all come to an end.

"We'll kill him," my man vowed.

I agreed with him, and I knew all of them would want revenge on Ofelia's and my behalf.

"I want him alive," I ordered as he took off my binds. I knew how hard it must have been for him to stay still and let the events play out. All of my men were given orders to stand back unless Estevan intended to shoot and kill me. Giorgio was a casualty that wasn't of my concern. I only hated that I didn't get to kill him, but by the end of the night, all of the demons would be laid to rest, and that I could live with.

We took off running only to find chaos upstairs. I was relieved when they told me the dancers had made it out safely.

"This way, sir!" my men managed to say amidst the smoke.

The fire had spread and fast. It was hard to see.

I removed my jacket and held the material over my nose, trying to get a barrier.

Just as we came up to the main hall, I saw two of my men carrying an unconscious Estevan.

I looked at the man who had once been my best friend, and I wanted him dead. Now that my life was in the balance, I didn't care if I did it or someone else. I just wanted him off this world.

"Throw him near the fire. Let him wake up when he starts to burn alive," I ordered.

My men would guard the doors to make sure he didn't make it out alive. Just knowing that when he did wake and felt surrounded by flames, he would go around to every exit and none would open. That would give me satisfaction, and with that I was able to walk away.

We were walking to the nearest exit when Paola came in running. She was frantic, trying to run past us, but my men stopped her. She didn't even care she was around men, nor that she was being touched; she was on a mission.

"Ofelia!" she shouted.

My heart fucking stopped with one single word.

I looked at the entrance to the auditorium, knowing in my gut that if Ofelia wasn't outside, the stage was where I would find her. I ignored the shouts from my men telling me the flames had spread. I didn't care, and frankly, that shit didn't matter. All my senses were fucking dulled, but I could hear my heart, its constant pitter-patter beckoning me to the person it belonged to.

I started to cough the closer I got to the stage, but I saw her. There she was, still fucking dancing. I didn't think. I took off running because there was no way I was living this life without her.

My eyes burned from the heat and smoke, but I didn't take my gaze off her. She had lived through hell once; I wasn't going to let it happen again. The moment she bent her knees, I knew what she planned on doing. I opened my mouth to yell, but words failed me. Fuck. She couldn't do this to me.

It felt like a thousand years had gone by when my hands finally wrapped around her waist just as she was about to jump. I didn't know you could feel relief at a time like this, yet having her in my arms calmed me.

We were both coughing uncontrollably as I dragged her out of the opera house. Once we were both outside, I pushed her against the car I had on standby.

"What. The. Fuck. Were. You. Thinking?"

She blinked up at me, confused.

"You didn't intend for me to die?"

It fucking broke my heart, and I swore I would make up for the last few weeks.

I grasped her cheeks and fucking kissed her.

"You're mine, little swan, and I don't plan to let you go," I breathed against her lips.

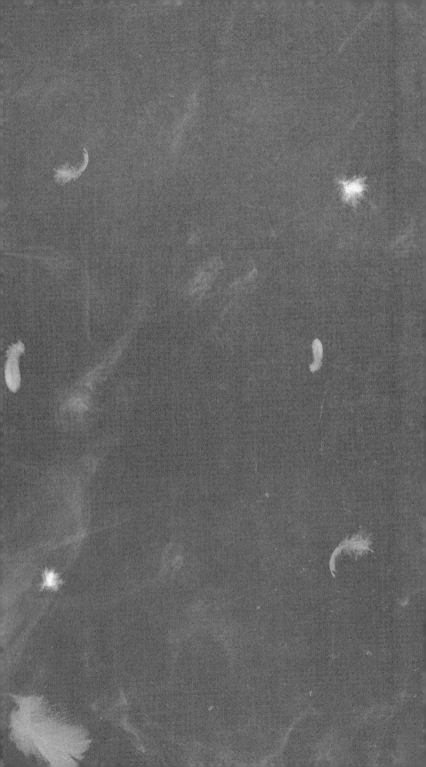

EPILOGUE

"AFTER TEN HOURS, THE FIRE FINALLY CEASED," THE female reporter said. "From what we are gathering, the prima ballerina, Ofelia Dos Santos, kept on dancing amidst the chaos and the flames while her father, Nico Dos Santos, watched."

The male reporter cut off the first one as the camera zoomed in on the theater's remains. "Dance of the dead," he murmured. "The macabre piece of art came to a fiery end. But, unfortunately, none of the other dancers have come forward, making the Dos Santos company all that more mysterious.

"Looks like the mystery of the infamous 'Dance of the dead' will die in this place. Ballerinas across the world have tried to get a spot in the play, but none have been accepted, leaving many to wonder where did Mr. Dos Santos get his talent," the female continued.

The television turned off, and Joker and Bane made their way toward me. A tan arm wrapped around my shoulders. A shiver went down my body when I felt Ofelia's lips kissing behind my ear as her arm started to make its way down my abdomen, causing my abs to constrict. I was tired as fuck, but I needed her more than ever.

"That's enough TV for you, *Daddy*." She whispered the words, and my cock instantly stirred.

I rested my head on the couch and looked up at her. She was gorgeous. Loose brown curls, tan skin that glowed with the sun, but the thing that I loved the most that got my cock hard as soon as I saw them was her green eyes. I tried to apologize to her, but she wouldn't let me. She just wanted to forget about everything and start fresh.

"Are you ready?" I told her as I looked past her to see what she would be bringing with her to the start off our new life.

She was a vision in the flowery dress she wore. Her body had filled out a little more now that she was no longer training rigorously. Her breasts were fuller, and her ass had grown. All of it drove me wild when I fucked her.

"I don't need much." She gave me a devious smile as I noticed she only had one suitcase with her.

"That's all you're bringing?" I asked doubtfully, raising a brow at her.

"Bikinis don't take a lot of space, and I figured I'd spend most of my time naked either way." She bit her lip.

I couldn't help but laugh. My hand shot forward, wrapped around her waist, and pulled her toward me.

"What am I going to do with you, little swan?" My voice came out gruff when she straddled my lap.

Ofelia held on to both of my cheeks. "There are lots of things you can do with me."

I reached up and kissed her, my hands making their way to the back of her hair and grasping two fistfuls of her curls. She moaned into my mouth, and I smiled as I pulled back.

"None of which I can do right now. We have to go."

Ofelia pouted but got off me. She made her way to pet both dogs.

"Come on, guys, it's time for our big adventure."

I stood up and looked around one of my many houses. No place ever felt like home, and I wasn't sure I could sit still after years of traveling the world.

"Is it a big boat?" Ofelia asked as she got in the car.

"Enough for us," I told her.

She grabbed onto my arm and rested her head on my shoulders. Joker went on the passenger seat while Bane sat next to Ofelia. My driver was now making his way to the marina, where we would embark on our new journey.

"I wonder who will join us?" Ofelia said, and I heard the excitement in her tone.

I couldn't help but smile back at her. She really did look young when she looked up at me like that. It did something to me, but I was too selfish now to give her up.

No one would ever protect her like I would. No one would ever go to the lengths I did to keep her sane. And now that she had come into her own, I was not about to let some dumb fuck come here and reap what I had sowed.

"Guess we will find out soon enough."

I kissed her forehead, then wrapped my arm around her shoulder as the marina finally came into view.

It was already dark, but it was better this way since the world thought we were dead. So it was okay to let them believe that. The truth would come out soon enough when the only bodies they would find were that of Estevan and Giorgio.

"Ah, we are here!" Ofelia said, full of excitement. As soon as the car came to a halt, she and Bane were rushing outside with Joker begging to be let out.

My driver chuckled. He leaned so he could reach Joker's door and let him out.

"Thank you," I told him as I pulled out a cigar.

I got out of the car to get our luggage.

"You didn't have to do that. As of right now, you are no longer in my service," I told the man who I had employed for the last few years.

"Thank you for everything, Mr. Dos Santos," he said as he went to shake my hand.

"Nico," I told him as I shook his hand back. "You ever need anything, Leonardo, you know how to find me."

It was comical how his eyes bugged out.

"You know my name?" he said with awe.

I chuckled as I lit my cigar.

"Enjoy your new life," I told him before I began to walk away.

I knew the names of every person who came to work for me. I knew the struggles they were facing and what my money meant for them and their families.

No one was more loyal than someone grateful.

Leonardo had been one of many. Since I was no longer going to be touring the country, I had to let all the staff go.

Thanks to Roman, I was able to get my various houses sold in a way that it would never trace back to me, and I'd still get to keep the money.

Now that Estevan was gone, I got to keep the money he had amassed. Since the slimy sick fucker got it from damaging the girls I tried to save, it was only fair to let everyone who ever worked for us get a share.

Most of the staff was let go since they had families, but they would get compensated. As for those who didn't have a place to go, they would be joining us. To say it had been a busy night was an understatement.

Ofelia was on her tiptoes, trying to see who had joined us.

"Let's go, brat," I said as I held on to the luggage with one hand, then grabbed her hand with the other one.

When we reached our ship, I stopped dead in my tracks, and Ofelia squeezed my hand. I blinked back the moisture that had gathered in my eyes.

"Wow," Ofelia breathed.

I couldn't believe that all the dancers and half of the men I had employed were ready to take off and sail the world with Ofelia and me.

"Mas—" Paola cut herself off right away. "Mr. Nico, we would all love to join you guys...that is, if the offer still stands."

"Of course," I told them.

"Please, after you guys," Ofelia said, sounding happier than ever. She extended her arm toward the walkway so they could all go first.

When everyone had boarded, I led Ofelia to the side of the boat to see the name of the ship.

"*The Swan*," she read out loud.

"Are you ready?" I asked her.

Ofelia turned around and wrapped her arms around my shoulders.

"I think the question is, are you ready, old man?"

I tugged her hair in a warning.

"I mean, besides wanting to get fucked all the time, I might get on your nerves, and I don't want you to drown to your death or anything like that."

"My little ballerina," I said as I pulled her closer to me. "You've been getting on my nerves for the last seven years." My hand glided down her back and under her dress, touching the cotton of her panties. "I think it's too late for me to jump to my death."

She gasped when my finger dipped into her pussy.

"Wet for me already?" I groaned as she moved her hips to take my finger deeper.

"You want to fuck me, don't you, Daddy," she moaned.

I pulled my finger out only to insert two right back in.

"Or you want me to fuck you while you lie in our new bed." She gasped.

I bit her bottom lip, and she smiled as she rubbed my hard-on.

"Let's go or they'll leave without us," I told her, before shoving both the fingers that had been in her pussy into her mouth.

"I love you, Nico," she said, her words low but sure.

I couldn't help but smirk into the dark sky as I dragged her with me so we could get on the ship.

"Aren't you going to tell me the same thing?" she said, somewhat annoyed.

"Did you say something, brat?" I looked down at her.

She glared at me.

"Fine, be that way." She was now annoyed.

As soon as we were on the ship, the crew got ready to sail away. Everyone came to watch as *The Swan* left the port. I think everyone hoped to find a better life, sailing the seven seas. Nothing would ever compare to the suffering they had on dry land.

Ofelia went to hold on to the rail as she watched the dock get further and further away. I came behind her, wrapping my arms around her hips.

"Contemplating jumping to your death?"

She snorted.

"Is this what freedom feels like?" she whispered, probably because she was trying not to cry.

I kissed her cheek. "Guess we'll find out."

We stayed there until the only thing we could see was the ocean, and the city was nothing but a small speck of light in the night. It almost looked like a star.

"Ofelia," I said, my voice sounding gruff even to my own ears.

She craned her neck so she could look up at me.

Fuck, she was fucking gorgeous.

"Are you going to miss dancing?"

She took a second to answer me, and I didn't know what I would do if she said yes. I wanted to give her the world, and if I had to sell my soul to the devil a second time, I would.

"Dancing was a lifeline, a distraction, and although I love it, it's not all I am. So, I'm ready to find out who I am without my ballet slippers."

When I didn't say anything right away, she did.

"You made me a star, and after what happened, I will probably be a legend. So that is more than I could have ever asked for."

My hold on her became tighter.

"Ofelia," I said again.

"Hmmm," she replied, already sounding exhausted from all of the events that had taken place.

"I don't believe in answering things that are already obvious."

A huge smile spread across her face.

"Come on, let's go to bed," I told her.

We didn't end up going to bed right away. Instead, she made sure that everyone who had boarded with us was taken care of.

"Oh God, I'm so close," Ofelia moaned as she rode me.

It never got old—the sight of seeing her naked and fucking me. I grabbed onto her hips and started to thrust into her, causing her eyes to roll back.

"Fuck, your pussy is so fucking wet for me," I groaned.

"Just like that, Daddy. I'm going to c—"

I flipped us and started to fuck her harder. My lips attacked hers while I held myself up with one hand, and the other got lost in her curls.

As soon as she came, I followed. Her pussy convulsing around my dick was more than I could handle.

I was trying to catch my breath when she started to giggle.

"What's so funny?" I asked as I nipped her neck.

"You love it when I call you Da—"

I bit the arch of her neck.

"Ouch."

"Stop being a brat," I told her as I lay down next to her.

Her head immediately came to my shoulder, and she threw half her body over mine.

"Delia didn't come," she said sadly, and I tensed. But then, my mind went back to the day in the sauna room.

It was getting harder and harder to be near Ofelia. Today, I had been pushed to my limits. Just the thought of her got me hard. I needed a release, and since I couldn't get it from her, my hand was the next best thing.

My hand was on my dick when she was in front of me. My dick jumped for attention, and I stroked harder. When I finished, she took a step in between my spread legs and dropped the towel.

It was late, and I was tired, and the usual shield I had against her was gone. My eyes greedily devoured her. The moment she bent and touched my knees, I knew I was done fighting it.

"Let me make you feel better," she purred.

"You should go." My voice was weak. It held no real conviction.

Ofelia just laughed as she kneeled before me and put me in her mouth. The moment she started to deep-throat me, my head rolled back, and my hips involuntarily rose.

When her nails started to dig into my thighs, I groaned and then wrapped my hand around her hair and pulled it.

Even though her mouth was fantastic, I needed her pussy.

When Ofelia got up, I thought she was on the same page as I was, except she was crying, trying to back away from me.

"Ofelia!" I shouted, worried that I had hurt her.

She didn't listen to me, and I started to feel sick.

I called her name again, and she fell.

Ofelia and Delia were one and the same. I always thought her disorder came after being raped, but no, it happened way before that. Ofelia was the naïve side of her, and Delia was the "evil" version of herself she had created.

"Did you fall asleep on me?" She poked my side.

"Who knows, maybe she will show up again," I told her, even though I doubted it. Every day, I could see both versions of herself merging. She might regain all the time she lost when she was "Delia," or just start to live her life the way she was now.

Whichever version of her I got, I could handle it.

THANK YOU

For taking the time to read Swan Song. My Dm's/ Emails are always open for you guys. I would love it if you have the time I would appreciate it if you could leave an honest review.

If you want a bonus scene to see what happened with Nico & Ofelia you can find it here:

https://dl.bookfunnel.com/ywdc74qcnb

WANT MORE?

Broken Dove

Welcome To The House Of Silence

I lived my life with darkness all around me.
Everywhere I went, I needed constant guidance.
I listened.
And obeyed.
I learned to dance so I could be freed from my gilded cage.
A dove who could not find its way home.
Then one day, I met Luke.
He made me feel happy—safe. Mending my wings so I
could soar once again.
All the while biding his time to rip me to shreds.
Because, at one time, I belonged to *La Casa Del Silenzio*.
If their whores weren't blind, they were mute.
Too bad for everyone, I could still speak the truth.
With him at my side, I could conquer my past.
But I don't think either of us expected my wings to finally
snap...

Preorder Now- mybook.to/brokendovekindle

ACKNOWLEDGMENTS

Thank you so much for taking the time and picking up another one of my books. I really appreciate it. I want to thank my girls for motivating me when I felt like quitting. Jenny, Becca, Ashley, you guys are the BOMB, and I love you guys.

Kristen and Sue, thank you for all your feedback. You really helped made daddy shine.

To my ST, you guys are awesome; thank you for all the support.

To my ARC team and Coffee Shop, thanks for continuing to be on this journey with me.

To Zainab, Sandra, and Cat, you guys slayed it this time. Thank you for helping me make this book something I can be proud of.

Another thanks to my PA, Ashley, who goes above and beyond. I'm so glad you came into my life.

To Jennifer from Wildfire, you are such a sweetheart; thanks for all your work on this release. It wouldn't have been the same without you.

And to my child who never let me get a damn word in. I love you.

ABOUT THE AUTHOR

Claudia lives in the Chicagoland suburbs, and when she's not busy chasing after her adorable little spawn, she's fighting with the characters in her head. After not being able to keep up with them, she decided enough was enough and wrote her first novel.

Claudia writes both sweet and dark romances that will give you all the feels. Her other talents include binge watching shows on Netflix, obsessing over 2D men, and eating all kinds of chips.

If you want to know more, you can always find her here:

Reader Group: Claudia's Coffee Shop
www.clymaribooks.com

facebook.com/c.lymari

instagram.com/c.lymari

amazon.com/author/clymari

tiktok.com/@c.lymari

goodreads.com/clymaribooks

Printed in Poland
by Amazon Fulfillment
Poland Sp. z o.o., Wrocław